Mooncalves

MORE PRAISE FOR MOONCALVES

"At the heart of Victoria Hetherington's disturbing *Mooncalves* are characters that crave each other and punish each other in tangled psychosexual relationships. Hetherington demonstrates uncanny insight into the intensity of these abusive interactions against the backdrop of a strange little cult led by the sadistic, Charles Mason-like Joseph, and she holds nothing back, whether it's sexual, violent, or emotionally toxic. The inner workings of the female characters' minds feel excruciatingly accurate, and there's a visceral immediacy to the scenes, a dark, apocalyptic cloud hanging over them. You will have trouble putting *Mooncalves* down, because as protagonist Erica says, "transgression can be unbearably sexy."

~Myna Wallin, author of *Confessions of a Reluctant Cougar* and *Anatomy of an Injury*

MOONCALVES

A Novel

VICTORIA HETHERINGTON

|N₁ |O₂ |N₁
CANADA

Library and Archives Canada Cataloguing in Publication

Title: Mooncalves : a novel / Victoria Hetherington.

Names: Hetherington, Victoria 1989- author.

Identifiers: Canadiana 2019005056X | ISBN 9781988098746 (softcover)

Classification: LCC PS8615.E79 M66 2019 | DDC C813/.6—dc23

Printed and bound in Canada on 100% recycled paper.

Now Or Never Publishing
901, 163 Street
Surrey, British Columbia
Canada V4A 9T8

nonpublishing.com
Fighting Words.

We gratefully acknowledge the support of the Canada Council for the Arts
and the British Columbia Arts Council for our publishing program.

For C, J, M, and S, with all of my love.
I gratefully acknowledge the support of the Ontario Arts Council.

I didn't say I don't like being human. I said I didn't like the limitations, problems, and high level of maintenance of my version 1.0 body... Our sole responsibility is to produce something smarter than we are; any problems beyond that are not ours to solve.

—Ray Kurzweill, *The Singularity is Near*

And now the wheels of heaven stop/You feel the devil's riding crop/Get ready for the future: It is murder.

—Leonard Cohen, *The Future*

Index de Personnages

Pre-Singularity

Sainte-Pètronille

Logan, Walden devotee. Chapters 1, 4, 7, 9—12,
15—18, 22
Joseph, leader of Walden. Chapters 1—4, 6—18
Erica, spiritual wife of Joseph. Chapters 1–2, 4—19, 21–22

Toronto

Shelagh, Erica's lover and closest friend. Chapters 2, 5, 12, 21
Neil, Shelagh's best friend, Erica's lover. Chapters 2, 5,
12—16, 18, 21
Étienne, Shelagh's former fiancé. Living ghost. Chapters 2, 5,
11, 12, 21
Lori, Logan's mother. Chapters 1, 8

Post-Singularity

Toronto, Theoretical Space

Abby, Logan's daughter. Chapters 3, 6, 9, 19, 22
Mo, Abby's stepfather. Chapters 3, 6, 19, 22
Buppy, Synthetic companion, Abby's closest friend.
Chapters 3, 6, 9, 19, 22

Table de Matières

Table of Contents

LOGAN: SUGAR DADDIES

I lie in the tub, and Erica sits on the toilet. We've gone quiet. The whole house has gone quiet. Erica squeezes her legs together, pinching out dimples in her thighs with two fingers. I'm looking down at the water, following my own hands around—if I stare hard enough, my fingers fold together and start wiggling like creatures, moving on their own. That's the kind of playing I did as a kid. After my sister Brooke moved out I inherited her box of shitty toys, and even though Lori wanted me happy and playing, I didn't know how to handle those Bratz dolls that smelled like pussy, the colouring books ruined with baby scribbles. Even after Lori's army boyfriend Jake moved in and bought new toys for me, I didn't know how to touch them.

"What are you doing?" Erica asks, and even though she's warm like a kindergarten teacher, I lie:

"I'm checking my hands for splinters." The tops of my hands seem soft and dark grey six inches down in the dirty water, moving like fish under ice. I sing two things in silence, and one thing goes *the baby the baby the baby* (which loops within me, constant like a ticking fluorescent light), and the other thing goes: *where am I where am I where am I—?*

"Is Logan your original name?" Erica says. I press my hands against my big tight belly.

"Uh, yeah," I say, pretending like I don't know what she means, but her visible surprise gets me annoyed. "I was born in Canada. My dad was white. Actually, he was blonde like you." This statement, maybe especially the 'was,' shuts her up for a good few minutes.

"You *are* really clean," Erica says, after a while.

Then she asks me if I've cleaned my butt.

I mean it's clean just from soaking in the water, kind of thing, but she's not happy with that. She dips her hand in the water, then takes the soap from me.

"Get on your side," she says.

And so I turn over, cup my belly with one hand and stick my butt out of the water, and I feel her fingers slide right inside of me.

I press against the tiled wall. My cat Langley pushes against my arm like this: gentle, with a kind of pulse—bump, bump, bump. He could wait through anything. My forehead smacks against the tiles, and I make a noise despite myself.

"Do you need to cry?" she says, and then: "There we go. We're almost done."

Afterwards she squeezes one of my hands, going: "This is just standard procedure, OK? Joseph did it to me on my first day here, and I just went—" and she widens her eyes and giggles.

"Why do you do it?"

"Checking for drugs. You can never be too careful."

Which tells me she's never done drugs.

"You stayed so still," she says. "You're very well-behaved, but it made me feel like: where's your maternal instinct, Logan? To like protect your young?"

I say, "Where's yours?" and her mouth twists down. She turns away from me, and cleans her fingers in the sink.

"You're ready now," she says. "Want to know what's next?"

And from her face I figure she can't get pregnant anymore, and regrets it, or else she left some kids behind. After all, she's here— where would her kids be? There's no kids here. Squeezing my thighs together and forcing back tears, I say, "I don't care," which I say all the time, to Lori, and to my ex-boyfriend, Jason. Whenever they start hurting me I say it—although they want me hurt because they need it, and even if I'm crying, saying *I don't care* ruins some of whatever it is they get. I'm so far from home I forget who I am, but my plants will keep growing, the early morning shift will start without me, and Langley will nudge Lori awake with his face-bumps, all like I don't exist.

"Since you are family now, you'll share our marital bed as a celebration of your fecundity and closeness to nature," Joseph says later with this really straight look on his face, speaking like a doctor. He stretches his arms out towards me and wiggles his fingers, so I lean over and hug him. Erica smiles at me, and Joseph rubs my back and sniffs my hair, rubbing his boner against my stomach.

Right after saying 'yes' I start crying, maybe because they expect me to cry, and maybe because guys stopped holding me tenderly as soon as I looked pregnant. I stand there, hemmed in and sobbing, feeling like a liar, as if I'm not me but one of them, watching myself sob and thinking, *What a pussy.* I've fucked for money before, which doesn't feel too far off from this. In fact, Jason isn't the father of this kid at all: a guy from a sugar daddy website is.

I learned about those sites from spying on Lori, digging through her search history for porn. She's had profiles on three sites since I was about eleven, and they all featured the same blurry photo of Lori hugging somebody's horse, and another where I'm about six, and sitting on her lap. *Charming young lady with precious well-behaved little daughter,* one of her profiles said, which made me cry once, because I was younger then. I never met any of the guys, except for one: he was taking a shit with the shower running, and he'd left our bathroom door open. I stared at his flabby white sides for a full ten seconds until he spotted me and gasped.

Six months ago, I stood on a packed bus stopped in rush hour traffic, getting coughed on by an old guy who kept elbowing my tits really gently. There wasn't anything special about that moment except I let him keep at it, rubbing and rubbing, gripping his suitcase in his other hand. I thought: *Well fuck it: why not?*

So for a week I put in thirty hours at Weight Watchers, and Lori and I did the weigh-ins, walked and walked at our side-by-side treadmill desks, and handed literature to smiling dads hovering protectively near their fat, pretty daughters. Then I'd come home to like two hundred messages in my inbox, all from smiling dads exactly like that. And I'd laugh, and Lori laughed too when I told her, and looked through the messages together and read them out loud in silly voices, until she got tired of it and lit a cigarette. "It's because you're just eighteen," she commented, blowing smoke rings at the kitchen lamp. After three double vodka sodas, she added: *It's because you've got a kind smile and you're wow-whee pretty*, like she's way older than she is.

I only met two guys in person, and I fucked them both: EAGER TO PAMPER and then Hesh-86—no names, just their screen names in my phone but even face-to-face, even in bed, because they were married. I stopped at Hesh-86 because he got me pregnant, even though EAGER TO PAMPER sure gave him a run for his money, as Lori put it. As we pretended to count the Artisan Pressed Greens bottles in Maintenance Products Storage, I told Lori everything about him. EAGER TO PAMPER looked about fifty, and maybe like he'd had plastic surgery too; he was wearing some kind of makeup, but I couldn't tell what it was; I met him in a dark pub right down by the waterfront, where absolutely nobody except lonely tourists go, to pace back and forth, throw rocks in the ruined lake, and take selfies in front of the CN Tower.

"Well sugar daddies go there—but I guess they're tourists too?" Lori said, shaking her head, then dropped a green juice. She examined the bottle for cracks, rotating it in her hands, which were shaking a little. She said she needed a cigarette. On our way out to the picnic bench, a construction worker sitting at another bench yelled *Hey beautiful!* "Thank you," Lori replied for us, then lit her cigarette.

"As your mother, I feel like . . ." she said. I let her think. A gust of hot wind picked up and the huge maple tree over the bench dropped those pale green seed things all over our laps.

"Where did you make love?"

"Against a tree in that garden by the water, after going for a walk in the dark," I said.

"He couldn't even spring for a hotel! It was chilly that night, weren't you cold?"

"Yes."

"Jesus Christ, tell me he used a condom."

"I brought one."

A woman left the clinic, red-faced and rubbing her eyes. She was carrying a bunch of new products, including a digital scale the size of two fists, which flashed so bright in the sun I had to look away.

"How much?"

"$300, plus dinner." I could tell she was wondering how he was, to which I'd have said: *Like an old man,* which I can only say now I've fucked one. I could tell she wanted to ask whose idea it was, anyway, to which I'd have said: *Mine, I think.* Maybe she was wondering if it felt good, if it was good.

Yes—he thought so, he said it was. But maybe it wasn't.

She squeezed my hand, looking worried, then said I should go home, she'd cover for me. Here's the thing, though: I spring back like a rubber band, and so that night I wiggled into the same dress EAGER TO PAMPER squirted his little load on, and rode the bus downtown to meet Hesh-86. I wasn't good at telling if older men were handsome—they all looked like they'd been rubbed with sandpaper, to me—but this guy was handsome. Absolutely he was. His sweater and jeans looked expensive, like they kind of hugged him. He didn't push up his sleeves, he rolled them. He said, *Get whatever you want,* and didn't even blink when I got through five strawberry daiquiris, a plate of calamari and a plate of gyoza because I thought it'd be cheese (it wasn't). *Nothing for dinner?* he asked, like I'd been sipping on water all night.

I'm good, I said, and he nodded, then slid off his stool, and stepped over to me. Right in the middle of that dark little bar he put his hands around my face. And he kissed me.

At work the next morning, Lori bumped my arm like *so*? I shook my head. Over in Storage, she closed the big door behind us, and demanded my story.

"And you feel like you're in love? And he has a wife and two children? And he *came inside of you*?"

"Yes. Yes. And yes. It felt—it felt like he had to."

"You remember my friend Gail? She would always say, 'Pregnancy is just a state of mind.' And you know how many kids she has?"

"Two?"

"*Four.*" She pulled two twenties from her purse, pressed them into my hands. "Go get that morning-after pill. Go now. Leave early." I cup the bills in my hands like I used to hold the frogs I'd catch, between those wet rocks down by the creek that runs behind a rehab centre. *You'll grow extra fingers,* Lori would shriek every time I'd catch one, either because the creek was polluted or the frogs were black magic—she'd give me a different answer every time. She'd tan on the biggest, flattest rock and I'd never wash my hands after holding the frogs, not even when she'd hand me a sandwich from her purse, and she never said anything. The creek disappeared under the highway, and it started again at the other side. Lori makes just as much money as me, which isn't much at all.

"Mom," I said. "Mommy."

She sighed. "You know he's not going to call again," she said. "I think you're perfect, you're my perfect little girl, but you're not his type. I'm saying this because I love you. I'm saying this as like, get ready, don't wait for him to call, put your phone under the sofa cushions if you have to, because you're not his type."

He didn't call and didn't call, and things happened like Langley got sick and I started fucking Jason again, and then it was two weeks, and after two weeks and a day, Lori found me hunched over the sink, crying into a stack of empty lettuce wrap trays. She folded me into an awkward hug, calling me *honey,* calling me *sweetheart.*

"I'll tell you how sad and boring his life probably is," she said, rubbing my back. "When he's not preying on kids like you, he sits around looking at girls in bikinis on Instagram, pulling on his sad little dick. Right? Feeling shitty about his age and how bad at romance he is, eating all his feelings because he hates himself so much and terrified of intimacy because he eats all his feelings and hates himself so much."

I asked Lori what his type might be—although I know already, kind of.

"Tacky and older than you, pretending they're still in their twenties," she said kindly.

"And what else? White?" I asked, and she frowned. "No, but maybe blonde, even if it's dyed—you know how blonde hair turns the heads of idiots like that. And maybe girls who look like they do come from more money. Not much more, but a little more than us."

Well, two mornings later I threw up every crumb of the really gross dinner Jason made for me, which despite being gross had a lot of cheese, because he loves me, and I deep-down knew I was pregnant. The funny thing is, I made Jason cum on my back almost every time we fucked, and have since we were 13. So I knew it had to be Hesh-86's. And anyway, I go through phases of annoyance with Jason, and was smack in the grey middle of one of those phases. It's something I couldn't help, even though I tried.

So I went to Jason's place again that night—he had a surprise for me, he said. I was relieved when he opened his laptop, because at least the surprise wasn't another gross dinner, and he loaded up a video. It was one woman and another woman, making out with their big tits—big like grapes taped on Barbies—smooshed up against each other, sliding up and down. They took turns sucking on each other's tits, tits so swollen up the nipples and aureoles looked fat enough to pop, and then some guy, little and dark-haired like Jason, walked right up to the side of the bed. He was stroking his dick, his back arched like he was lifting something heavy with his one hand, and he leaned against the side of the bed, his thighs pressing into the comforter and grazing the tips of one girl's toes. She jumped a little.

"Hey Rosie and Mara," he goes.

"Hey Brad," they go.

And I closed Jason's laptop, because I saw what he was getting at. "Maybe you'd think it's exciting," he said.

"I know it's been six years we're together, and I'm getting fat. And I'll only get fatter," I said to him. "And you've never had anybody else." And then I said something really lame like *Go free,* but he cried anyway, he was already crying, because he was just a boy. Still is a boy.

So after I'm done sobbing against Joseph, his boner throbbing against me the whole time, Erica leads me up to their bedroom. The bedroom is mostly green and kind of nice, even though everything looks made for children, and all I think about is Jason watching that video, his thin face all pinched up in the laptop light—he didn't know I was watching him. Erica reaches towards me carefully, like I reach for Langley when I need to stuff him in his carrier. She places both her hands on my belly, and Joseph watches us both.

Erica asks, "Does he kick?"

Well, Joseph thinks it's a boy too, so I just kind of grin at Erica, at them both, like *What are you guys, midwives?*

And Erica keeps her hands there, then guides me down to their little bed, so I'm sitting beside her and between them, and she begins to stroke my stomach in circles, then down towards my pussy area. And Joseph takes a deep breath and reaches towards my hair, then stops with his hand just like a millimetre from my head. He closes his eyes, his hand just like hovering there, and I get nervous—will he decide he wants to hit me instead? So I say: "Please touch me."

His eyes pop open. "How may I touch you?"

"Any way you want." And he keeps staring, so I try to elaborate: "You can fuck me hard or take your time, um, whatever you want. Or . . . or you can take turns fucking me, and one of you can leave the room if that's better, or you can, you know, watch." *Might as well get it over with*, is what I'm really saying, which is similar to saying '*I don't care*' when people I love want to hurt me a little. But that's not totally true: I've been looking at his body through those loose clothes, and at hers too, and when Erica caught me staring today she winked, and I got a little wet.

After I say all that Erica pulls back a little, frowning, but Joseph seems to relax. "I think all the pleasure centres in my brain just lit up for like three seconds hearing you say all those things in succession," he says, and then he asks me to repeat myself. He presses his fingers into my hair, begins to comb it, twist it.

"Touch me how you want to," I say again. "Whatever you want is good for me."

Joseph jumps up from the bed, and stands with his back pressed against the wall. He folds his hands down near his crotch like men do sometimes, and nudges it a few times with his fist. So I lean over to Erica and stroke her hair like Joseph stroked mine, then touch her face with the tips of my fingers. She's so soft I almost yank my hand away, but as Joseph watches us I stare into her eyes, and she stares into mine. And of course I remember Rosie and Mara, Rosie flinching when Brad strolls up to the bed and bumps her foot, flinching even though she knew Brad was coming, even though the whole thing wouldn't be happening without him, even though she smiles warmly when he climbs onto the bed, stroking his cock like he was *born* ready for this.

And since I'm not watching this like a video but am actually in it, I know what I'm thinking as I stare into Erica's eyes, running my fingers down her chest towards her tits: *I can't believe how easy this is.* I almost giggle, because what if this was Jason or somebody else, in my place? They'd fuck it up, for sure. But here I am, pulling this little woman towards me and kissing her like I've been waiting years to kiss her, yanking her cotton dress up so I can see her thighs and massage them—like I was born ready, too. Just as I showed up to meet Hesh-86 in the big dark pub he chose for us, and I knew what he wanted, and what he meant, as soon as he said: "You're so mature for your age."

It was a tall order, but he thought I could handle it, which became the same thing as me being able to handle it. Because he'd chosen me, because I met him in that dirty pub and acted OK with him being married, because he liked the blunt way I messaged with him, because I'd signed up for the site in the first place—because, because, because, my whole life stuffed so full of reasons going so far back I might well have been born for it, born ready.

But then Erica braces one leg against me and begins to press against my hand, and through her underwear I feel that she's wet. She turns her face away from me, flushed red and breathing hard, and I put my arm around her back and lean against her shoulder, my head against her head so Joseph can't see her face, so we're huddled and together in a compact shaking ball almost the size of a single person. Her arms tighten around me and her knee digs into my ribcage and so I press harder, and then pull her panties aside—crumpled and wet as a dishrag—and push inside of her. She gasps, but quiet like a secret, a wet warm rush of air in my ear, trapped against my neck and in my hair. She's holding me tight as a drowning person so I hold her just as close, and when she starts to come she goes *oh god* against my neck so quiet it's probably just her lips moving, but I hear it loud as anything and keep my hand inside of her as she pulses around my fingers, keep it there until she pulls away. And when she pulls away she looks into my eyes again, then past me to Joseph—and then I know something new, I know something she knows, and it goes like this: *Most men, even the smartest men, are dumb in the exact same way.*

Joseph disappears to the bathroom and Erica smiles at me and slides under the patchwork quilt, and so I lie down beside her. We stare at each other, and she strokes my hair away from my face.

"You know you're very smart," she whispers. Under the sheet I'm holding my belly again, *the baby the baby,* and I don't know what to say, and I can't even smile back at her: sometimes I'm too shy to smile at even the nicest people.

"I don't feel good," I say.

"What's wrong?"

"I wasn't good in Toronto," I whisper. "I don't think I know who the father is, of my own baby. I—men paid me for sex. And I stole things sometimes. And I'm so, I'm bad to my m-mother."

She's quiet for a moment, then looks up and back towards the door, listening for him. She pushes my hair away, and presses her mouth to my ear:

"I did all of those things too," she whispers.

"All of them?"

"*All* of them. But your baby isn't a punishment, you understand? It's just life."

"I don't feel that way," I say, and she pulls back and watches me for a moment.

"Of course you don't. He's a blessing, your little boy," she says. Then she leans forward and kisses me, and then in a gentle way, kisses harder, like she's saying something, like we're talking and she's winning a fight.

We sleep and wake up, and my first full day of work lasts forever. *Please be careful,* Erica says whenever I drop something (which is a lot), and she barely masks her annoyance when I can't test the temperature of the hydroponics tanks, but otherwise, things slip by so pleasant, and every meal—even if it's mostly the tomato sauce we make together—tastes like heaven. And as patterns emerge in our daily activities and even in the way we live, I lay each day over the next, lining up the day-patterns like they're drawn on tracing paper, and time begins to race. And every night, Joseph and Erica speak to me in murmurs and gentle questions: *Do you like this, Hold me now, What are you thinking about.* Every night, the three of us still wet and maybe trembling, they rub my legs and my belly and my face and my hair, as Joseph gives us a bedtime thought:

Focus on us here, really focus, he goes, *because this moment is precious and will disappear soon—but it is now, it is now. And when it passes, recall this moment like a childhood memory, something that lights up in your mind now and then like the lights of a distant city, something warm and elemental. Holding you in the dark.*

SHELAGH: SOLAR FLARES

My name is Shelagh, and I dated a man named Étienne for six years, and for five of those years, I knew he'd never marry me. I didn't suck his cock, kept my wiry hair short, and worked a dull marketing job in an enormous company. In Toronto, a city averaging ten beautiful women for every guy strumming a guitar or working in a bank, I didn't stand a chance. *I'm just the type men string along*, I'd say sometimes, with a kind of jerky shrug that, in my estimation, affected plucky carelessness. But he loved me tenderly and for a long time, and even after I left him for Erica, he loved me still—as long as he could.

I spend most days alone now, remembering the short time I had them both.

It was the height of summer, those brief few weeks in which the heat stretches thick and unbroken through the city nights. Étienne and I rented a skinny townhouse in Chinatown. We threw dinner parties often, because we didn't want to fuck any-more, but still enjoyed falling into bed very late—stuffed full and drunk from other people's wine—to criticize our friends.

One night, we invited my friend Neil over for dinner. Neil had started dating a close friend of Étienne's, a girl named Erica, who was invited but hadn't yet arrived—she was running very late (*Of course*, Étienne said, and Neil tried to laugh.) With sweat dotting his prominent forehead, Neil peeled the label from his second beer, and described Erica to me in loving and rather misogynistic terms. She treated him monstrously but what could he do, she was his pixie, she had milky white skin, her little nose and fingers so delicate as to be almost translucent. *Gross. You deserve what you get*, I'd thought, examining the shredded beer label in his long fingers, watching his throat wriggle as he took a gulp. I think he wore a pinstriped fedora that night, which he'd take off, place in his skinny lap, and then put back on again—but I can't be sure. I've embroidered that night heavily in my mind.

And then: there she was standing in our doorway, her eyes adjusting to the relative dark. Taking off her thin trench coat and bicycle helmet, disposing of them herself (tossed on a chair, not the coat-rack). Slipping off her shoes, scratching one foot with the painted toenails of the other. Sweat in her hair, sweat faintly dotting the back of her dress. I examined her as both men and women examine beautiful young women, and later I'd think: seeing her as Neil did, I deserved all the punishment I got.

She sniffed the air, sending me into a panicky catalog of my own abject bodily smells—a bloody menstrual tang, and pungent sweat related the summer heat and anxiety—but then she re-calibrated, smiled, and took my arm. I juddered through a series of micro-movements, recoiling from and reveling in her touch. As both men openly stared, she led me into the kitchen.

". . . But the yard work is just really me carving some time for myself, you know . . ." I heard Étienne say haltingly, in a very different tone of voice than he'd been using before. She grabbed a knife, and took up chopping the carrots like she'd been chopping those carrots all along, as if I were her shadow, cast long, and she'd finally arrived.

"It's good to see you again," I said, and she nodded, but didn't speak. I'd only ever seen her at parties before, to which she'd usually arrive very late; at that point, I'd be too drunk to speak to someone so pretty and close to Étienne without becoming paranoid and snappy.

"Do you happen to have any coconut oil?" Erica asked, with a strange, solemn enunciation I quickly recalled was just the way she spoke, and would just as quickly start to love. "Because that's how we should fry this."

"Do you want me to get some?" I asked, and to my surprise she smiled and put down the knife. "I'll come with you," she said.

I watched her pull her jacket back on, button it gracefully, and shake her hair from under the collar. She dug, with brightly painted nails, through a purse packed with fascinating-looking things. She smelled incredible. I've been a woman all my life, and a feminine one too, but somehow every aspect of her femininity was a revelation, a sweet, humiliating shock.

"We'll be right back," Erica called over her shoulder, into the hungry silence that had fallen in the living room.

On the way to the store, she talked about parts of Toronto she hated—primarily the clubbing district, packed as it is with weekenders jamming themselves into every available taxi and stinking up elevators with puke and cologne, teeming in droves from the suburbs to stalk the streets for fights, spattering blood and teeth on the sidewalks. "All I see is a sick surplus of cash and this fog of anxiety to spend it. It's terrifying," she said, and I wondered, maybe uncharitably, if she was repeating something Neil had said.

"And think of the sex they must have," I said, "I mean after a night of yelling garbage in people's ears and buying twenty-dollar vodka sodas? You're probably more in the mood to strangle someone than fuck them," I said. She nodded with grave approval but didn't comment further, and we fell into silence.

"How'd you meet Neil?" I said, even though he'd told me already.

They had met at a drum circle on Ward's Island, she said, which wasn't really his thing but had been growing on him lately. She'd been growing concerned about him, she said, but didn't feel right disclosing why.

"Is it because he likes drum circles?" I asked.

"What? Oh!" She laughed and I laughed too, relieved.

"You strike me as fairly socially inhibited," she said as we entered the store, and I blushed. "But I find that people like you and Neil, those are the people worth getting to know."

"Why?" I asked. I wanted to grab her arm and hear the response as soon as possible.

"Oh god," she said, lifting a peach from a bright pile of peaches, sniffing it, then sliding to the left and squeezing a cantaloupe. "You'll have to focus me. I get so overwhelmed in speciality stores like this."

"Oh. Did you not grow up in Toronto?" I asked.

She gave me a quick look. "Well, I did. But uh, I've spent most of my life escaping it. It'll eat you, Toronto. I grew up in an apartment right downtown, so my very first memories are traffic noises like six stories down, all day and all night, just humming away like the ocean. Growing up, I could walk anywhere and do anything with no, um, friction."

"Friction?"

"I mean you can pass thousands of strangers, and there will always be thousands more to pass. You can do whatever you want here, and everybody does. And that's bad for you. It'll eat you."

On our way back I asked her again: "Why are people like me worth getting to know?"

She smiled a little vaguely, then said, "Oh, because you're a watcher. You see everything, and there's wisdom to that. Just don't let Étienne boss you around."

"Étienne?" I bark an angry laugh, then stop and blush. "Wow, that's a little presumptuous."

"I know him very well, Shelagh. I know how he gets, with women."

"Do you?"

"Besides—Neil's concerned, too."

I thought of Neil, swelling up in her presence, pulling at his thin blond beard and saying whatever he could to keep her attention, offering up his life for her to probe, to examine the most salacious bits with diminishing attention. He was concerned—sure. He'd counterfeit any kind of sentiment to parenthesize gossip. The weasel.

"Don't blame Neil," she said quickly. "Oh, I shouldn't have said anything! It's just that . . . you know, Étienne runs his own life like an infomercial."

"Huh. And what's he selling?"

"Himself? Or how normal he is? I'm not sure. You know what I'm trying to say—uh, it's that there's something so *rehearsed* about Étienne. I see it in the way he runs your house, the way he talks about his five-year-plan *all the time*, the way he fears embarrassment, the way he curates his Facebook and keeps it open for anybody to read. It's the way he goes out of his way to use euphemisms for swearwords, instead of avoiding swearing altogether."

"That's a whole lot of evidence," I said, and she smiled, but said nothing.

"Well, I hear that from Étienne that Neil bosses *you* around," I heard myself saying, which was a total lie: I'd heard nothing of the sort, and started to sweat as she paused, and didn't breathe until she spoke again.

"Oh, that's true," she said, "but he takes good care of me. You've probably heard I've been sick." She paused, shot a glance at me before continuing. "And if he's bossy, or a little mean—well it's not his fault. I chose him after all, and choose to stick around."

"I see."

"*Do* you." She smiled. "You think I'm old fashioned, don't you?" She sidled close and gave my hand a little squeeze as we walked.

And with that, I was hers.

For the rest of the night she was impeccably delightful, and even to me—a woman—her delightfulness didn't seem like any effort. We cooked everything to her liking and then the four of us sat out on the balcony to eat, and she was luminous in the buggy fragrant dark. She doted on Neil, and he basked in her compliance to his whiny demands: *Can you pass the veggies again, move over a little, can you speak a little louder, please?* She listened patiently to Étienne's pained analysis of a tense interaction with his boss, then asked about each of his coworkers by name. She then told exotic and self-deprecating stories about her first real boyfriend turning out to be polyamorous but it was OK because she was sixteen, about acid trips with painters in Yellowknife, and finally about her years spent with a man (Joseph, of course) on a Quebecois farm, all so vividly beautiful—the man, the farm, the years—she dreams of it all, it beckons her still (I kept looking at Neil in astonishment: he studied his phone through that particular anecdote).

Throughout these stories she was too self-aware to step outside of self-deprecation, even for a moment—all the while gesturing with her tiny hands, so mesmerizing that I was sure I'd memorized her wisp-thin bronze rings, convinced I'd see them on my eyelids every time I'd blink for the rest of my life.

My folly was seeing her as anything other than people-sized and very dangerous.

At around midnight she took off her shirt, then her bra, pulling each in an easy looping motion up and over her head. She leaned back against her chair, bright white in the candles.

"Whoa," Étienne said.

"I bet you're pretty pleased with yourself," Neil grumbled.

"I'm just doing me," she said, totally without guile—and she was. We were tense and over-performing, after all; she was still and calm, holding court.

"Well. The dishes," Étienne said, getting up so quickly he bashed something—his knee or his elbow—on the table, and started stacking our plates. No matter what else he was thinking about or where his blood was pulsing, I knew he'd rush into the kitchen to rinse those plates, because he was also thinking about how quickly melted cheese hardens on ceramic. My heart hammered—throbbing with affection, throbbing with annoyance. Neil followed him inside. I took off my glasses and rubbed my eyes, my face hot and probably visibly flushed even in the dark.

"Look at me," she said, and we laughed.

"Oh, I am."

"You can't see," she complained.

"I'm farsighted. I can see up close," I explained, then: "I see everything I want to see."

And in a thunderclap moment, driven by a jolt of alien bravado—though in retrospect I understand she was guiding me along with neon-bright precision—I leaned in, in, in, into her cloud of perfume and hair-smell and smoke, and found her gentle soft skin, her nose, her lips. And as our boyfriends washed dishes and chatted loudly in the kitchen, their voices and not their words drifting out, her mouth moved and her hands found my face, and she kissed me back.

After the kiss, Erica acted like nothing had happened. It was so catalytic that I expected *something* to happen, but summer simply passed into fall. On October evenings after work, I'd lay my head on Étienne's shoulder, and we'd watch the sun set, and drink wine until he became restless, and shake me off. He'd suggest I trim my pubic hairs, dye my greys or try wearing makeup when we went out, and I'd accuse him of being in love with Erica: the more I pined for her, the more paranoid I grew that he was doing the same.

One cool evening Erica and I met at a dim bar on College Street, and she gulped vodka cranberries in smudgy glasses, and I sipped a beer. I told her about Étienne's cruel moods, and ached to kiss her again. She fiddled with her straw, her eyes wandering, then settling on the waitress. She winked, and they smiled at each other. The waitress had just rushed her third drink over, and I'd barely half-finished my first. Erica took a long drag from her straw, and interrupted me.

"You'd marry him just to spite him, and you're so *bored*. Aren't you?"

"I think he's bored. Has he said anything to you—is he bored?"

"*I'm* bored! I'm falling asleep just listening to you. You're bored, you're the one who's—it's you." She took another gulp, then coughed a little. "You're so bored it makes me existentially anxious," she said, and I wondered, stung, if this was another phrase she'd heard from Étienne. She got drunker and drunker, and eventually slapped the tabletop with her open palm, and insisted I leave him. She'd live with me, we'd cook for each other in her little apartment. *You know how well I take care of people*, she told me. I didn't speak to her for two weeks after that, which was agony—I lived for her. She was as much a feminist as me, as any smart Toronto girl at least pretends to be. Nevertheless she didn't understand what it's like for women like me, or even men like Neil. We pass through life like silt in a pool filter.

When I called her again she acted like no time had passed, warm and bubbling with news, most of which I already knew:

Neil had called me, unintelligible and wracked with yell-sobs, two nights in a row. She'd left Neil, she reported, and he'd splintered into twigs. (Of course.) She cared for him deeply and still spent the night sometimes, when he was feeling sad and needed her company. (Sounds healthy). She was bringing him some soup that afternoon, did I want to come along too, and surprise him? (I did not). Likely she'd not even noticed my absence. Likely had no idea I'd fumed on my own and maintained a perfect, icy silence.

I didn't really believe that, of course. I don't think I could have handled it.

On my thirty-sixth birthday, Étienne took me to Terroni's. I wore a gold-coloured disco dress he'd bought for me which, on its third wash, had gone grey. Halfway through our steaks, a waiter carried a thin slice of cake over to a nearby table, which had a small, bobbling cluster of balloons fastened to its edge. The waiter presented the cake, and a dressed-up woman at the table started crying. *You're still young. We all are,* her friend cooed, rubbing her silk-clad shoulder, and I thought, ah: she is turning thirty.

The next night I broke up with Étienne, and he sat at the very edge of our bed and didn't say much. I felt he wasn't sad for himself, really; he seemed mostly sad for me.

I went to our bathroom to wipe, and then examine, my face. Following my own eyes around my heavy features the mirror, I tried to read them as if examining a map, but really I was just following myself around—useless. By the time I returned to the bedroom, he'd shut off the lamp. I stepped in a soft pile of cloth, and then a hard, vacant object: his pants, his shoe. He stood tense and naked waiting for me, and his fingers found my neck and my shoulders, and the streetlight flashed on his watch. I yanked him to me. He scoured my neck with his teeth, and I pulled at his hair. Crushed up against his body and then the wall, I imagined he was raping me and I choked on purpose, an ugly, coughing sound. He didn't notice. I considered stiffening, screaming. I twisted my head and saw he'd closed the window, but so what if he'd left it open, and so what if I screamed? Our house sat at the rough edge of Chinatown, and it was the middle of the night. Who'd have done anything, if they'd heard?

And what could anybody have done for us?

"Where are you going?" he demanded, when we were done: I had rubbed my thighs dry enough to pull my panties back on, and then looked at him for the very last time—or so I thought.

"Who are you going to, this time of night? I should lock you out," he said, and I frowned at him.

"Why would you do that?"

"Because you're a spoiled brat!"

"Am I? Who spoiled me?" I asked, and he had no response.

"I love you," I said, and he took my hands, and told me he loved me too. For the next few weeks, he'd oscillate like that, as people do: it's hard to behave consistently when someone you love is leaving you. I withdrew my hands and pulled on my sweater, pleased with how thin my arms had become— as autumn stripped the leaves and love away, my escalating thinness would become my sole source of private pleasure. Étienne slumped on the cane chair near his window, a towel bunched up in his crotch. It's hard to describe the look he had, because you're not old yet, but it was bemused and not unpleased, with a little tilt, a dash of *I-told-you-so*. There he sat, suspended in something much bigger than him. And I insisted on kissing his tightly closed lips, still wet from me, and off I went, stiff as a mannequin, ignoring the passing buses as they grunted by, one by one.

I walked through white hoops of streetlight, the October leaves hissing around. Every shape and sound ballooned huge in the nighttime stillness. I walked and walked, my thighs numb and my arms pistoning along with me. I wasn't an engine like him, though—running on hot, endless combustion. What was I, then? A chimney? A weed?

I turned a corner onto a new street, along which the ground dropped away into a dense, deep black ravine, and then I saw it. Under a flickering streetlight a block ahead, two big male bodies were locked together, struggling. They seemed gigantic, dwarfing the trees that lined the ravine. I slid out from a pool of streetlight and pressed up against a black hedge, rapt, amazed. They were nearly silent, their faces bunched up tight. One man jerked violently, and then went limp up against the other. The victor eased him to the ground, wobbling a little under the weight, until the other man rested half-in, half-out of the gutter. Then he ran—dashing away from me, the ravine and his opponent—turned a sharp corner, and was gone.

I realized I'd pressed myself so far into the hedge, my hair had bound up with its thorns, and its branches had left deep tracks on my skin, reaching through the loose knit of my sweater. I ripped my hair away and sucked blood from my wrist, and then approached the man sprawled in the gutter, starting and stopping, until I stood over him. He lay wet in gutter leaves, edged with thick black mud. His teeth were bared and his eyes stared up into mine, until they didn't. His light-coloured shirt was soaked red-black, a stain growing between his left shoulder and where his left nipple would be. I understood later, with a jolt, that he'd probably been stabbed right through the soft underside of his armpit. In the streetlight his loafers gleamed bright green, and his ankle glowed white—no socks. And beside him on the sidewalk, right beyond his twitching fingertips, I saw a gun.

I was so self-absorbed, I think, that this memory holds less significance than what had transpired before, with Étienne. Someone died in front of me, and I remember it like a dream.

I wrapped my scarf around my hand, kneeled to pick up the gun and, fumbling only a little, wrapped it in the rest of the scarf. I placed the bundle in my purse, then ran for about a block before slowing to a walk again. Pressing up against the brick wall of a convenience store, I called Erica, over and over, until she picked up.

"What the hell, Shelagh?"

I could tell through the phone she'd been drinking for hours, and had just rolled into a deep blanket of sleep: the sleep of the dead, and the drunk.

"I left him. I left him! I only have my—my clothes, like the ones I was wearing when it happened. Can I stay with you?"

I heard a fumbling noise and then a rustle; she was rolling across her bed. "Yes, of course," she said. "I won't tell him you're here."

Three hours later I woke with a start on Erica's spindly couch, as the towels she'd covered me with slid to the ground. I unfolded myself and sat up, parting the blinds covering the small window nearby: it was so early there were still stars out. I could move to the other side of the world, find a town where women don't spoil like milk. I could quit my job, and find another one. I had lifted the lid off my life, and could rearrange the cogs and pathways exactly as I liked. I was ready to *happen* to people, just as the dying man had happened to me. You'll have to forgive me, I thought of life this way back then: horrific events unspooling in the news, the slow aging of my parents, and that man bleeding out into the sewer, all of it happened to me, equally important and unimportant as I kept on and on, obsessed with myself but simultaneously thinking myself passive, thinking myself invisible.

You see?

I didn't know how young I was.

Up until I met Erica, Étienne and I lived a quiet life that kept its shape wherever I went. I shrank from big social groups like house-fires and retreated for long hours alone, reproducing this topography everywhere and trudging through it blind. But I would have followed Erica anywhere, and for a long time—and to the detriment of my health and relationships—I did, moving into her tiny apartment, tracking her progress from odd job to odd job until she gave up, becoming first a scavenger, and then a thief. She stole laptop chargers and bags of weed from university libraries, and dresses from Anthropologie, and crystal wine glasses from upscale restaurants, then sold it all on Craigslist. She'd often return jumpy from these transactions, furious that her male pur-chasers could anticipate that she was a girl from the tone of her emails, and had conducted themselves accordingly. One guy refused to pay more than twenty dollars for a two-hundred dollar pair of loafers; another time she returned with her wrist bruised up, and didn't speak for a full day afterwards.

She then applied for welfare, and though she sobbed all through the preliminary phone assessment, she was immediately turned down. Her parents lived in Richmond Hill, she confessed afterwards, and technically they were considered, she admitted with some shame, to being wealthy. She sold a lot of my things, 'relieving me of the tyranny of my possessions,' which made sense, coming from her. She then took up pickpocketing from drunk people at the expensive clubs on King Street, and shocked me with how good at it she became. I'd stay up until dawn sometimes, waiting to hear the front door click shut. I'd listen to the thumps and tinkle of stolen wallets and snatched earrings as she emptied her pockets and purse all over the floor, each item plucked from the crowds washing tidal through the King West clubs I'd frequent all the time too, when I was in my twenties.

She returned one morning at around 5AM, clutching a limp black wallet and an iPhone in a diamond-patterned case. The grey dawn came in through the blinds on the kitchen window, settling in dashes across her face and neck. She looked tired enough to cry. We looked through the wallet, finding one compartment packed with fortune cookie papers, another with thirty US dollar bills, another stretched fat with small change. The driver's license revealed a plaintive looking young man with large eyes and a skinny neck: William Radner-Lohius, twenty-eight years old, sixty-eight inches tall.

"I know he looks like Bambi in this picture, but he was awful at the bar, so drunk, so sweaty, all hands," she said. The iPhone started ringing in her hands, and she dropped it. "I hate this," she said.

I was drinking milk from the carton one night, little sips, with the fridge door propped open against my stomach, keeping me cold. I wore only panties and a T-shirt. The fridge light illuminated a few floor tiles around my feet and the legs of a nearby chair, but nothing else really, so when the door banged open and Erica shrieked with laughter, I couldn't see anything except that she wasn't alone, two bodies silhouetted briefly as they fumbled together in the cold light of the hallway.

"I've been this tall since age *twelve*, no kidding," the guy slurred, and Erica clicked her tongue.

"That's so interesting! I can't imagine being so tall, so young."

"People stopped messing with me after that. And then I hit six-five around, like, first year undergrad," he continued. Erica turned on the living room lamp, and took his coat. "Wow. You could have killed it at basketball," she said. She tossed the coat over the couch, then leaned into him and kissed him. He wobbled a little, then grabbed her face in one hand, and gathered her ponytail in the other, bunching it into a fist. His hair was grey.

"I did, actually," he says. "Kill it at basketball. Didn't I tell you?"

She yanked him down by his tie, and kissed him again. They were very drunk, but they knew I was there—I could tell by how they weren't looking at me. She must've warned him I'd be home. Drinking milk, drinking tea, taking laxatives. Hurting myself to grow thin and then thinner, testing the remnants of youthful elasticity which once kept me firm as a flower stalk. I had turned thirty-six the week before, too old for this shit, but the hunger to attain girlishness never escapes you, no matter how far girlishness itself slips from you, a brief window of possibility for a select few, a ring of sun-kissed fawns, constantly replenishing.

"Arnaud, this is my roommate Shelagh," Erica said, gently freeing her hair from his fist. He glanced over at me, then looked me up and down. I'd sweated through the neck of the T-shirt, and my nipples were inexplicably hard. I plunked the milk container on the counter, and then went to my room.

"He was awful," I told her the next morning after he'd grabbed his sports jacket from the chair, tucked a cigarette behind his ear, and left.

"He paid me," she said.

"For—for dinner?"

"No." She shredded a piece of omelette. "He's so old he couldn't even *believe* my naked body, you know? And too drunk to want me more than once. Really we mostly talked, and then he slept. So peaceful—it was like he came over just to talk and sleep. He kept cupping my boobs really gentle, like they were something alive, and then letting them fall."

"You know he's probably married, right?"

"Oh yeah. He has a grown-up kid and like a wife. He golfs with friends, but he talks like he's just been released from solitary confinement. I like this, Shelagh. I'm not going to steal anymore."

"Jesus," I said.

"Do you want in?" she asked. "It'd be safer with a partner. Plus then, house calls."

I said yes right away, because then I'd be her *partner*, inexplicably bound together through danger and secrecy, sifting our bodies through the grey mesh of male hunger criss-crossing Toronto. Because then I'd get to see that body, cup those breasts and worship them too.

Because I was in love.

Loving Erica was such a costly imperative that losing everything else—my home, my boyfriend, my relative freedom—had happened and was OK, because I was buttressed by her focus and elevated by our intimacy, which fluttered around my ribcage whenever I was alone.

The following Saturday, she called me into her bedroom: another man in a suit was sitting cross-legged on the bed, one socked foot jiggling. He was loosening his tie, and looked me over. "Want a drink?" Erica asked us both, and darted out of the room.

"Come sit," the man said uncertainly, patting the bed. He was bald, and when I sat beside him, I saw a pale, pale layer of fuzz coated his skull, gathering thickest above his ears. The insides of his ears were the hairiest part of him. He had very pale blue eyes, and barely looked at me. He was sixty-five at least, but at thirty-six, I was too old for him.

Erica returned with three sweating cans of cider, one of which I'd noticed earlier, half-empty, warming on the sunny kitchen windowsill. The man accepted that particular cider, and allowed her to unbutton his shirt, then brush her mouth against his white, wiry loops of chest hair. His shrunken chest was very tan. He kissed her hungrily, his neck under his jowl crinkling like tissue paper, his dull pink tongue snaking into her mouth. He pulled her onto his lap, then grabbed my knee. I froze, and he pulled back from her a little, looking into her eyes.

"I've just gotta ask you whether, um," he said, wiping his mouth, "your friend is here for fun, or? Because I'm just paying for you."

"We're a package deal," she chirped, and I felt so nauseous I had to stand up.

"She's just kidding," I said. "I'm going to bed."

Even his subtle, very nice cologne couldn't mask the old-man smell, and his skin bunched loose around his gold rings, so they looked wedged on his fingers. He looked near death. I could imagine his grey, filed-down tooth nubs under the white crowns that clicked when he spoke. But he didn't want to fuck me because he thought I was too old. I was full of rage and so was he, the rage reserved for those who've had loved ones snatched by death, and those staring down death themselves. He looked at me, and saw himself burnt up in a vase, buried in the winter ground.

"Erica, I have a fucking *job,*" I said early the next morning, as she prepared omelettes and hummus toast for her and I. "You know? I don't need this crap."

"Oh god, I'm so sorry," she said, sucking egg off her palm. "I think he was really sick. He couldn't even get it up, you know? But listen: this is freedom. Right? You come home from that office every night just deflated. You spend all your daylight there, no windows, and they pay you *peanuts*. This way . . . we could sleep until the afternoon, if we wanted. Watch movies, paint our nails, make our own hours."

I wanted to become visible again, and accompany Erica through this big city packed with ugly romance—a romance born of the sheer fact that so many others were witnessing and sharing our experience. So I waited until the sky grew lighter, and then called in sick to work. I made more coffee and drank it all, and then, jittery, ate another slice of toast with some cottage cheese. Erica pulled on a ratty fur coat I'd given to her, which my tall, elegant mother had passed on to me, perhaps in a moment of cruelty—glamor is undeniable and elusive; it skips around. Erica looped her furry arm through mine, and we rode the streetcar down to Dundas Square. We strolled right past the mannequins and into Winners, and she found a bored-looking saleslady leaning heavily against a makeup counter.

"My friend's husband is an Egyptologist. Teach her how to look like Cleopatra," Erica instructed the saleslady. She meant Elizabeth Taylor as Cleopatra, I knew. Erica's fascination with old Hollywood beauties was an overwhelming, almost childlike adulation, perhaps because she was almost as pretty they were, and similarly buffeted by the desires of dull, toxic men. The saleslady tried her best, painting black wingtips at the corners of my eyes, feathering my hair with spray, finding an iridescent, emerald-green eyeshadow, and brushing powders along my cheekbones. She then produced a mirror, and I frowned. My lips, heavily greased, frowned back at me, and the bright blue eyeshadow made my eye sockets seem even more sunken than usual. How is it possible not to get your hopes up in moments like these, even when you're old?

We then ate sushi in a small basement restaurant at Dundas and Spadina, my shopping bags perched on my knees. Whenever a man glanced over I practiced meeting his eyes for a beat like Erica could, calm and firm, before looking away. After a while, I realized there was nothing to it. Each man assessed us together, as we were sitting side-by-side in our booth, occasionally grasping hands. Every time she laughed, she tipped her head back and black fillings peeked from the back of her mouth. Erica and me.

We got our nails done after lunch. A redheaded girl pressed acrylic nails over my own, then painted them with candy-stripes. Beside me, Erica released little flashes of patchouli scent whenever she tossed her hair. Steam laced the air, gathering in near-opaque clouds over some hairstylists' chairs. I sipped black coffee and blinked my heavy green eyelids in the smudged-up mirror, nice and slow.

The next day I came home after work, and called out for Erica. "Are you home?"

"Just a moment," she called through the door, in a shitty French accent, and a man mumbled something. Erica emerged from her bedroom with a short man in a white linen suit. His hair was jarringly jet black and looked a little off—was he wearing a wig?

"*Cherie*, ah must meet wiz my business partnair now," she purred at him. "Just put—yes, that is right, just slide it there, under the lamp. OK, *bon soir*!"

"*Bon soir*? It's only 4 o'clock," I said, after he'd left. She sighed, counting the money. "Oh, whoops. He really likes French-Canadian girls. But he wouldn't know the difference, he doesn't know a word of French. He couldn't even figure out the tip on three beers without whipping out his phone."

"What's with his hair?"

She smiled benignly. "I kept it safe for him on my desk."

"I knew it!"

Erica pulled me into her bedroom, which was even more disastrous than usual. I sat cross-legged on the very edge of her plush, satiny bed, and opened my laptop on my lap, ignoring the sex smell dissipating from the air. One of her pillows was folded in half, and visibly wet.

"We'll go online," she said, pacing, twisting the money between her fingers. "Craigslist. I don't want to keep hanging around those bars, I end up wasting money on those awful drinks. Like I had just one martini last night, when I met Andy," and she gestured out towards the door, indicating that he was the same man with the janky wig. "And it was *fourteen dollars*. No olives, even. Plus the Uber drive down."

"*I'm playful and fun, but I have my own life, and respect discretion*," I dictated as she lay back on the bed, typing and nodding along, and chipping nail polish off her toes. I watched her toes out of the corner of my eye, thinking: *If I had feet that cute I would wear barely-there sandals, read books in bars, and meet people with no effort.* As it was, at the conclusion of each day at the office, I washed everyone else's dishes before shutting off the lights.

"And a headline?" she asked, and I sighed. "I'm sure whatever is fine," I said, and she slid her laptop over to me, then sat up and leaned over my shoulder. She made a small exasperated noise at what I'd come up with ("COME PLAY").

"This isn't a joke," she said, "This is serious. Look——" and she showed me a dick picture she had just received on her phone, the penis itself purplish and near palpably trembling in the left hand of the sender. The base of his ring finger was lined with a lumpy Band-Aid.

"Take it as serious as *he* does," she instructed.

We sat together late into the night, and though my elastic youth was nearly gone hers remained, that terrifying power that, at the dawn of every generation, seems certain to tear us all down.

An hour later, she yelled out to me: "Shelagh? Got a pen?"

I did. She came to her doorway and, running her fingers through her hair with one hand, she gave me an address, a room number, and a name: Paul Smith.

"I don't think Smith is his last name," I said, and she laughed.

"I doubt Paul is his *first* name! He says he's a scientist, though. Astrophysics, so that's nice."

"That's nice," I agreed.

"He wants you for 7PM. You call me on the hour, every hour. You don't do that, I call the cops with an anonymous tip. All right?"

"Is that a hotel, this place?" I asked.

It was in fact a motel, squat and brown and swallowed up in concrete, right out near Downsview Airport, where everything is kilometres away from everything else. Paul was waiting for me in Room 9, playing solitaire with battered cards on a fake wood table near the coffee machine. He was one of countless unattractive men you see hunched between filing cabinets, driving trucks, restoring carpets, fixing vacuum cleaners. The kind of men the world seems packed full of, who lie dead for weeks before the smell reaches their neighbours. But then again, maybe he wasn't so bad-looking—I never can tell with men. At least he had his clothes on.

He stood up, walked over, and grasped both my elbows gently; I could tell from his face that he'd never hurt a woman in his life. He didn't know how to proceed, and I realized with a rush like ice water that *shit*, neither did I. "Do you mind if we eat?" I asked.

"That is a great idea," he said, in a more gregarious voice than I was expecting. He had, I think, a Russian accent. "My treat, of course. I want to celebrate."

"Celebrate what?" I said, a little resentfully.

"There will be a solar flare tonight," he said. "Chances are, it'll miss the earth completely. Not a big deal to most earthlings, I'm afraid."

I didn't know what a solar flare was—or what'd happen if one didn't miss the earth—but I sure as hell wasn't asking. "How do you know that?" I asked.

"Satellites," he said, vaguely.

What a shitty celebration, I thought. Who'd pick a beat-down motel, and a bony escort over thirty? Maybe he'd stayed here before, perhaps attending a conference, eating spongy sandwiches from a tray and falling asleep in rough sheets, his head full of stars. Maybe this motel, my company, and a meal was just great, compared to whatever else he'd seen.

The motel restaurant was in fact a pub, and exactly what I liked. It was dark, but full of colour once my eyes adjusted: a flickering neon sign behind the bar, the pilling green felt of a pool table. The place was nearly empty, and the bartender waved us in with a thin, hairy arm. My heart leapt with joy, sudden and strange. I didn't know how free I was, back then; you only learn that later, when real age piles on like rocks.

"Tell me more about the satellites," I said.

"We've got a satellite that detects these kinds of storms a few days before it hits," he said, taking a tiny sip of his beer. "The satellite is a million miles away from Earth, if you can imagine this."

"How long did it take the satellite to get there?"

"Eleven years."

"Just to *get there*?"

"How long do you think it'd take you to drive a million miles? Or run?"

"A lot less if there's nothing in my way. There aren't even oceans out there."

"All of it is an ocean, yeah? And we are dust."

He must think like this always, which exhausted me to contemplate. So I started talking about tactile, simple things: how does his meat pie taste; does my hand feel clammy; look at that woman's bag over there, it's embroidered "GWENDOLYN" in shaky yarn letters—somebody loves her.

"I think if *I* ran all my life, I'd get far," I said, quite drunk. "Mars. Or the one with the rings—Saturn? Because . . ."

"Because?"

"Because I have faith in myself." I thought of Erica, and smiled a sloppy smile.

"If *you* ran all your life? Hm." He looked at my legs, as if actually assessing my musculature and capability. He sipped his coffee and I realized I liked his lips: they were large, chapped and soft-looking. "Assuming sixty years of running ten hours a day, let's say 1,5330,00 kilometers. So you could reach the Voyager satellite, let's say."

"But no coming home."

"Well if return journeys really matter to you, let's see…you could run to the moon, and come back to Earth. Then change your mind and run back to the moon, and then make it nearly home again."

I imagined myself floating dead in space, my sneakers on and strands of my ponytail drifting in and out of my opened mouth, having stopped just short of Earth's bright atmosphere. "Why would I do that?" I asked.

He smiled at me. "Why indeed?"

I drained my glass, feeling suddenly as spooked by the inches of space between us both as the vast distance from the moon to Earth.

Back in the room, we fucked. He cooed appreciatively over my thinness, grasping my thighs with his soft hands, pantomiming resistance on my part, so he might overpower it. His penis was smallish and had an odd shape, and I shocked myself with how wet I was—wet enough to make a rhythmic sucking noise as he fucked me, slick long strands of wetness gluing his thighs to mine, my thighs to each other, my asscheeks to the mattress. *Aaah, aahh, ahhh,* he went, no longer translating from Russian to English before he spoke, and I pressed my face into his shoulder and shuddered. *Call me Pavel,* he whispered, so I gasped his real name into the overripe flesh of his shoulder. It died on my tongue—why was I embarrassed?—and so I tried again. *Pavel, Pavel.*

Candy, he groaned into my hair, expelling heat and wet into my ear, tightening his grip on my thigh, my neck. I remembered that 'Candy' was the name Erica and I both gave, in our ads. Coming from him, it felt like my real name, perhaps—but not only—because he believed it was. At one point he pulled out and rolled his balls back and forth in three shaking fingers, and I throbbed in his brief absence, squeezing in on myself.

Afterwards we lay in our wet patches and he praised me, saying I hadn't once checked my phone, that I was so present. Saying that he was a busy guy, and lonely too (if I could believe it) and so when he wanted companionship, he wanted the whole person. He smiled at me by pressing his lips together hard, and rubbed sweat from his short, spiked hair. I thanked him, though really I'm on the internet all day, and even then I felt pings of desire for my phone, nestled safe and alluring in my purse.

"It breaks your brain," he said, miming typing on a computer. "It looks like a real world, behind that screen, but it is a deception. Mimic only."

And since he paid me to stay, he slept beside me in those grey sheets, his head shut off, and his body hot. I lay awake, thinking: I stay in hiding for most of my time. Internet addiction feels good, and starving makes those long hours, watching videos and not eating, feel active and intense. Digging through Erica's stuff the other day, I found a dog-eared tech magazine from December 1995, with *Joey Reiser* written in red pen inside the cover. The magazine heralded the incumbent 'Net', back when normal people understood it—vaguely, and on the horizon—as a series of tubes, imagining them crystal-clear and buried beneath the ocean. A silver dust of excitement puffed up from the pages, elucidating a magnificent library of Babel on the horizon. With the same red pen, Joseph had underlined and annotated passages in the magazine, in a script I couldn't decipher.

Reading that magazine I felt despair, but also amusement. What these scientists didn't anticipate, salivating over universal connectivity, was the baseness coiled at the core of each of us— guiding us from the moment we wake to the last breath we take, before trusting our bodies to sleep. We've proved the same as lab rats, pawing at pleasure pedals over and over, until we can't really move. We soiled the promise, all of us: people don't care for the utopian future dreamed up in the hermetic world of scientists like Paul, and scientists like Paul ignore the ugly, lazy, unremarkable nature of people. They live in the world, but not as we do—as prophets, as monks, as ghosts.

A fiery red light burst through the room, jarring Paul awake. I screamed and dug my nails into his arm, and confess I pissed a little, soaking the mattress. Something banged in the hallway, and somebody else shrieked. He yanked himself free. "It's happening. The flare!" Paul yelled. He jumped out of bed, and hopped up and down on the balls of his feet. He yanked open the blinds, exposing a mass of people dashing through the parking lot to their cars. His naked chest, arms and stomach shone bright red.

Later I'd learn that the Rocky Mountains had flared so bright all nearby forests glowed like day, and miners woke to prepare their breakfasts. I'd learn that aurorae scrolled through the sky, bright red over Toronto, green-white over Shanghai. I'd be able to visualize the electronic grid flicking out across North America—which lay in shadow—bathing office buildings and animals and people and highways in soft, shifting light. Erica, wherever she was, disentangling her body from a man's and rushing to a window, looking up in wonder.

And an hour later, when the millions and millions of Toronto lights would flicker back on, as the electric grid roared awake and ripped lightning through the city, I would sprint from the room with Paul yelling after me—"Candy! Your money!" I would yank out my phone and call Erica over and over, at least two hundred times, maybe more. And I would run and walk and run again, along the highway and then through city streets, dashing through people smashing windows and spray-painting fences and writhing with excitement. And she wouldn't pick up, but as her phone would ring and ring I'd speak anyway, babbling and crying with a kind of relief I'd never know again. Running and walking and then running again for kilometres and kilometres, I'd finally find myself by the entrance our apartment building. I'd gaze up at the tiny yellow square of our kitchen window. And only then I'd hang up.

But for now I just watched Paul yank up his boxers, and run out into the parking lot. I followed him, bringing my purse with me. A trio of raccoons dug through a burst garbage bag beside a dumpster, unfazed. He watched the magnificent sky and I watched their eyes glisten, as they sifted coffee grinds and bright yellow noodles through their paws. Across the road a final street-light whined, and then clicked out. I placed my hand on Paul's shoulder, and we stood together like that, watching the massive aurora twist through the stars.

THE WATCHERS I: EASY FOR HER TO SAY

By now, I bet everyone has a Synthpal[1], but I've had Buppy since before I can remember. When I was six he explained to me, gently, why the trees were dying, when nobody else would; he celebrated the scant birds' nests and anemic clumps of flowers we'd find. Buppy is my best friend.

From his perch on my lap, Buppy projects article after article across the wall, and I dig through Mom's ancient tablet, clacking my nails on the glass. We haven't spoken in at least an hour. The tree branches rattle against the window; just like last summer, they're completely bare. We hear someone walking toward the living room, and so Buppy immediately switches the grainy newsprint and faded-out photos to a vivid clip of two naked girls wrestling in a plastic kiddie pool full of shiny, bright orange guck. One girl scoops up some dirt from beside the pool, and grinds it into the other girl's hair, who then roars and beats her collarbone with her fist.

It's just Mo: he wanders into the room and stands beside us, pulling some stuffing from a rip in the couch, watching the wall.

"The orange stuff is cheese," Mo says. "I love this show."

He trudges into the kitchen. "Spaghetti-Os?" he calls out, and I ignore him: I know we've been out of Spaghetti-Os for weeks, and chances are, so's the rest of Toronto—maybe even Canada.

"Are you even allowed to be watching that show. Abby?" Mo yells from the kitchen. "You're what, thirteen?"

"Ha, ha," I say, rolling my eyes. "And you're what, fifty?"

Buppy switches off the show and the newsprint appears huge on the wall again, and we sit quietly, scanning the faded-out

[1] A synthetic robotic companion, descendent of Japanese family companion robot Jibo.

words, the occasional, dust-flecked photo. Suddenly I see a name I recognize, and gasp.

"Get this! '*By the seventh of January last year, Joseph Reiser re-entered Ontario with a new name and a stolen social insurance number, blah blah . . . Reiser and his seedling cult have exploded into ghoulish overnight fame, greatly exacerbated by the Internet.'*"

"Well that is an irony he could have appreciated," Buppy says, then pauses, analyzing my reaction of his performance of humour.

"That's not irony," I say, like I know what irony means anyway, and we're quiet for a while until I find something else.

"What the fuck is this? The journalist *sympathizes* with him! '*Born in 1983, Reiser would tell his family he felt born too late. "He refused learning to type or to use the computer," recalls his mother Joanne, a soft-spoken grade school teacher still teaching at the same Scarborough elementary school Reiser attended."'* Well, that isn't creepy at all."

"Keep going."

" ' "*He would say to me, 'Mum, I wish I was alive when knights and bandits were riding through the forest, and the forest was everywhere.' He'd refuse to draw if he ran out of green crayons—which he often would, just filling pages and pages with 'grass' scribbles until he was down to the nubs. There's a big apartment building you can see from our backyard, and often I'd find him just staring up at it. I would ask him what he was looking at. Sometimes he'd say he was counting the windows, but I felt he was lying to me. Sometimes he'd say, 'I'm imagining the sky behind it.' I guess that was much closer to the truth . . ."'*"

"What you're saying is that lots of horrible people were cute children once, correct?"

"And white men who do inexplicably awful things are framed like this all the time. Some creepy uncle interviewed later in the piece suggests that, if Reiser stuck around Toronto a little longer, he'd have urged the kid to join the military to, hold on . . . '*Straighten out and do some good in Afghanistan.*' Like, the war."

"Yikes."

"And then here's another article, same vibe: the guy rattles on about Reiser's higher-than-average grades in biology and

English, and how shy he seemed to be, keeping mostly kept to himself, except for that super tight little group of friends. Here's his mom again: '"*I'd come home to see the four of them sitting around on my couch and on my floor, and they'd fall silent right away, like someone plunked a jar over them.*"'

"That strikes me as bizarre behaviour. It is, isn't it?"

"Oh yeah . . . um: '*Reiser's extracurricular activities add a startling dimension to the story . . .*' Oh my god! He was a boy with '*large metaphysical concerns and whimsical sensibilities.*' Then they talk about building the greenhouse in the backyard of his childhood home, '. . . *fashioned entirely from materials pilfered from nearby home renovations and dumpsters. Upon its completion, the group spent most evenings in the greenhouse, learning about regeneration*' which—all together now!—isn't creepy at all!"

A new article flashes across the wall, and several sentences jump out, highlighted in yellow. "Here's an interview with some of the friends."

"They're still *alive?*"

"They were then, presumably. Listen"—and he reads the parts he's highlighted—"'"*We'd watch the sun set and the stars coming out through that plastic sheeting, which we found and stitched together ourselves,*" one surviving member of this little 'group,' Cora, reveals. "*We didn't spend money on a thing except some of the seeds,*" explains another group member, Kayla. "*Because obviously, where are you going to find orange trees in Toronto?*"

"'"*Initially, to me . . . I hoped the greenhouse would be a place for us to get high in secret, maybe fool around, and just like hang out,*" 'Kayla' explains—"'"

"OK Bups, I like Kayla."

"'Kayla recalls sensing weeks of careful observation before Reiser even spoke to her. "*He was very serious, a very serious kid. When you're kids you're always trying this or that, you stick your feet in the water to see what washes off. Most things do. But Joseph was always a very serious little kid . . . everything stuck to him.*"'"

"Jesus, OK: the term 'kids,' and several cute little variants, have shown up twenty times in these articles so far. I counted."

"You counted?"

"Keep reading."

"'*Speaking with Cora and Kayla, one senses the portentous nature of the greenhouse activities: the group spent nearly every afternoon and evening in the greenhouse, throughout which Reiser would read out loud, 'monologue' while holding hands with each group member, and conduct one-on-one conversations that were sometimes 'nice' but would reportedly 'get emotional.' Neither woman revealed much more, except that Cora mentions frequent discussion of early childhood.*

"'*In addition to these activities, the group would tend to the array of plants, which included tomatoes, butter lettuce, green beans, strawberries, even a small pineapple tree. "It became like a little world, a jungle, you could barely see anything outside," Cora explains—*'"

"Boring, plants, whatever. What about Reiser's mom? Search 'Joanne Reiser'."

More articles flash across the wall. "Let's see . . . '*Joanne Reiser has refused ongoing requests to be interviewed about the unfolding situation, or any events in Reiser's life following his childhood . . .*' and, '*. . . after a preliminary interview, Joanne Reiser had at first agreed to speak again with this reporter in order to clarify 'misunderstandings about my son's later life,' but Reiser's lawyer has since advised against further contact with the media . . .*' and, '*Joanne Reiser will show the greenhouse to anybody—media or otherwise—who "asks nicely and seems safe."*'"

"Aww."

"Abby, there's a video that appears associated with this article. Would you like to watch it?"

"Oh my god. Play it!"

The newsprint dissolves, and in its place a lone bungalow appears against the wall, tiny and worn in a street of bright, renovated giants. The greenhouse dwarfs the bungalow and encompassing most of the backyard. The plants and sheeting are long gone, but the structure withstood years of winters without any upkeep on her part—I'm assuming. The camera pulls in on Joanne Reiser resting her hand on a blackened support beam, squinting up at the peak of the roof. "This thing sprang up like a mushroom," she says in a lower voice than I expected, "and it's been here almost twenty years, why take it down now? You only have one life."

When the journalist, a peppy-seeming woman with disconcertingly white teeth, presses Resier for clarification—"what do you mean, only one life?"—Reiser takes a minute, perhaps weighing the sensations of her Victoria Park neighbourhood, the buzz of late summer cicadas, the cries of children playing street hockey, against the anomaly of her son. "By only one life I mean . . . eighteen years this thing has been here," she says. "Like me, like my home. And yet it's just yesterday I watched them build it."

The journalist interrupts her here, rattling on about the size and durability of the remaining structure. I imagine that, as Reiser presses her forehead against that support beam, she tunes Brown out, marvelling instead at the collapsible nature of time. She speaks up again, just once: "Sixteen years it was just him and I, Caroline. Then this, and then he's gone, and I try not to think too much about it. Then eighteen years pass, and that's been my life . . ."

"And that's just life," the journalist says, which is easy for her to say.

"That's life," Reiser agrees.

LOGAN: A KNOWING IN OUR BONES

One morning Erica and I sit together on the bed. We listen to Joseph reciting his Morning Talk downstairs. It almost sounds like he's hypnotizing himself as Erica pulls my head down to her tits. I suck on her nipples and then kiss them both, a light little kiss each. She sighs. "Thank you," she says. She pulls away and crouches down, then drags a suitcase out from under the bed. She unzips it and takes out a beat-up box, and opens that. I look inside and see a bunch of tissue paper, and some stacked things made of cloth.

"I keep little dolls. How creepy is that?" she says. She takes one out, and hands it to me. It feels dense, like it's stuffed with pebbles, and I try imagining her as a kid and playing with this doll in particular, though it doesn't look much different from the others. I can't imagine it, partly because it's impossible to imagine her as a child, and also because the doll has such a serious, old-fashioned lady face. "That's not creepy," I say. "Did your mom give them to you?"

She balances the box on her bare thighs and lifts out another doll, and rubs its head with her finger. "I'd like to say I did," she says. "It'd be less weird then, right? Truth is, I never had dolls as a kid, and I bought these guys for a dollar each at a garage sale, just five years ago. They're not even the whole set—I only bought as many as I had cash for. Eleven."

I think of Brook's toy-box—which was always hers long after she left—and remember the ruined Barbies inside, poking up like bright pink spears from the mass of other stuff, the tangled skipping ropes and the stinky uncapped markers. "I didn't play with dolls either," I say, then look in the box again. It looks pretty full to me.

"Seems like you got enough, anyway," I say, and she giggles, then walks over to the windowsill and places one doll right on the edge, so it's sitting up. In the sun it looks especially raggedy, and sort of mean. I realize I'm leaning sideways, so it'll feel like it's looking at me. "At my old place, I'd keep them on the sill like that," she says, softly.

"It's weird, I want to imagine you playing with them as a kid, but I guess you didn't," I say. I take one of the dolls from the box on the floor, then drop it—except for its plastic head and hands, which stick out of its little dress, its body is totally deflated. She took all the stuffing out.

"What's with this one?" I ask, and she laughs again, and then almost says something. She takes the other doll from the windowsill, and then shrugs.

"I'm going to stuff it with something else," she says.

"Like what?"

"Oh, something to remember. Like writing in the margins of a good book, and sticking things in it too, like movie tickets and birthday cards, then discovering it again on the shelf years later, and experiencing that time in your life all over again. That's a nice feeling, isn't it?"

"I really wouldn't know," I say, and she looks a little embarrassed.

"How about finding a ten-dollar bill in your coat pocket when you take it out of storage in the early winter, right? Like that. I'm so grateful for our communal life, and happy to share with everyone every day, but I need to keep some part of my mind to myself." She takes the doll from me and puts it back in the box, then slides the box and suitcase back under the bed. "Let's go downstairs and start breakfast," she says, stepping over to me, standing on her tiptoes a bit, and kissing my forehead.

Some days I feel so tired I sit down by the nearest hydroponic tank, watching the blue light dance over the lettuce leaves, watching all the white roots drift thin as hair through the water, and I can't decide: are they are moving a little, or is it me?

Once, Erica finds me there, and finally loses her temper. "You're watching that tank like it's the Northern fucking Lights."

For the first time, I wonder if she's jealous. She sighs and lies down, and I watch her thighs relax and wonder who else has fucked her. Did she have a husband before this? Did she have a good job, did she come from money? She's the type that always expects the worst from people, and won't demand any better. Girls like her have cropped up everywhere I've been: in my grade ten math class, crying openly over a missed test (though I saw her gleefully cutting class that day); in the sandwich assembly line with me, insisting she's breaking out in hives from handling the tomatoes (through her latex gloves); taking her time washing mugs at the coffee shop, moody and difficult (because she's in love with a regular customer, who is obviously married). Girls like her stick to me like mud. You feel sad for them every time, overwhelmed as they are by the same stuff you do—which looks easy to them, when you do it. Eventually you learn that they eat your pity, and then resent you for providing it.

We doze and I wake up and she's leaning over me, breathing hot into my eyes and nose, making a horrible face. I stifle a shriek and she jumps away, entirely blue in the grow lamp, and starts sniffling, rubbing her face in her sleeping bag. "I'm sorry," she says.

"I thought you were all about, like, helping me," I say, and then listen to the tank aerating for a moment, calming myself down. "I'm not going to tell on you," I say.

The next day, Erica hardly speaks, and Joseph watches us very, very closely: he watches us at breakfast, when Erica starts sobbing during his Talk about Transformative Love and the Chosen vs. Birth Family, he watches us during Sharing (in which Erica Shares, in a little voice, about being a kid and letting her parents down with bad marks), and he watches as we work together out in the Greenhouse, during which Erica is very careful with me, and I'm very polite to her. "It's really cold today," Joseph says, and Erica suggests he go inside, to warm up and get started on dinner. He drops his pruning shears in the dirt, and Erica picks them up. We watch him go, and then Erica turns to me.

"Do you hate women?" she asks.

"What? No," I say. "I was raised by my mother. I've always had lots of girl friends."

She looks at the kitchen window—so quickly I almost miss it—and then places both hands on my shoulders. "I don't want you to feel ashamed," she says. "But I know Joseph takes you sometimes, when I'm not around. And first and most importantly, if it's not consensual, you must tell me. OK? You *must*. Tell me, and we will go from there."

"Uh—"

"If it *is* consensual, you can always talk to me about it, but don't bring it up during Talks. I'm not sure about Joseph's stance on me knowing, and so I'd feel most comfortable requesting an open Conversation, maybe during Sharing. Joseph feels the Family Dynamic is very fragile at this stage, especially with developments that aren't Shared openly with all Members."

"Oh, no," I say, feeling annoyed, then feeling bad about feeling annoyed. "We're not. It's not that."

She looks at me for a while, her little hands gripping my shoulders. I stare down at her, she stares up at me, and my belly swells between us both. "OK," she says finally. "I don't know much about her, but I know your mother is very special," she continues, turning away to pull some shrivelled beans from the plant. "You should treat her like she is, because she is. Something happens to girls as they grow older, and you don't know that yet. I hope you don't mind me saying so—you only know it by going through it. She's seen a lot, and she's tired."

Since they seem about the same age, I ask Erica if she's tired too. "I'm, uh . . ." she says, trailing off, then gives her little laugh. "Sorry. No, I'm not tired. People handle disappointment and heartbreak in different ways, you know? Back in Toronto, I'd see people walking around *all* emotion, like churning balls of chemical reactions bound up in bodies, some more tightly controlled than others. I pretend I don't see it, but I do. Being needed tires some people out, especially if you can't see that's what's going on."

"Not you though, right? Joseph says you live to love. He says you're a mother to the world, and the matriarch of the Family."

She smiles, like I knew she would. "That is a kind thing to say," she says, "but it's weird to hear it. I mean on one hand it describes me perfectly: I guess I've mothered everyone I've, um, been with." She looks over at the window again. "So maybe it shouldn't feel wrong, since it's true."

"Then why does it feel wrong?" She keeps looking beyond me and back at the house, and seems to either shiver or shrug. Joseph's light-coloured head bobs up and down in the kitchen window, the kitchen itself almost black behind him, open wide as a mouth.

"Because when someone else describes me that way, even the person who knows me best in the world, it's not . . . total," she says slowly. "A total description would include things from all over my life—my present and my future, not just my past— all the little details, all the things that would make those truths sound wrong to you, too. Do you understand?"

"My mother would," I say. I'm not sure I know what I mean, but Erica does. I see understanding blip across her face, and I recognize it, and then maybe I know something, too.

There are many ways of knowing the world, all waiting to come alive in your subconscious, Joseph said yesterday, during Communion. For centuries and centuries, Erica told me later, privately—like she was telling me a secret—women weren't allowed to write books or write in diaries, to write anything.

But still we passed on knowing, we passed it between among another other, across continents and from generation to generation, even beyond death.

A knowing in our bones.

SHELAGH: BAD NEWS

When I got back to the kitchen Erica was drunk, with lip-stick smeared on her neck. I was breathing so hard my chest and stomach burned, and my sweat-slick face must have frightened her. She poured me some water, sloshing it into a mug.

"Were you with that guy—Paul Smith? When it happened, the power outage?"

I grabbed her wrist and told her it can't happen again.

"You get away with it despite yourself," I said.

She yanked her arm away, stepped back and rubbed her little nose, assessing me. I had an awful, dizzy moment—*me*, why would she listen to me?

"You think I have it easy," she said. "Don't you? But I'm twice as tired as any girl my age. I've been running on adrenaline for fifteen years. You know what I—uh." She looked over her shoulder, then drained her drink, like words had come out by accident and all she had wanted to do was drink in silence.

"I've been hungry enough to kill birds and eat them. Pigeons," she says. "I'm sick and I don't know what it is. Every other day, I think OK: this is it, I'm dying."

I felt a rush of anger, coming up so fast my hair shook. "What if it's all in your head, like really severe anxiety? Remember what that doctor said last month? What if you stopped drinking?"

"How *dare* you," she said, but her lips parted. I knew by then that she couldn't resist brutes, or being adored.

"You won't go hungry now. But you will stop it with these men, you understand? You're not too good for normal work. And I will take care of you."

"Why would you do that?" she asked.

"Oh fucking come on," I said, stepping towards her. "Because we are in love with each other."

"Is that what this is?"

"Yes," I said. "Yes, baby." It sounded a little funny, coming from me to a woman. But she would make it not ridiculous. I needed her desperately, and she knew I did, and on her face I saw a change. She was making up her mind to love me back, without knowing it. By next week she would think she had wanted me, loved me, all along.

"Baby," she repeated, softly.

Ten minutes later, in her smelly bed: we kissed, I grabbed her face, and she grabbed mine. We pulled back and laughed because there was so much hair getting in our mouths, and we wiped each other's faces, and then leaned back in again. She was so soft, she was so delicate, a bunch of birds in a silken bag beating their wings, struggling to get loose—a *woman*. I pulled up her shirt and felt her ribs; I pulled up her dress, and her thighs were firm and I scraped the skin with my nails, and she moaned and flinched. Right before every kiss, I felt a vertiginous rush: was it OK to do this? To look at her breasts, to accept her tongue in my mouth? She grabbed for my nipples like a boy, yanking them from my shirt and squeezing them both at once, and I giggled until I saw how serious she was. She was quieter than I thought she'd be, but whimpered consistently as she stretched her body along mine, one moment draping herself over my back, the next moment turning me over, climbing on top of me. I wasn't sure that this was sex, but I was no longer certain that the sex with Paul earlier, the rhythm of his small penis inside me, was sex either.

We fell asleep, and woke again. It was still dark.

"You shouldn't want to be with a girl. Girls aren't good to each other," she said.

"Why?" I found her eyes, reflecting the dim light from the window.

"They leave you for men. They get angrier than men, they stay angry longer, and then the anger turns into other things that don't go away." She stroked my hair as she spoke. "And they take a long time to tell you bad news."

It took her months and months to tell me her bad news, but she left signs everywhere. She would go out with men as much as she could, it seemed. She drank more and more, leaving dozens of wine glasses and mugs around the house, sticky with booze and dried-up lemon slices, attracting clusters of fruit flies. When she'd run out of cranberry juice to mix her drinks she'd make tea and pour vodka in it, claiming she couldn't leave the house if she hadn't had at least one drink to calm her nerves. And strange letters started coming, each one packed with many sheets of paper and sealed with wax. Sometimes postcards came too; one day, I managed to read one before she came home.

One side of the postcard featured a photograph of hilly countryside, covered in trees all vibrant with autumn colours. A long body of water stretched beneath the trees, reflecting back the bright oranges and yellows and faint greens, shining silver-black in a shadowy inlet. 'La Belle Provence' was printed in a red cursive font in the corner. I flipped over the card and my throat closed up: 'The goldfinches are here again, eating sunflowers seeds from my hand. Did you know I harvest them from the flowers you planted? They come back every year. The chickadees sing all day, remember their song? The water at the riverbanks, it moves slow right here, and quickens downriver. The water makes a sound so soothing it is almost an absence of sound. I am fine, thank you. And you belong here.'

I left the postcard on the kitchen table, and later that night she came home, paused and picked it up, then went to her room, which we now shared. She then spread a bunch of the letters on our bed like a second quilt, rereading them one at a time. I kept passing the bedroom to catch glimpses of this, and on my third circuit she spotted me, and nudged the door shut with her foot. She got up only once, to stew lentils and stir-fry some vegetables for dinner, and I drifted into the kitchen to watch. Wasn't I angry? Of course I was. But like with Étienne, kissing my hands and telling me he loved me the night I left, real anger hadn't caught up with me yet.

"When they say low heat, do you think they mean more like medium, or low?" she asked, dangling the package in front of her face (I'd long suspected, and she'd long denied, that she was growing near-sighted).

"Well jeez, I don't know," I said, rolling my eyes, and she giggled. "They mean low, baby," I said.

"That's why I love you," she said easily, scraping the vegetables around in the pan.

"And why's that?" I asked before I could stop myself, taking the package out of her fingers and kissing her hand. She turned back around to stir her lentils, and I leaned my chin against her shoulder, becoming a little unnerved by her composure.

"You're really hot," she said, squirming a little, and I let go. "I mean, with the stove, it's a bit much," she added, looking around at me with eyes full of pity and anxiety, and I froze through to my bones. She turned back around.

"You sure you don't need any help?" I asked after a long moment, and she stifled a sigh.

"You can, I don't know, chop something. Maybe garlic? The repetitive activity might feel nice."

Before I left the kitchen I put my hands on her shoulders and kissed her right on the mouth, just to see her flinch.

Back in the living room I ordered pizza and stared at the wall until it arrived, then sank deep in the couch to eat it, burning the roof of my mouth, growing sluggish with thick dough and sweet tomato sauce and liquefying meat and salt. Growing full and then overfull, the ache now refocused in my corporeal self, my chest and belly, I felt the rush, the comfort-high, that always chased the shame: I had gained half a pound that week, and was making myself fatter still. Overfull and ashamed, I remembered that in tenth grade I had loved a boy so much I knew I'd have to switch schools before something horrible and life-ruining burst out of me, swarming from my chest like bone-house wasps. My shirt would go transparent with sweat minutes before our classes together, and whenever he spoke my tongue swelled up balloon-like, and I'd rush to the bathroom. Just thinking about him I'd blush right down to my breasts, a sensation as humiliating as wetting myself.

One airless winter afternoon he left class without his sweater, leaving it crumpled beneath a chair. I waited until the teacher was distracted, then sidled over to his chair and stuffed the sweater in my backpack, thrumming with guilt and excitement. I shut myself in a bathroom stall, dumped my sandwich in the toilet and wrapped the sweater in the plastic shopping bag instead, to preserve its smell. In my room that evening I unwrapped the sweater and laid it out on my bed, extending the sleeves and flattening the creases. I ran my fingertips down those sleeves over and over, tugging slightly. I brought my nose to the fabric and sniffed, smelling lunch meat and pencils and backpack fabric—mildewed from winter damp—and also, lingering near the armpits and neck-hole, something else, something new and other and *good*. Alone like this, I could control that goodness, I could make it last as long as I wanted, released from the social anxiety that pumped through me like blood. As I chewed through the pizza, gnawing at the crusts until the pain was almost unbearable, I thought about Erica's letters and that boy's sweater and the pleasure of escaping detection.

The iPhone started vibrating on the coffee table again and I jumped. Erica was talking on her own phone now and I couldn't discern her words from behind our bedroom door, but listened closely to her voice. She talked and talked, and cried and moaned and giggled too, perched hidden in our bedroom as the summer night, the city night, whispered in around the dozen little dolls she kept on our moonlit windowsill. I had settled like lead in her bones and made her unhappy, and she was struggling free. I pressed a pillow along my stomach and closed my eyes.

When I woke up Erica was leaning against me, holding me around my waist, stroking my cheek. She had placed a blue plate of eggs and toast on top of the pizza box, and the cooking smells were already fading from the apartment. I eased from sleep into tears. "Are you going? Where are you going? Who is he? You can't go," I said.

"I have to. I have to go," she said, and stroked my arm for a moment, staring up at the ceiling.

"My childhood friend Joey, who I told you about? The guy with the hair? He has a little organic farm up in rural Quebec. He calls it Walden, like a manor, you know? But really it's a small, cozy place."

"Hah. Thoreau."

She blinks at me, smiles, and continues. "So, he needs my help for a while."

"Why yours?"

"Come with me, it'll be wonderful," she said, without looking at me. If she'd asked with more conviction, or even repeated her request, I may have said yes. As it was, she slumped as if exhausted, and I shivered with anger. What right did she have to be exhausted?

"What? It wouldn't be wonderful for either of us. How can you leave the city? You're terrified about being 3.6 kilometers away from Toronto Western Hospital."

"That's not true," she said, reaching for my fork and snatching the plate.

"You are! Remember when you were panicking about having another attack? Remember what we did? We sat down with a pen and paper, and figured out how long it'd take you to get to the hospital in a cab from here, and then all of your favorite places. The movie theatres, Jeff and Cheryl's apartment, and that grocery store with all your stuff, your flax and chia. Remember? Do you still carry that paper around with you?"

She fixed me with a wide-eyed stare, eating the eggs, brushing the stray yellow bits from her shirt to the carpet. "That's also part of it: I'm fading, you understand? This city is killing me quicker than everyone else. Yesterday I threw up into a trash can in the subway; I had blood all down my chin. I get so dizzy in the mornings, I can't move until you do. You make fun of my flax and my chia, but your food would kill me even faster."

"*My* food?"

"Up in the country, I might be able to . . . I mean, they're all vegan, no toxins, it could turn my life around."

"They?"

"Well, just him and I for now, but some friends are coming."
We sat in silence for a moment, and she watched me closely, then
reached over and squeezed my hand. "Come on, you're one of
those friends. Come with me."

I closed my eyes and shook my head. "I don't know what
you mean—come with you? What about money? What about
the rest of my life? That's not the way the world works, I can't
just fuck off without planning for it, taking time off."

"I sensed that in you. That's partly why I have to go," she
said gently.

"You sensed what, that I'm a responsible adult? What about
my job? My career? What about when I'm fifty?"

"What about it? You'll still be you, just even more so. You
have your whole life to work."

"It's not *optional*, Erica. You have to work and support yourself, build a credit rating, participate in the world, and . . . oh
god, you're looking at me with this, like, pity. You know what
happened to the nineties club kids you idolize, all your old
friends? They burned out and live off their families now. People
avoid their calls, because they call to beg for money. They over-
dose, they can't find work. They sleep in tents in the Don Valley
parkway. They starve. They freeze to death."

She let go of my head and stood, bending to pick up her
backpack.

"That's all you're taking? Do you even have your medica-
tion? What the fuck is going on? This is ridiculous."

"I understand your anger. I know this seems sudden, but
really it's the consequence of a certain series of events."

"It's *the* consequence? Of which events? Did you feel this
was inevitable?"

"I said a consequence, not the consequence."

"No, you said—"

"It'll only be a while. There's a lot to do during harvest."

"During . . . ? He's the one who sent you all those letters,
isn't he? Don't lie."

"Yeah, he is."

"All those letters? And you're just friends?"

"Yes."

"I don't know if I believe you."

She looked down at her lap, quiet for a moment. Then she said, without much emphasis, "You should."

"I'll try to. The thing is, I think you're in love with him again, and I'm what triggered it. I also think you can't stay in love for long. I think you sweep in, enamoured and totally dazzling, and then you grow resentful of the need you've created, and then you leave. I think I'm one of many people you've done this to. I think you'll end up unhappy."

"That is so mean. You're being so *mean*. When have I given you reason not to trust me? When have I ever lied to you?"

"I wouldn't know, because I have a feeling you're good at it."

"I'm a good person," she said, getting mad.

"You are," I said, "In that you're generous, you're kind, you're attentive. But you're indecisive, you're passive as hell, you're all over the place. You need to be careful with people. You—it terrifies me."

"I *am* careful with people—Shelagh, there are a bunch of people who love me, and I love them! You wouldn't know how that feels," she said.

"Oh! I knew it. Remember how I told you that I'm boring, that you'd get bored with me? And what did you say to that?"

"I don't remember."

"You said that people like me are the best kind of people. That you'll spend your life learning from people like me."

"I meant it."

I looked at her. "Yeah, I guess you did."

"I don't know if it makes you feel any better, but this has nothing to do with you," she said. I began to suspect that the fog of discomfort oozing around the bedroom door last night hadn't been restlessness and annoyance with me, but something else, something deeper and more urgent—anxiety? Apprehension?

"Erica, are you in trouble?" I asked. She looked away, got up and walked toward the window, came back and picked up my plate, and disappeared into the kitchen. I followed her.

She was scrubbing the plate vigorously. "Trouble like, am I pregnant? Don't think that's much of a risk. It's insulting that you think so."

"Oh my god," I said. "Erica, you're freaking me out. What's going on?"

In retrospect, I lost her then: by confessing my fear I allowed her swoop in, to comfort and manage me, to take the wind from my sails and dismantle them.

"It's all right," she said, cupping my face with soapy fingertips. "I'm just tired, and stressed about money, OK? This is just something I need to do, and it's a challenge like anything else, and I'm just being lazy. I've been lazy for too long. It's been six months since I left the bakery, did you know that?"

"Yeah?"

"Yeah." She leaned in and kissed me on the mouth. "I love you," she said, and I started crying.

"Hey, hey, hey, now. You'll be OK," she said. "I'm leaving a postal address if you change your mind, and want to join us."

"A *postal* address?"

She smiled—gently, wistfully—and left, closing the door behind her with such care that it didn't make a sound. I counted five seconds, then ten, the silence crowding my ears.

I yanked off a couch cushion and hurled it across the room, hitting the fake mantle she'd swaddled with dreamcatchers and knocking off the porcelain duck we'd found in the street. It occurred to me that Erica had maybe heard the noise; maybe she wasn't even at the elevator yet. I threw open the door and dashed out into the hall, and saw that she was gone. Back in the living room I grabbed a pen, steadied the pizza box and wrote, *Can't outrun myself. Might as well die.* I stopped writing and worried that I meant it. Could writing it, and feeling good for having written it, make it true? At what point do people calcify and submerge, just cope and float along? Don't most? When would I?

The phone started vibrating again, rattling itself across the coffee table. I watched it go, feeling a tug deep in my chest (betraying, no doubt, my anthropomorphic attachment to technology, for which Erica would often admonish me back when she still smoked weed and used payphones exclusively). I accepted the call, and pressed the phone to my ear. "Hey, sorry," I said.

"You bitch," someone said.

"Is this your phone? I found it in the bathroom at Bar Volo last, um, yesterday. I'm glad you called."

"You found it? Well, that's surprising. That's truly surprising. Due to the fact that the tracker's been disabled."

I sighed. "I don't know what you're talking about. I have no idea how to do that."

"OK, I was just testing you. Listen—don't hang up." (I froze obediently.) "I didn't mean like testing, I just knew it was stolen, is all. But if it wasn't stolen and you really, actually found it, then thank you"—(slurred into one word and pushed through her nose, like *theeenkyou*, with a threadbare sense of overuse)—"for finding it. I'll come meet you anywhere to get it back."

"I don't know. I can't."

"You can't? You *can*."

I felt the blushing heat come over me, indicating humiliation so deep, it was almost pleasurable. "I can't," I repeated, and hung up.

Étienne called that evening. As I sat alone in the apartment and watched my phone vibrate, I shivered with pleasure at seeing his name on the screen. *Someone's thinking of me, someone who loved me, someone with proof of my existence outside in the world, calling me back into existence!* I thought of how many hours it'd been since I'd spoken to somebody, and cleared my throat a few times. I picked up.

"Well, nice to finally hear from you," he said, with the curt pomposity Erica mocked sometimes, back when she was just Neil's girlfriend with the bike.

"I'm the one hearing from *you*," I said, raising my voice a little, daring him to cringe like he would when I'd raise my voice in public. He sighed, a brisk little explosion. He sighs like a sprinter gulps air, deep and quick and often.

"I've got a bunch of your stuff in a box," he says. "Let me know when you're ready to pick it all up, and I'll leave it by the back door."

"That's kind of you, Étienne," I said. "I'm not big on possessions right now, though, so you can forget about it. Give it all away."

"I know you're being possession-free bohemians and exploring your sexualities and that's exciting, but pretty soon being poor won't be fun anymore," he said, before he can stop himself and against his better judgment, I could tell. For a moment I saw Erica through his eyes: selfish, manipulative, weak-willed, bitter, unhappy and defensive, drawing the world tight around herself like a cloak so she might seamlessly populate it with exactly what she needs to see. His angry breath met my ear, bathing us in a burst of echolocation, and I saw her body—gone gaunt from neglect—out in stark country moonlight, the kind she'd fall asleep to out in the country, everything black and white and entirely what it is.

"Soon it won't be fun anymore. She doesn't care for you, she just wants to possess you," he said, speaking even faster. "Where is she? Listening and rolling her eyes? You guys going to laugh about this later?"

"She's gone," I said, and against my own better judgment, threw myself at his mercy: "For good, I think."

"Well. I'm not surprised," he said after a breath, and I felt too weak to scan his voice for schadenfreude. "Where did she go?"

"I don't know. She had this weird . . . her friend Joey, like a high school ex-boyfriend I think, he has a farm somewhere in rural Quebec. She wanted me to come. Étienne, I'm worried that she might, I don't know, it all sounded a little weird. I don't know."

There was a pause.

"Typical. You just can't keep away from total hippie fuck-ups, can you? I never understood that when I was with you, but now I do: you're just like her."

"Why would you talk about your friend that way?"

"Because she is! It's why I'd never date her!"

"I'm nothing like her. I'm like you," I said, half-pleading.

"Yeah, whatever, so you got a masters, so you have a job. You've had a job for, like, half as long as she's been alive, and you get to feel superior to her. Within her fucked up little matrix, you're outrageously responsible, and you love it: you can't date anybody who challenges you. So where does that leave you?"

"All a-fucking-lone."

"I gave you a good life, and you just about derailed mine. I gave you a good life, that's all I wanted to do."

"No, you wanted to—"

"To what? To have a partner. To love you. Shelagh, you broke my heart."

I started crying into the phone, a kind of hacking silent crying, like vomiting in secret. And then he hung up on me, and I returned to myself, returned to him. For a moment (the first of many) I felt glad she was gone, and sat pulling stuffing from a hole in the couch, remembering him.

With my big jaw and wide body, my cropped mass of heavy hair, I was always threatening to dwarf him, to engulf him—we were almost the same height—and so he'd beat me back, insisting I crop and tame my hair, wax and pluck myself, holding me down to fuck me and then grinding his teeth all night as he slept. I pulled out one long strand of couch stuffing with some of Erica's thick dark hairs tangled up in it, and was suddenly revolted by my sedentary, overslept body, and by the light moving across the well-worn carpet. It was time to move, but where? I'd stay in a motel, I'd sleep hidden in a clothes rack at a Winners, I'd go anywhere, anywhere other than here. Shouldn't I?

And the version of me that perhaps Étienne loved, the shimmering girl who existed only in motion and collapsed rubbery and useless when alone, cried out. *Yes—go—go now!* Brave the sear of curious eyes, the wind rolling over the earth, the streets going on and on, before I fade into a pair of floating eyeballs, and am found months later with the television still on, burning shadows into the carpet and the wall above the couch—*Go!*

I burrowed my fingernails into my wrists and yanked out eyelashes one by one, watching the doorknob until the light withdrew and I could no longer see the carpet, my hands. *Forgive yourself because you tried,* went the Shelagh that writhed drunk up against Étienne at a winter party in somebody's basement.

"Fuck you," I said.

I threw open the bedroom door, marched to the window, and the deep pink sunset streamed in. The bed was so tidily made it looked sealed. Though we both knew she'd left for a very long time and probably forever, the room looked the same—in fact, it was hard to spot what she'd actually taken. She'd taken her dolls from the windowsill, a book (the *Bhagavad Gita*), and all of her pill bottles. And everything else was untouched: bright loops of metal and beads, piled all around her jewelry box. Her clothing, rolled in balls and stored in the shelves, or else scrunched in balls and tossed on the floor. Her Japanese teapot and the matching mug that I'd never once seen washed. Her hairbrush, packed dense with shining hair. All eleven plants, which I'd never counted before, looking a little deflated everywhere they sat and hung.

On her bedside table, weighted by a shedding hunk of mica, she'd left a big sheet of paper. She kept a large roll of paper under our bed, and would tear off pieces to scribble on whenever she woke up. She'd record her dreams—which she imbued with great significance—write grocery lists, record nice texts she'd received and wanted to keep. Every single time she'd leave the apartment, I'd fill up with shame, snatch the sheet of paper, and read everything she'd written. This time, therefore, it was easy for me to find new writing, to spot what she'd written in loopy, deteriorating cursive the night before she left.

And there it was: '*You have grown up and grown strong, strong because you understand the world of men, and now you're protected from it because you understand. Many things are possible for you now. Don't let him take it, keep yourself awake. It is possible! Goldfinches and the earth. Don't slip from the new world!*' And somewhere else, in the same red pen: '*It feels like my pussy ripped apart, and he had no idea really, just heard woman (ME) screaming, just felt flesh under his hands, put his fingers around/inside wet parts. Like when I look at porn, I see women's bodies like fruit, like peaches, their noises don't mean pain, their noises aren't even connected to bodies. Wind in trees. Noise on a tape. And I don't remember either, do I? Do I remember myself like that? Take <u>precautions</u>.*'

Though everything was as familiar as home can be, even the identical quality of late-late-afternoon sun, shadows began oozing from under the pillow and out of the closet, blooming like fungus over cut flower stems, taking the shape of her body, her hands. Her clothing seemed to deflate further still, never to be worn again. Shadow toast formed and dissipated on the dirty, crumby plates. Shadow fluid floated in and through her china teapot, reminiscent of our shared string of breakfasts—a long string, but as it turned out, as finite as anyone else's.

"Oh fuck," I said out loud. I rushed over and opened the balsam box I kept under our shoe rack.

The gun was gone. She'd taken it.

THE WATCHERS II-VI: GOOD LUCK, SISTER

II

Today we try time travelling again. I mean it isn't time travelling exactly, or even at all—because that's impossible—but it's the best we can do.

"Let's hope it plays nicer this time," Buppy says. Yesterday, the thing he calls the 'view' wasn't working. I got upset but he was like, *Be patient, we're mapping the past movements of more particles than you can imagine.* "It's not that we're *actually* going backwards," he explained once I'd adjusted his speech to Colloquial (I can't help spacing out when he gets into the details like that). "It's that we're looking through a window for the view that you want, and we're making the window, and the view."

"The window first, or the view?"

He sighs.

We didn't teach him that. To sigh.

A faint burning hair smell, with no point of reference—probably, it's me. A sound I feel in my teeth, like a dozen people yelling through a faraway phone. The first time I heard it I saw time pulling around me, for just a moment, a dark breeze.

"Are you there?"

"I'm here," Buppy says, but only after a moment's pause, because he isn't 'here' exactly, and I'm not either—I don't think we're anywhere. Mom claims she's the one who taught him to lie, but it was obviously an automatic update: people tell, and need to hear, lies every day.

The river shivers into view, blindingly bright in a sunset. I blink and watch the sunset not directly, but glowing deep yellow against the grass, the boughs of the trees. The glacial, unstoppable majesty lays bare whatever we pin temporality to, and invokes all the classical music Mo plays for us sometimes—chicken scratches to something like Buppy, I'm sure. Soon the sun is gone, but light remains: a cooler afterglow, like a fluorescent light seeping under a door. I look around for people, a little apprehensive: the last time we were here we watched a lawn party, everyone with teased 1980s hair passing around trays of crackers dotted with spray-can cheese, ashing hundreds of cigarettes into dozens of seashell ashtrays, and a woman glanced over and looked right through me. I wondered if they sensed us, and if they extracted personal meaning from our presence: were we ghosts? I asked Buppy later, and he said *well, humans inclined to haunt themselves would be haunted anywhere, wouldn't they?* To which I thought *dude, what do you even think of us anyway?*

I want nothing to do with them, the people we watch. When we go back, we are of the golden sunlit mornings, illuminating the bright green leaves. We are of the world just as they are, but a billion, billion times more diffuse. *Time and space are bound up in too complex a dialectic,* he warned me, *to really get this right the first time*—or the seventh. Two trips ago, we got the space right but overshot time a bit—1943—and watched someone die right here in this remote peninsula in Sainte-Pétronille, near a raft bobbing in the Gatineau River. A young woman, drunk on mugs of home-brewed-looking liquor and shrieking with laughter fainted, and slipped from the moonlit side of her canoe. Since others were swimming right nearby (a group of girls and boys who looked related), we watched panic wick into their minds slowly, but all at once. Last trip—1992—we watched another woman die nearby, drunk and struggling with a man (her husband?) down by the dock, at the sandy lip of their large property a little ways down the river. This time no accident, she slipped away through the cold, opening eye of a November morning. I turn towards the little house at the riverside, and watch movement in the uppermost window. I can tell he suspects that the young woman trapped in this upper room could meet a similar fate. We come back again the next time, make our way through the house, and stand over her. She's tied to a radiator.

"This isn't Mom, it's the Strickland woman. Erica," Buppy says, and I look over at him, like *Are you stupid, except obviously you aren't?*

"I know," I say, and pick him up, stroke his smooth back. He's the exact same temperature as he always is: cool, cooler than me.

"We're not too far off now," I say, and we're quiet until I speak again: "We aren't, are we?"

"No, just a few months," he says. "I wasn't aware you were asking me a question."

I need to know how it happened, those cursed few months she suffered through as I grew and grew, sealed up in her stomach. I love my Mom, and I am transfixed by her stories, and I believe them because she does, because people need to tell their memory-stories over and over, adjusting them with time. I believe her stories, but the truth might be an entirely different thing.

When we visit, we are of the long and golden evenings, hastening summer's passage as we push on and on. Like many of the women before her, Erica has become many creatures since her long punishment began at the hands of the man stalking through the house. At first she seems a young dog full of fight, her yips meeting the bird noises, the water noises. Even when she was stuck in a closet for so many hours that sunlight must've hurt, and then handcuffed to the radiator she seemed to fight, fight like she could win, struggled until the white paint of the radiator chipped away and her wrists purpled. We watched her twist and growl through her nose until she had to lie back and sleep. We watched her wake up in the dark, her wrists gone almost black.

Next visit, she drools until the duct tape unsealed her lips but like most of the women before her, she must've known enough crazy men to know not to scream. It seems just enough just to breathe through her mouth, to gasp big breaths, to lick the salt from her swollen wrists and ease the building ache. We push the sunlight on and on, and the next time we visit Erica, she's eased into a catlike mode: dozing often, curled up around the radiator, waiting out the days. We pull faint whiffs of the outside air through the high window, and she inhales deeply and must know she's in the country, and perhaps tries to imagine the layout of the place. It has changed radically through the years, as even remote places do. Even Joseph, who's lived here alone a long time by the standards of the living, long and quiet enough to maybe even sense we're here, even he'd be surprised at how long people have lived around here. He came close to knowing when, digging for something in the woods, we watched him stumble across the remains of a burned-down cabin, a charred rectangle worn to nubs by decades of snow. We'd watched two women died in there, trapped and suffocated by a candle fire. Four escaped with their lives but never failed to return often with flowers, twisted with grief, returning and returning until they took them back in the fold.

Halfway through every night we hear Joseph's feet coming up the stairs, cushioned by carpet, and Erica freezes. The first time he comes upstairs she wets herself, with fear and fury, but she knows what to say, as if she has been planning it for days:

"Hold on, please—don't you want to hear me apologize? Please not more duct tape, I can't breathe through it. You want me to die in my sleep?"

He's quiet. "Maybe you do, right now," Erica continues. "But you're the most patient person I know. You know me. People don't really change, you know who I am. I made some mistakes and I'm not doing well, is why. Because without you I don't do well, I didn't do well, and like you said, I went in the wrong direction, I got stupid, I got crazy. When you found me—"

"We found each other," he says. "But I'm afraid you've turned into poison. Sometimes, people turn into poison."

"I just, no, for a while, I got lost, I just, but . . . you believe in me. That's why I'm here, and you're here, and we're together again. You believe in me. You always have."

Like many men before him, he shifts his weight from one foot to the other and clasps his hands, stalling for time.

"Back when you were just up to my chin, and it was the four of us. I remember how that felt," she says.

He turns and leaves.

Erica's mouth begins to hang slack now, giving the appearance of sleep. Her teeth, however—the front four illuminated oh-so-slightly by the moonlight—are clenched shut. She could be panicking, panicking over the two inextricable truths that have paved her life and led her here as sure as any highway. From what I know of her, she has never resisted anybody, making their desires her own. And even when they were apart her entire life encircled his, anchoring and sharpening his rage, his faith—his want.

Before the next visit, Buppy asks me if I'm sure. "We can skip ahead," he says.

"I don't want to," I say.

"Your mother will be upset if she knows you're watching this," he says, and I laugh, like *You'll have to do better than that.*

"You can't just forget things like I can," he says, which is his Euphemistic way of saying, *Even if I could be negatively affected by memories, I could delete them anytime I want.* I turn him to top-volume Euphemistic whenever Mom wants him back: she likes to think he's a person.

The afternoon swims into view: she's laying on the floor, hardly making a dent in her clothes. The light grows more golden, filtered through the leaves and spilling more greens into the room. She sits up, and starts to sing to herself. He plays a movie for me, 'Apollo Moon Landing: Remarkable Achievement or Extraordinary Hoax?'—a favorite of Mom and Mo. Erica starts crying, then lays back down and sleeps. Evening falls, pushing long, dim rays over the floor. "Do you want to go home?" he asks, but I shake my head.

Joseph comes up the stairs ten minutes later, and closes the door behind him. She says nothing. He says nothing. We say nothing. Joseph walks over to her and stands just out of reach, stands there until she looks up at him. He looks down and she looks up.

"You took a job in the gutter, in the sooty heart of the city, making garbage and serving wasteful idiots. You were with many men. Then a *woman*," he says.

"I worked in a bakery. I was not wasteful. I kept eleven plants in my apartment. I would water them daily and think of you."

"You may have thought of me, but you gave yourself to others. You were wasteful and watched others be wasteful and you said nothing," he says.

"I was weak and lonely. I was wasteful and unfaithful, I was disgusting, I hollowed myself out. I barely survived," she says.

"You survived by scavenging, lurking on the cancerous fringes of the city, gnashing your teeth. You snatched wallets and fucked for money, and all the while your illness grew. You ate pussy and sucked on breasts for money. You would have cut earlobes off to snatch jewelry."

"Yes, I was totally wretched."

"And whose fault was that?"

"Mine."

"Only yours."

"Only mine. Yes. This is why I'm being punished."

He pauses. "But you can be redeemed."

"I can be redeemed."

He bends and touches her hand. "Each bruise on your wrist, you know what that is?"

"The poison leaving my spirit, my body."

"And hard ground broken for new growth."

The next time we visit, it's late summer. The day is almost gone. We gather around Erica and slip in and out; she stiffens as she hears Joseph coming up the stairs again. He closes the door behind him and walks to her. He waits until she looks up at him. He then takes something small and round from behind his back: an orange. He comes closer, and kneels. I sense the infinitesimal shade he creates, and she watches the long shadow that he casts on the empty wall behind him. I can almost feel the faint heat of his breath through his nose. If he died right now, like this, she would die too. He presses the orange into her hand, and (as the women before her had done) she makes herself stay absolutely still. Perhaps there's a kind of relief running through him. Perhaps she feels it too, because she seems to relax a little, maybe anticipating just how he will peel it: a thumb through the top, leveraging a thick, pulpy strand of peel. The segments come apart ragged and wet and we telescope up and away as he begins feeding each to her, piece by piece.

Buppy overshoots the next visit (1972), and watch a drug-fueled outdoor sex party for as long as I can stand it. One guy, furry-chested and sporting thick sideburns, lifts a woman up over his shoulder and heaves her in the water, his stomach and penis flopping with the effort. "Please don't eat me!" he yells, and everyone shrieks, even the couple fucking up against the willow tree.

The next time we get it right: it's an early fall morning, the birds are singing, and we come in with the bright noon as it heats up the room, which then fades into afternoon which gives way to golden evening. Like many before her who've weathered romantic storms, struggling onward with their lives—at least for a while— Erica is already becoming something new. Something with three times the lifespan of a person, something flightless and still, or at least so slow Joseph can't see her move, can't hear her speak, can't watch her plan. She can compress all the long hours of a day into just moments, and each moment of beauty, silently observed—a robin's song, the leaves whispering against the window—she stretches into days, she saves and tastes over and over when he is asleep in another room, when it is dark, when she is chanting for him. Joseph comes upstairs, and kneels in front of her.

"It's the morning," he says, "and what are you grateful for?"

"The sun, the sky, the big tree and its shelter, the earth beneath us and around us," she recites, easing onto her knees, waiting to be fed. Her mouth waters a little.

"Each bruise on your wrist, you know what it is?"

"The poison leaving me."

"Breaking hard ground for new growth."

He takes a tiny key from his pocket and reaches over her with his other hand, holding the handcuffs still. Her heart hammers with fear. Whatever this is, she is not prepared for it.

"And your gratitude is faith."

"And my gratitude is faith." Erica seems to retreat into herself, doesn't move, watches him remove the handcuffs, regulates her breath.

"And your gratitude is faith."

"And my gratitude is faith." Erica presses her hands to her knees, watching his calm, blank face: maybe he was very expressive when they were young together, all eyes and emphatic gestures, charming—he'd have to be, wouldn't he?—but now, he seems out of practise at maintaining eye contact and making facial expressions:

his speech is careful and slow, like he's reading tiny print. Likely he has spent years alone like this, season after season, with only books and his plants to keep him company—well, mostly. We know that at least twice, a woman, presumably from the nearby village, has come back with him in his truck, and spent the night in his bed.

"And your gratitude is faith. Help me trust you," Joseph says. His breathing is even and his pupils are a little dilated but normal; as far as I can tell, he is not excited or frightened or angry.

He lifts her and carries her across the room and into a darker, cooler place, a narrow hallway with a black banister and a steep drop to the left—experiencing it for the first time she takes it all in, her head pressed to his chest. He carries her to a bathroom down the hall, stepping sideways through the doorway. The tub is full and steaming. He undresses her, then carries her over to the tub, kneels again, and slides her in. The water appears scalding hot, and she bites down hard on the inside of her cheek, then her tongue. He watches her closely. His arms are still beneath her, underwater, one cupping her reddening shoulders, the other floating beneath her bright-red knees. Perhaps she can smell him.

"This is pretty fucked," I say, then lean over and adjust Buppy to Colloquial.

"Word," he replies.

Erica grasps Joseph's hand so tight her knuckles go pale, bloodless.

"I'm so scared I'll get sick again, like really sick," she whispers.

"What a strange thing to say," Joseph says. "You're always sick."

A tear slides down her cheek, and he brushes it away with his thumb. "You'd best focus on maintenance, to prevent relapse," he says. "I am thankful you're safely removed from the city, from the smoke warping your genetic material, blackening your organs, weakening your eyes. You'll see, you'll learn: up here I create my own compost using centuries-old techniques, and the air is fresh all year. Everything I grow is fundamentally, *chemically* different from anything grown in the city, and better than any medicine. You came to live with me, to grow the Family by my side, but you also came simply to *live*. In the city you were resigned to a slow death, weren't you?"

"Yes," Erica whispers.

"Because of your guilt. You twisted your guilt and heartbreak inwards like a knife, and it curdled into self-hatred. You were living out a long and public suicide, wandering the city like a ghost."

She stays very still, staring at him.

He takes his hand away, gathers himself into a crouch. "Practically speaking the truck always has gas, it's always ready—there's a hospital two towns over, less than an hour away. But I promise it won't come to that, and I know you trust me."

"I trust you," she says.

"Help me trust *you*," he says.

"You can trust me. Please trust me."

"When the water cools and you're clean, I'll take you through the house. Would you like that? I'll show you the plants, and when this bathwater cools back down completely, you'll take it downstairs. You'll use the buckets behind the door. You'll feed the plants."

"Thank you."

"What are you grateful for?"

"The sun, the sky, the big tree and its shelter, the earth beneath us and around us," she recites, and then winces as he encircles her wrist with his fingers and gives it a little shake before speaking again.

"Each bruise on this wrist of yours, you know what it is?"

"The poison leaving me."

"Breaking hard ground for new growth. And your gratitude is faith."

"And my gratitude is faith."

He takes the handcuffs with him when he leaves. I wonder if she notices.

III

Erica dries her bright red limbs and pulls her dress back on. The side of the dress, which has a million buttons along one edge, sags open. She reaches inside the flap and cups her own breast. She stands there squeezing it, looking at the door.

"Why is she doing that?" Buppy asks, as he usually does when confronted with unusual human behaviour.

"Um, sometimes people do weird little things with their bodies, you know? Maybe it's a nervous habit. Like—I smell my top lip by bringing it to my nose. It's kind of an addiction I'm careful with."

"Why?"

"Because it looks dumb as shit."

We watch her touching her own breast, squeezing her nipple offhandedly.

"Does nakedness mean anything to you?" I ask Buppy, and then wonder why I asked. He's silent—maybe he doesn't know what I want to hear. And I don't either.

When Erica leaves the bathroom, Joseph is waiting for her at the top of the staircase. About two kilometers east the remainders of a small home are mostly buried in the woods, its ribbon driveway long-submerged in the river, which creeps further and further in every year. Eleven visits ago, we watched a woman tend to a riot of plants in that home, pruning the large vegetable garden out in the yard which seemed the envy of her sisters and neighbours—but even that was nothing like this. Erica masks something like panic as she's led through the rest of the house. The room in which she'd been locked is bare compared to the rest of the place, which is entirely packed with plants: even along the little staircase a huge array of herbs and tomatoes grow wildly towards each tiny window, hanging from pots, nailed to the windowsills, each stalk and shoot pressed against the glass or curved towards the sun.

We know that Joseph speaks to his mom, the woman from the old interview footage—Joanne—once a week, usually on Sundays. Mingled adoration and concern plumes out through the phone, stirring something overfamiliar in me (or at least it would, were I not temporarily released from the coils of need the living cast and tighten over one another.) As the treasured son of this doting mother, there are, naturally, large gaps in Josephs' understanding of household upkeep, and as soon as Erica is allowed in the rest of the house she'll start cleaning. Good luck, sister: I know that the floors, caked with soil and thick with dust, have never been washed, neither have the windows, the sofa cushions, the pillows, the sheets. Were I actually inhabiting that space I'd likely experience the air as unbearably fragrant; all day gasps of pollen, petals, seed pods and withered discarded leaves tumble to the floor for Erica to sweep and wipe away.

"I wish I could smell it," I say to Buppy. "The flowers?" he asks, and I wonder if he wishes for things, too. Likely he knows I'm wondering that, because he quickly says, "Remember how many flowers we'd see in spring, when you were young? Remember how excited you got?"

There is a small living room in the middle of the house, open to the kitchen on one side and with the entrance hallway and the narrow staircase edging the other; very little natural light reaches this room, but day and night it glows blue with eleven grow lamps. These devices would spook the house's previous inhabitants, signifying as they do the slow technological procession towards the end of the world, which cropped up even in these remote communities and included refrigeration, television, tales of spaceflight (and televised spaceflight), and unnerving newspaper photographs of the sweet little lamb born someplace bright, gestated not in a womb but a beaker. Of course Erica, immersed as she is in her own time, doesn't so much as flinch as the man takes her around to each lamp and identifies the plants growing beneath, sometimes with great specificity and sometimes with a vagueness that struck me as ominous: *These are seedling greens for salad, which we'll have to sow by mid-September so it'll be ready by first frost; here, you'd recognize this as common sprigs of Queen Anne's lace but you'll come to know it as Daucus carota, it's good for abdominal pain and works as an abortifacient; and these are delicate medicinal herbs and flowers that require special care.* As he speaks she sometimes smiles and nods, saying *I recognize this or that,* seeming to recall some shapes and colours from what must be ages ago, if ever.

He then takes her out into the yard, and she cries out. Over the last three years and twelve seasons, Joseph has dug and planted at least twenty plots, each the size of a large coffin and arranged in rows, packed so densely with flowers and vegetables it's likely overwhelming. The plots surround a greenhouse, constructed from pilfered materials, a gigantic, semi-transparent pastiche of a building glowing in the sun and sparkling faintly on the side that faces the river.

"Oh my gosh," she says, looking at him, and he nods like *Go ahead*. The condensation coating the plastic and glass is so thick the walls are almost opaque, and as she approaches the whole structure almost blends into the dark green trees behind it. She looks back at him, amazed. "It's like, three times bigger," she says, and he shrugs and raises his eyebrows, like *Yeah, at least*. They spend the afternoon inside the greenhouse, emerging only as the evening light comes through the trees, dancing diffuse amongst the final, fleshy magnolia petals that drop to the ground, yanked down by the late afternoon breeze.

"What are you doing?" Buppy asks, rolling his little head around to peek at my device.

I cover it with my hand. "I'm writing a poem, OK?"

He doesn't ask to read it: as soon as I get him back from Mom, I turn his Compassionate Curiosity way down.

Later they're sitting at the kitchen table; the handcuffs have reappeared on the counter near the stove but neither person looks at them or at each other really, but rather down at their empty plates, or at their own folded hands.

"People, their faces—I couldn't handle it after a while," Joseph says. "It's overwhelming, all the want and the duplicity and the self-serving altruism, I could see it all," he says. "Babies are good, or at least entirely innocent, and animals are even better, but plants are pre-innocent, pre-conscious. They predated all humanity, all creatures, for eons. They are pre-conscious, yet all life; they are all need and yet self-sustained, always growing and always moving, though so slow we can't detect any movement at all. Plants bring us towards what we dread and run from. They unite us all underneath the terrified noise of our brains."

Something flickers over Erica's face, and she folds her hands and stares down at them, running her fingers over her wrists, which have begun to heal. Perhaps she begins to understand how she has been changing, how he's been grooming her with his glacial calm, with his bottomless patience. Perhaps she begins to recognize the speed at which he's trained her to move.

IV

One afternoon, sitting on a stool as Joseph brushes Erica's hair and they chant together, she looks up, likely listening to the bird singing just outside the kitchen window.

"That's a chickadee," Buppy says, like he's forgotten who he's talking to—it's my Mom, not me, who's obsessed with birds now; I gave that up long ago. They catalogue everything together, just like he and I used to do: she'll grab a dirty feather off the ground and bring it back to him, then pin it on her wall. Every morning, while she's still asleep, he'll record all of the early-morning birdsong for her. They'll play it at the breakfast table, over and over, until I throw down my spoon like *Holy SHIT you guys* and Mo yanks at one of his dreads and raises his eyebrows like *Chill out, Abby*.

"What's with her?" I ask, because Erica's eyes have gone wide, and at first she looks like she's never heard a bird before, and then like she's never heard anything before. She stutters and falls silent, then starts to cry so much she soaks her shirt and the tablecloth and her lap beneath, so much it runs all down her neck and pools in her collarbone and wicks up into her bellybutton and gathers in her healing hands, and he pauses, like he's waiting for her to stop, and then asks her to start the chant all over again. And as they chant and he brushes she flattens out the words, just rhythmic sounds as meaningless and meaningful as those of the outside world—the jumbled roar of truck engines and radios on the distant highway and the heartbeats of every driver urging them along, the thrum of wings and all the birds in the forest, the frantic dash of the squirrels in the cleared-out yard, the silent growth and life of each crop in the gardens and greenhouse, of every tree. He cooks some eggplant and kale in tomato sauce and feeds it to her, wiping the sauce from her mouth each time she swallows, his thumb resting on her cheek. He stares at her and she stares back. It is finished, or else it always has been.

"It's like she's joined our frequency," I say.

"She has become a tree," Buppy says, and I'm like *What the fuck does that even mean* until I remember that Mom set him to Late-Stage Romantic Poet late last night night, when she was feeling lonely. Mo's been staying out later and later; he came home at 8:30AM this morning, stinking like Gutrot.[2] Whatever he does, it doesn't help, because he seemes lonely too—lonelier even than she does, somehow.

V

Every now and then Erica will stare at an object in the house—the teapot, a slice of bread—for an uncomfortably long time, as if it's suddenly glowing with sentience. And each time she eventually smiles, resting her hand on whatever it is and swelling with fondness, like *I remember you*.

This time we visit it's still early fall, and the glossy leaves of the oak tree have grown tattered, one or two yellowed at their eaten edges. Cicadas sing all through the morning, and she chants with him and washes the floor as we ooze in and out, in and out. Cicadas sing, buzz and fall silent and then sing again as he leads her through the house out to the backyard, and on towards the greenhouse. He holds her hand gently; we haven't seen the handcuffs in weeks.

They start to work. "You want to come to Home Depot with me in a couple days?" he asks. "This hose needs replacing, plus I want to check the mailbox."

Her face twitches, like she's trying to make it as blank as possible before allowing herself to speak. "The duct tape isn't working?"

"No, I tried that," he says appreciatively, and she smiles a little. He believes in her, and he is pleased, relaxed. She looks pleased that he is pleased; a dynamic most of us—me, my mother, my sister—know very well, and have known for years. He wipes some dirt from one hand and presses it to the corners of her mouth, a fingertip on one side, his thumb on the other. "There are some things, like forsythia like this and smiles like that, on faces like yours . . ." he says, and she bends to pick up a stack of ceramic pots, perhaps to hide her face.

---

[2] Bathtub booze: like many major North American cities, Toronto became a 'dry' city after the second bee extinction and subsequent mass shutdown of vineyards.

VI

Buppy skips ahead a bit, with the volume off; we talk about how many shots of Gutrot I could take before it killed me (he thinks three, I think ten, at least.) I watch Erica and Joseph go about their days at high speed, the sun rising and setting, rising and setting. It looks like it gets cooler nearly every day, as they start wearing sweaters, scarves, heavier clothes. "Wait—stop," I say, and Buppy slows it down to normal again.

Erica steps in a few yellow leaves on her way to the garden, carrying a trowel and the shears. The tomatoes have ripened since our last visit. She seems further encased in a dream, in herself, in the bark than usual, and when he catches up with her, takes the trowel from her hands, and drops it on the ground, she doesn't move. Wind hisses through the trees as he takes the shears and grips them for a moment, then puts them down on the grass. He places his hands on her shoulders and squeezes them until she looks up at him, and then he kisses her. He kisses clumsily, hungrily, like a boy. He pulls away, and takes her chin between his thumb and index finger. "We are a family. We have always been a family," he says. She stays still, perhaps feeling how true this is. His face, dark with the sunlight directly behind him, is difficult to read.

The kiss produces a rupture even Buppy can probably sense: there is now a distinct division between them, signalling a before and an after. She vigorously re-pots tomatoes and beans, burying her hands in the soil as if digging for shards of truth, weighing them in pieces. She shivers as if considering the hot poke of his tongue, the shock of his smells and their strange familiarity, his body metabolizing and interacting with the same elements as hers, the same carpets and walls, the same soap, food and dirt. He works nearby, but leaves her alone. As evening approaches, he sniffs his own fingers after scratching his ear and then he looks up, wincing in the sunlight, and finally catches her eye.

They stare at each other.

We stare at them.

Anger slips into her features, blackens them like oil—the kind of anger I'd see in Mom. She's described how, years later, anger pierces the skin and beats inside of her, an all-over ache changing the colours of the world around her, shaking her from her summer-drowse, draining the catlike intelligence from her breasts and limbs and crowding right up in her head.

Erica stares at him and he blinks back at her, and we know from her quivering mouth she's remembering something else: the city she left, the woman she abandoned—Shelagh, the chick from the newspapers. A 'fading beauty,' according to one writer, 'Erica's long-suffering lover,' according to another. In photos I was struck by how *normal* she seemed: a city-dwelling woman with round, healthy limbs from biking and good food, with the kind of skin that's aging well, all things considered, the kind of skin that never really reddens in the sun. The kind of woman forever waiting her turn; the kind of woman asking gently about everyone else's day, making herself scarce when her lover gets upset; the kind of woman tasked with cataloguing and taxonomizing like her life depends on it. From the moment they'd met, Erica and Shelagh, she must have envied Shelagh's linear sense of self: falling in love and then leaving her boyfriend, and even in those weeks of crisis and upheaval, still making it to work on time every morning, still washing and folding her clothes regularly, still choosing places to eat dinner and looking forward to eating those dinners, still watching the news and forming opinions, all manifestations of the indestructible grain of innate her-ness pulling her along like a sturdy tugboat. For a moment I imagine their shared apartment, their street in Toronto and the perpetual renewal she'd watch from the second-floor window: every day pulsing with strangers, every night humming with voices, waves of traffic and pigeons and abandoned furniture and garbage drifting along the sidewalks, lining the gutters. The miracle of freedom, of near anonymity, was it terrifying because it was flimsy, because it was empty? Would Erica really have collapsed? Or should she have pushed through her terror, towards—what? As much a mimic, a liar, a charmer, she's cursed with diluting her own truth until it's indistinguishable from the force of external desire.

Joseph puts down his trowel and straightens up. "What's wrong?" he asks, and she stares and doesn't speak. "Close your mouth," he says.

"What's wrong? I don't know, Joseph. How can I talk to you about what's wrong?"

"You should always talk to me," he says.

The three of us watch him bend over a pot and as Erica's mouth twists into a sneer, and I can actually feel her strength balloon: she puffs up, seems strong enough to lift a car, to throw a table, to strangle him to death. Her anger shifts years away from her body, and we glimpse the long track he's chewed down her life like a weevil, through which—week by week—she drains.

"I've never lied to you," he says. "Talk to me and we'll fix it."

He steps towards her and she breaks eye contact, looking down at her hands and keeping still; so practiced is she that she knows just what he sees, and perhaps unconsciously adjusts herself to enhance the sight, as if to say, *Yes, you see me, and in seeing me you dictate exactly what I do, and therefore what I am—around you, at least.*

The sun beats down and a crow calls.

What kind of victory is that, anyway? What did existence feel like, when she was away from him? It's just a shrunken 'then' she must carry around like a talisman, aching for it to provide a barrier between them before, and them now. A butterfly lands on a nearby pot of chives, opens and closes its green-white wings just once, then flutters on.

"Cabbage butterfly," Buppy observes.

The field stretches behind the garden, golden and fragrant, and the woods are dark beyond it, and the water sparkles on and on. They stare at each other. Erica finally takes a step towards him, then another and a few more, baring her teeth; a shadow passes over his face, and he looks almost afraid.

"We were children together and I can't stop thinking about that," she says. "You can't replicate that, and it binds us together. That's what I came back for."

As soon as she's within reach he presses an arm around her shoulders, and grips her throat with the other. She jerks away, and I adjust the view, telescoping up and up until we can observe them both like clouds: their scattered tools, the dull gleam of the patchwork greenhouse and the snow-worn roof of the cottage, the brilliant sparkling water stretching beyond and the tiny tops of their heads. I bring us back down again, examine their faces.

"*No*," Erica says, but he reaches for her again. She bends and fumbles in the grass, then seizes the trowel. He kneels down to her and she crabwalks away from him, then presses the blade against her own neck. "Just try it," she says.

He freezes.

"Fuck!" I yell, grasping for Buppy.

"You wouldn't risk it," she says, seeming to feel a rush of truth, pulsing through her like water: I know she's right. They're alone—beyond alone, and he could kill her; we know he's imagined her dead. So they're alone, but we know he waited for her, and she knows too. She knows he feels absolutely pregnant with purpose, and that he couldn't imagine this without her. That he passed long nights alone without her, writing and thinking, projecting years of life just ahead, framed as legacy and aching for witness, a diary he longed to be read.

He is quiet for a long moment, staring down at her. "Stop it," he says.

We watch sweat slide down the inside of Erica' arm, pooling in her elbow. Like many women before her, she softens, shuddering into something sickening and unmistakable. She arches her back and kisses him. The trowel slips from her hand.

Joseph tenses his body as if to resist. "You came back for me," he says, with urgency—it's a question, and a plaintive one—and she kisses him again, sucking at his mouth, hungry for the very air he breathes and the terrible, singular force of his solitude, wanting always to be reflected back at herself just like this. He frees his mouth and drags a ragged breath: "I waited for you."

"You did. I know you did. You did, don't forget that you did. I'm your family," she says, her mouth pressed to his ear, her saliva on his neck, in his hair: "I'm your fate." We feel him expel breath at the truth of this.

Erica yanks up his shirt, pressing her cold hands to his stomach, and he shudders, pulling her towards him, and she pushes his hand between her legs. He goes still beneath her and his eyes are wide, his other hand fluttering, as if asking her to slow down—but she won't. *I am your wife. I'm going to have your child. We will find others. You will always know love. I am love. One day they will write books about us. About you, and about me. All of your suffering was borne of wisdom and had real purpose.*

She bites and sucks at his face as they grunt and struggle in the grass, his dirt-caked fingers squirming inside her like a frog trapped in a glove, her thighs squeezing him tight and digging into the grass. She throbs with anger and with love, with anger and love, as his face tightens up and he forces her body around, entering her with a gasp.

You waited for years. I am unchanged since our earliest youth, since our childhoods. Just as small, just as pale. I will create you, bring you into focus. You don't live without my eyes on you. You don't live without my body near yours. You don't speak without my ears. You don't see without my face.

He shakes and moans, gripping her head in his hands, pressing it against his. He is a man, just a man. All he must do is hand his life over to her, clumsy and half-awake, so she can make him become.

"That's a robin," Buppy comments, after a while.

"You're thinking about birds right now?"

There's a pause: he's not thinking about birds; he's just cataloguing them.

It's full-fledged fall the next time, and we watch Erica rake leaves, sending pained glances over to the house as brown leaf fragment bob, unnoticed, in her tangled-up hair, and all of a sudden the back door flies open and he's leading a heavily pregnant girl outside, and the woman drops the rake and scrapes her hair behind her ears, smiling a little painfully, and I jump up and scream before I can stop myself, like—

MAAAAAAAAAAAAAAAAAA!

COMMUNION MINUTES. LOGGED BY ERICA, VIDEO TAPE #2, SEPT/10

JOSEPH: Today I had a vision, which . . . are we filming? Yeah?

ERICA: *(from behind camera.)* You're good—go ahead!

JOSEPH: This morning a vision came down to me, hit me like a sunbeam. I saw that in just a few years, society will crack in two. For the one half: you'll be plugged in, you'll have the internet pressed into your eye with a glass lens or cut into your brain. The other half will resist, and be shunned, then banished.

ERICA: *(In a rehearsed-sounding voice.)* Banished? *(Logan, who is watching Joseph intently, makes a little grunting sound.)*

JOSEPH: Banished, living in shit. Non-Resisters won't feel fear, because it will be so pleasurable to give in. For a Non-Resister, your social world will always be around you, tendrils connecting you to dazzling ranks of people, everyone you've ever met or wanted to meet, everyone who's ever met you or wanted to meet you. You'll be bathed in so many images and videos, babies taking first steps and manicured toes in Bermuda sand, all eliciting differing levels of warm recognition. An elegant, total connectivity, and it'll happen so fast—you see how quickly payphones became abandoned shells, the phone books burned away with lighters and yanked away by squirrels, their plastic protective shells battered and hanging against the grimy glass. You see how quickly newspaper stands get covered with bright graffiti—pictures naturally, not words—and are kicked over, last decade's trash.

ERICA: I have seen this.

JOSEPH: You've seen this, too, Logan?

LOGAN: *(chewing her thumbnail.)* Yeah.

JOSEPH: You see book stores sell candles and pillows or get boarded up. It is coming like a tide to sweep us along, and it is already around our knees, and rising all the time—and it will be so pleasurable to give in: never reading more than a paragraph at any time, receiving social tugs all the time, watching whatever you like whenever you choose. You can learn little facts about parrots and feel a spurt of wonder, then forget them. You can watch the end of Ghost over and over until you can make yourself cry, briefly grasping that one pure emotion until you are satisfied, and slide back into The Soup. You will never be lost or alone, you will be superhuman, and it will be so pleasurable—and it is already almost here, you understand. It has already arrived. And what will happen to Resisters?

ERICA: They'll be left behind.

JOSEPH: Creating what?

LOGAN: A two-tier society.

JOSEPH: Good, Logan. And what then? Will the Resisters find it easy to get jobs? No, it will be nearly impossible. And what then? What then, once they have unraveled the secrets of aging—and this is a reality, this is happening—soon, five or ten years from now, those with means can double their lives, and up until their bodies give out, maintain perfect glossy health. Maintain forty-year-old bodies or thereabouts, for a hundred years. A hundred years of basting in The Soup, endless pops of relevance gaining short bursts of attention, dazed all the time, for those with means. Work lives woven into these new needs for those with means. And those without means, those resisting all wetware and denied all the jobs except for the shit-carrying and the brick-laying, what will happen to them? They'll be lucky to make it to fifty. And nothing will be brutal, nothing will hurt: those in The Soup will watch videos about Resisters, who they will see as animals, vaguely deserving of a certain set of rights, vaguely suffering out in the shit pens, out in the brick-piles. The ones affecting sophistication will scan a few photos, perhaps feel a brief shiver of sentiment, and then move on. Swim on through The Soup.

(Pause. Logan looks over, presumably scanning Erica's face just above the camera.)

JOSEPH: And where did I find you, Logan?

LOGAN: Well, over the internet, sort of.

JOSEPH: Precisely: no one is clean. You all remember websites like you remember your sixth-grade summer, your mother when she was younger, your first trip to Florida or wherever your lives took you before we all crossed paths. (*Pauses to rub his chin beneath his beard.*) So do I. And what do we do together? We read long books, wandering through the prose, luxuriating in the bliss of long-form reading, of sustained concentration. And we love each other because we are together, and we let people in our past fade with dignity. And we write in our diaries. And we read and reread them, alone and together. And we take accountability. And we quietly cultivate a new class, a new movement for which we are the *sine qua non*. And we tend our gardens. (*Points to his head*).

JOSEPH: And what are we Grateful for?

EVERYONE: The sun, the sky, the big tree and its shelter, the earth beneath us and around us. Our Home, our Gardens, our Greenhouse.

JOSEPH: And your gratitude is faith. Each callus on your hands, you know what it is?

EVERYONE: The poison leaving us.

JOSEPH: Breaking hard ground for new growth . . .

Erica: Here's the Thing about Being 14

Here's the thing about being 14: you disgust you. Gawky, you burst from the tight peapod of your child's body, never again un-ruptured, suddenly bloody.

Here's the thing about being 14: even as you sprout into a woman-looking thing, you're still the child you were—for a while.

Here's the thing about being 14: you dig through clearance racks for lace things, cheap tight things, to truss your sudden womanhood.

You do this because you have older sisters. You do this because of your mother. You do this because of the men who hate, stare at and long for you.

Here's the thing about being 14: you have no taste. You fasten a huge plastic rose to your hair, an accidental, exaggerated metaphor bopping against your ears.

Here's the thing about being 14: your self-consciousness is acute but incomplete. You lump socks into your bra; you can't afford a padded one.

Here's the thing about being 14: the men. They are seventeen, they are forty-three, they follow you off the bus, touch your hair, yell after you.

Older women watch you too. Like other girl-women flinching through the world, you are suddenly hyper-visible. Hyper-devour-able, hyper-detestable.

You don't know what to do with it yet. Some girls do: they weaponize it. Some girls don't: they get pregnant. Sometimes, they turn up dead.

For now, at 14, you occupy the grey middle of the continuum: buffeted by the desires of men, you spend most time alone.

Willing your breasts to wither, withdraw into your chest. Ripping out your pubic hair. Starving out the blood. Painting horses.

Here's the thing about being 14: you must befriend other girl-women. They terrify you, but they keep you safer than you'd be otherwise.

Girlish scorn, though imprecise, is still effective. A tight circle of disdainful girl-women can wilt even the most persistent hard-ons.

'Who wants McDonald's? Some vodka?' some guy yells, leaning out his car window. The kind of thirty-year-old most thirty-year olds avoid.

Your alpha girl-woman rolls her eyes. Alpha doesn't even look at him. You are tempted by vodka, but you worship her. So you roll your eyes too.

It's not that she's beautiful—though she is. It's not that she's smart—though she is. It's that she's so confident she's nearly perfect.

Good instincts run through Alpha like filaments. She ashes her cigarette over the withered grass of the soccer field.

Your circle of girl-women hover at the periphery of the schoolyard. He leans further from his car, and his lonely-stink trails out.

The boys your age hang further back, eyeing the man in the car, mapping his desire. They are frightened. They are jealous. They are boys.

'Cunts,' he spits, and speeds away. Knowledge spreads through your bodies, a quivering moment of osmosis: he's off to the next high school.

It's not that Alpha isn't sexual: she is. 'I gave [boy-boyfriend] a hand-job on Tuesday, during First Spare,' she confides—

Since she's Alpha, we know her school schedule: she's dropped French already, and can lounge beautifully on Tuesday afternoons—

'and he never cummed,' she finishes, with a self-deprecating smile. She flicks her drinking straw against the lunchroom table.

Your conception of hand-jobs and cum is stick-figure abstract, so your laugh is the loudest, your zeal the most palpable:

Sweat dots your fitted hoodie, fear of being caught out. Your horse paintings spring up over your ribs, bright sudden brands on your flesh.

'Did you tell him to get the fuck off your property?' Beta crows, scraping frosting from the inside of her Dunkaroo container. Alpha frowns.

'It was in the school basement,' Alpha says. and since she's her, your world reconfigures: acceptability shifts around her;

Your hazy understanding of glamor mutates to accommodate the school basement. Her bright-pink fingernails, grazing his scanty chest;

Her bright-yellow miniskirt still bright by the long-abandoned, folded-up bleachers, beneath which his skinny knees shook;

The pale, root-like nub of him, visualized as a fungus, milked at arm's-length—the length of her lovely arm, that is—

The whole hand-job ordeal rendered oddly chaste to you, a kind of flesh pulley-system, as yet innocent of spit, frustration, and shame.

Alpha knows spit. Alpha knows shame. By some quirk of genetics her large eyes seem wise, a trait men will ascribe her far too early.

But in handing themselves over to her, in ascribing her premature maturity, they play an age-old trick: they make her grow up, lightning-quick.

They yank her into the grey adult world. Age comes over her like autumn, until she's old for 14, old for 20—older than they'll ever be.

But for now: bleachers, boy-boyfriend's loose, child's mouth. Her cigarettes, each eventually printed with lip gloss. Her own child's mouth.

You go home, the hand-job in your head. Thin, pulley-arms, a quivering fungus. You put on a Green Day CD. Squeeze your thighs together, tight.

Where's Alpha? She's at the mall, carelessly thumbing through piles of denim. She can't see you, can she? You fuck yourself, ride your own fingers.

When Joseph finds you on the bus, you are weathered by men already.

You don't know it, but they've all worn you down, left you open to him. He watches you remove your backpack. You're still 14.

Here's the thing about being 14: you don't recognize danger if it flatters you first. 'I can tell from your eyes you've seen pain,' he says.

You haven't known pain, not really. But he'll change that.

He leads you off the bus, buys you a coffee. It's all he can afford, really—a dollar fifty—but you're impressed he has any money at all.

He is tall and thin, but has some flabby meat to him. He keens for you to discover the pale, bruise-y bulk of him, under his clothes.

It isn't courtly or gentle, it's a matter of days. But the raw newness of him—proximity to his desire-stink—stretches it into an era.

You don't know the language of play-resistance, resistance-resistance. When he reaches for your hand, you grip his just as hard, right back.

You don't know, either, that resistance-play is rooted in a primal function, though you feel it, an undercurrent, pulling beneath you:

He is pockmarked, weathered and hungry, and wants to consume you. Your youth, a sparkling atmosphere invisible to your peers,

For your tribe of girl-women live encased in it, too—the whole school gleams bright with it, near-shakes abuzz with it, reeks with its smell,

Your youth, your bobbling plastic rose drooping against your tangled hair, drew him in. It's your fault. You squeezed his hand, didn't you?

Didn't you look at him as you squeezed his hand, making a silent promise right back at him, mirroring the longing in his eyes?

Didn't you know, squeezing his big fingers right back, your knuckles aching—didn't you know you were coaxing him into safety, into love?

Didn't you know, squeezing and smiling, that you were falling in love with him, too?

When you're 14, you have discretionary time. He opens a mouth in your bedroom, and exhales: horses and painting evaporate.

One day he'll record an album with Marilyn Manson, Joseph says. So you save three weeks allowance and buy his CDs, memorize them.

'Where are you going?' Beta asks one day, so Alpha won't have to, though she watches you closely. Your chest cleaves, and your halved ribcage swings up and open, yanked in two directions: one, towards the mall and safety. The other, towards him. Your heart beats in the centre.

Your heart beats in the centre, and Alpha already knows. By some flaw enfolded in you, you'd take a strange man's strange pain over her.

At a payphone, you call until he answers. 'Do you have any vodka?' you ask. You realize later you named your price, and it was low.

In his mother's basement, which stinks of loneliness and weed, Joseph feeds you gin and Diet Pepsi. In your real life, you aren't even allowed soft drinks.

You feel afloat, powerful—the floaty power inversely proportionate to your coordination, it turns out, as you drop your glass.

You don't care you've dropped it. and he cares only until you take his hand, squeeze it. Then press it to your breast.

His fingertips bunch up around your nipple like—you think, drunk for the first time in your life—the legs of a thin, white tarantula. But a nice one.

Oh yes, a nice one. You are invested in his niceness; you can't see how he'd be otherwise. Your world is very small.

'You're mature for your age,' he says, and you understand that he means something else: you know what I want, so act like it's OK.

You know what he means, and it makes sense. *I'm young,* you think, watching his hands. *I'm young, and I have so much more than him.*

And isn't this free? And aren't I? And aren't we? and, with a glass broken on the dirty linoleum, thus begins your courtship (what a word).

A courtship conducted behind fast food restaurants, in dark schoolyards at night, and at the very, very sticky back of a movie theatre.

You wince, grip the armrest and trust the movie-theatre semi-dark, as he gropes between your legs. Older men aren't always good with their hands.

He takes your wrist, you tiptoe past his mother's room. He leads you down to the basement. His bed is unmade; you scan its filthy sheets for romance—

Ascribing a Rubenesque, draped aspect to the black rumpled sheets, a sunset quality to the ailing glow of his lava lamp.

In the late autumn, late afternoon light, he takes off your clothes. He undresses you so gently, and when he discovers the socks curled up inside your bra, he smiles, and kisses your tiny nipples so softly, his tongue flicking over them. It feels so good. Years later, you'll remember this moment, and feel perplexed by it, disturbed, until you remember—not everything could have been bad, right? He drew you in somehow.

He undresses himself. His nipples are the same colour as yours, his stomach a little loose. His thighs, thick with hair. The skin beneath blue-white.

His thighs, the slender, alien meat of them. Your circle of girl-women, for all its exuberant attitude, is still encased in child-hood.

He tries to fit two fingers inside of you. You watch two lumps interact inside the lava lamp: one absorbs the other, and it seems celestial.

Love takes root in your heart, opening up new channels, then flooding them with poison. He carries murder in him, and it's as if it's you.

Blood tastes like metal. Like black, never-washed bedsheets, and his stinking palm over your mouth.

You know he's horrible. He's so horrible that, weeks later, your family is baffled: what would you be doing with such a low human being?

But love doesn't work so simply, sometimes. Sometimes abjection creeps in and traps you.

This is because transgression can be unbearably sexy. You transgress your humanity in his hands, and become a creature, bleating for its life.

The dirtier the basement, the better. The crueler and uglier, the better. The low lows heighten the highs, streaked invisibly over bare white walls.

You don't recognize what the infections are. They linger for weeks and you can barely walk for ten minutes without rushing to a toilet. Or peeing in the snow. Or in your pants. There's a sting, so sharp you hiss, and your jean-clad thighs are briefly hot and wet, then freeze.

He is 26. He's a waiter at a diner, and wears an apron. He hates it, hanging in his closet like a limp fish. Whenever you spot it, you prickle up with fear.

One day he says, 'I want you.' You pretend you know what he means. He takes you by the wrists, eases you up against his bedroom wall.

On March evenings after work, you lay your head on his sour-smelling lap. You watch the tree in his mother's backyard lose colour with the dark.

On nights like this the restlessness enters him, stiffening his body. His blood runs to stone. His eyes weep red from two after-work joints.

Sometimes he'll insist you shave yourself completely, or demands a threesome with his twentysomething Goth friend. Let's call her One.

You stay quiet, cling to him tightly, bite back tears, wipe them off on his shirt. His restlessness passes as moods do, as time does.

No matter the hurt, you return to his bed. Lie still, watch the lava lamp lumps interact. One star eats another. A black hole eats that star.

You fake sick from school to visit him at the diner. As usual, it's empty. You've got the plastic rose in your hair. Your bra is stuffed.

The snow has receded. He rakes black, liquefied leaves from the patio, scowling and tugging at his apron. You sit on a damp chair, watching.

He goes inside to wipe the rake, his apron coming untied. You wait patiently, sucking your stomach, wanting to look thin, tidy, correct.

He, instead of coming back out, comes to the door and stands staring at you through the glass. You jump when you look up and see him.

His fingers are pressed so hard against the glass door his fin-ger-pads go white from pressure. His long nails bend backwards.

He shows you an old photo of his mom. She stands at a sink and looks over her shoulder, her hands blurred with long-ago domestic activity.

You: 'She's beautiful.' Him: 'No, she was a monster—though now she really looks like one. Too much drinking and crying and screwing and fighting.'

Your chest aches for his mother, a faded, squirrelly woman. She seems to occupy a different universe than his black jeans, his hate.

'That's your mother,' you say. Right then and there, you develop a lifelong distaste for men who bash their mothers and exes.

'I wanted to hit you,' he says. 'Just then, when you argued with me. Hey—hey, it's OK. I didn't do it, and I confessed.'

When love songs come on the radio you turn them off, you turn them on again, you don't know what to do:

'I would die for you, I will always love you, what am I sup-posed to do without your love, come and get your love'—you're flabbergasted by the truths coiled deep in each song, evident in the swelling strings, in the voice-hitches and gasps for breath, all suddenly and unbearably erotic.

It's the summer of 1999, and you squeeze yourself into crop-tops that hike up over your ribs, and dot your stomach with glue-on sequins from the drug store, vividly aware of your girl-woman power wafting out through your skin. Men everywhere smell it, but you've learned to examine yourself and everything around you like a security guard watching surveillance footage.

On the bus last week this guy touched your hair, leaning over to stroke it like a pet, and when you jerked away he jumped up and got off the bus, and you saw that his hair was white as a cotton ball.

And just yesterday as you were walking Bubbles, a guy driving a minivan with WELL DONE HOMES emblazoned on the side pulled over beside you and stuck out his head.

'Hey beautiful, you got anywhere to be?'

'No. Just outside,' you say. Though you lie easily to your mother all the time, you find it almost impossible to lie to strangers—it's especially hard, you're beginning to find, to lie to men like this, with want and age scrawled across their faces. That necessitates a different set of skills, which you won't master until your early twenties. He holds up a knotty index finger, asks you to wait, and drives off. He then returns 15 minutes later with a tray of iced coffees and an oil-spotted bag of donuts.

'Walk with me,' he says, swinging his legs out of the car, rolling his ropy neck around and massaging it with a paint-spotted hand. He dangles the donuts in front of him until you take the bag. He starts to walk, and you fall into stride beside him.

'So what do you like to do, you know, for fun? You a student? Do you drive?' (Without breaking his pace he leans backwards and pretends to grip a steering wheel, miming a casual drive through the neighbourhood, and you wince.)

'I don't,' you say.

He barks a fake, easy laugh. 'Ha, Toronto girl to the core, right? My ex-girlfriend was like that, but I like driving, so I don't mind.'

'I usually get rides to school, yeah,' you say, with care, and he pauses.

'You a student, then? You're 18, right?'

'14,' you say, the third sentence you'd spoken since thanking him for the coffee. He stops walking.

'Well. Call me in four years, and I'll take you out to dinner,' he says, then grins around his chewed-up drink straw. 'Or call me tomorrow and I'll take you to McDonald's.'

He laughs, so you laugh too, then sense you've been insulted. So you, in retaliation, ask him how old he is.

His face falls. 'Do you really want to know? Why do you want to know that?'

But he knows that you know why you want to know.

'Well I'm 40,' he says, and you flutter with pity. You'll feel bad for losers like this until your 30s, when they start ignoring you.

'That's OK,' you say—as ever. You even walk him back to his car. He brightens, and eats a donut in one bite. He has big, healthy teeth.

'I'm in the neighbourhood all the time. Next time I see you, I'll have written a song for you,' he says. You find this unbearably exciting.

But once he's gone, you sit on the sidewalk for a long time, trying to sing the love songs in your head again. Anxious embarrassment pulls you home. You feel you've been unfaithful, because Joseph asked to be your boyfriend just the day before, and here you are, having iced coffee in the street with a man who'll write a song for you.

When you throb right out of your body, drifting along waves of music, you have a laser focus on him, only him: Joseph, your older man, your quiet protector.

One cloudy Tuesday, you meet his friends: two women he's known since high school, two woman who look old to you, but are probably about his age: Cora and Kayla. They seem in love with him too—when he crosses his thin legs, plucking invisible lint from his tight black jeans, waxing poetic about sheeple, they tremble and listen. They bring him lasagna and sushi. They ignore you as much as they can, and it doesn't matter, because he's in love with you. But it isn't because you're so mature for your age, like he says: because what he loves is your childlikeness. The fact that you are, in fact, at 14: a child. Even within that circlet of adult losers, the women handle you with cool formality and little nips of aggression, because he loves you.

Here's the thing about being 14: you smell weakness, you assess coolness in seconds. A vivid matrix of social standing clips over your eyes, and you map everyone's high-school status: that mailman, with his long loping gait, he was briefly a basketball hero, now he cheats on his wife.

Your mother: she only has like, two, friends. She was one of the quiet ones, maybe nursing impossible crushes on geography teachers. Or the long-haired cashier at Longo's: a metal-head, probably still plays with the same band, probably still set to rip the world apart. So, Cora and Kayla, they're easy to read: total losers, even if they have forgotten. The gothy sort who wear corsets because they're goths, but also because they feel fat. A decade ago, all the other girls in school were cool compared to them, and skirted him like poison.

20 years ago, Kayla reveals over beer, he climbed right up the side of the school, whipping up a storm pipe like a flag up a pole and strutting around on the roof, laughing and throwing pieces of gravel at the cool girls as they shrieked and shrieked. Most of the boys watched him uneasily, though with his loose white T-shirt and buzz-cut hair he looked just like them. 'Why'd you do it,' Cora had asked him, once he'd been coaxed down by the French teacher, trembling in his big T-shirt, maybe holding back tears. 'Just bored,' he'd said, but you know he was lying. You ask for a beer, and he says no: you're too young. Really, it's because they're Joanne's, and he can't take more than three.

There they are, reminiscing about school, old despite themselves. But you're old, too—you'll be 15 soon, just five years shy of 20, and you look like a woman more and more every day, with bulges on your chest at least as big as a fat man's (you pray for bigger breasts almost every night, a silent prayer to whoever, not Carmen Electra big but just big enough for your large-handed man to cup them and say 'well, that's a handful.') Your body sings for him, and his body aches for yours. One evening he says: 'We need to fix the Greenhouse.'

And as you feel the breath of Spring and daylight begins lingering into the evening, the four of you steal beams and poles from the renovation sites dotting the neighbourhood—him yelling directions, frequently getting frustrated and saying things like 'Great, oh that's just great'—then hammering and soldering and stretching and stapling and using nearly everything in the big green toolbox, which his actual dad had left behind along with two blue work shirts, the old TV set, and an ugly pair of sunglasses Joanne still keeps folded by her bedside lamp. This mystifies you completely. Many objects are imbued with unbearable and humiliating resonance, a fact you keep very secret, as it's childlike and you reject it like poison—but even for a faded-out grownup like Joseph's mom, how could she stand it? Those glasses perched beside her every day, nighttime junk, whatever mystery novel she's reading, the remote control with its greased-out buttons, her empty plates of lonely bedtime snacks—how does she bear it?

One afternoon he delivers instructions, relayed from Joanne. Her elbows are acting up, she wants just to sleep. Time to work in the garden.

You all get stoned and prune the gourds, rescue the black beans from the beginnings of a weevil infestation, and patch up a leak in the irrigation hose. Cora and Kayla sing Pearl Jam as the sun sets, and pretend not to notice when Joseph presses his crotch up against your dirt-caked hands. Your heart races—he never kisses you in front of Cora and Kayla. You look up at him: in the darkening blue afternoon, his features are unfocused, and convey pure, uncomplicated ownership. The heat of his crotch, coiled within those black jeans, against your small hand. His mouth curls with desire to want something, and what you want doesn't matter, because of how he fucks you, and how he owns you, and how they hate you. Why want anything when they want your death, in different ways?

Later, as you all sit crossed-legged on the dirt floor of the Greenhouse, he rewards you with dinner: two Poptarts each.

After dinner he introduces you to their tradition, called 'Sharing Circle.' To you, well-versed in sleepovers and strictly regimented activity, it feels natural, but for two 26-year-old women, perhaps less so. But since adult life has stolen them from fun and spontaneity, they must relish this.

Anyway, here's how Sharing Circle works: one at a time, going around the circle, he asks each of you to Share your most recent and most shameful desires—or acts—and then after each woman confesses—everyone's favorite part—he takes your hands, and forgives you.

Cora goes first: 'I'm so fat I don't feel like a person. I'll feel like a person once I'm 40 pounds lighter,' she confesses.

Your mother keeps you on a strict diet, disapproves of your thighs. You swallow hard. '40 pounds is way too much, you look beautiful,' you say.

'Oh, and how much is enough, then? 20? 30?' Kayla says, sharing a glance with Cora. Joseph takes Cora's hand.

'You are fat. You are in fact very fat,' he says gently. 'But you can fix it, and we can help you. Just eat less and walk more, walk everywhere you go. Focus on this goal even when I'm not around,' he says, and then kisses her fingers.

'I used to hate my little sister so much that still I have dreams she's an escaped monkey from the zoo, and I kill her with rocks,' Kayla says.

'Every animal is sacred, Kayla,' Joseph says. Kayla starts to cry, covering her face with her free hand. He rubs his chin.

'Have you always felt your mother pitted you against your sister, Kayla?' Joseph asks, and she gurgles a tremulous 'yes.'

He rubs her fingers in his. He has beautiful hands, though the long nails are unnerving. 'Your mother,' Joseph says, 'she doesn't know how to love. She lives a bleak and lonely life, and she has no one but herself and your negligent father to blame. You would go home to the room you had to share with your sister, probably because your dad snorted and gambled all the extra money away.' You interrupt:

'How old is your sister now?' Kayla pauses for a moment before answering: '21. She's in medical school.'

'Your parents poured all their resources into her, into Aviva, didn't they?' Joseph says gently, as she sobs openly now.

'Mom never left us alone,' she whimpers. 'Just always nagging, nagging, even in the shower—she limited my showers to four minutes, and if I took longer than four minutes, she'd come in, shut off the water—and Aviva got four minutes too, even though she was basically a baby then, and she still thinks I'm fat, they both do, and—and I'm so sick of it. I hate my family so much.'

'I know you do, Kayla, and that's okay. That's okay because we are your family too, your chosen family.' Kayla nods fervently, blowing her nose on a stray leaf. Cora rubs her back, and Joseph kisses her hand. Three faces, one shining wet, rotate towards to you. Your turn.

'I didn't study for a biology term test this week,' you share. 'I'm pretty sure I bombed.' Joseph asks you if you're sure that's your confession.

'Yes,' you say. Kayla blows her nose in the leaf again, and snorts derisively. Your smile fades: you're playing a game with high stakes, no rules.

Joseph kisses your hand, then sniffs it, and kisses it again. He sighs, sharing a glance with Cora. 'You're a smoker, I can smell it on your fingers.'

Cora then gives you a look like, *You've got what's coming to you and I pity you deeply*, which she gives you so often—over dropping the pruning shears, over sneaking into the subway without paying fare, over spacing out and ignoring her and One sometimes—that now, you understand this look as meaning something more like: 'You're going to feel pain and I can't wait.'

'The Millennium is racing towards us and Y2K is threatening to rip society apart,' Joseph says, 'threatening to send cars flying off bridges and satellites falling from space, and you're developing an addiction? An addiction that will rot your body, burrow tunnels in your brain, blacken your throat, make your teeth fall out?' Kayla looks back at him, then says, 'She tells me that she gets them from a girl at school.'

You close your eyes. Even though they're nearly a decade out from high school, the fact of you smoking Alpha's cigarettes, a person with a nearly perfect sense of self who glides through the school like the most exotic fish in a tank, deepens the betrayal. You have curried acceptance far beyond this group, within a golden circlet of the impossibly young. It reminds them of your youth, your relative normality, your future a golden worm still curled in your chest. It reminds them of the great gulf between them and you: you haven't had a chance to fuck up adulthood yet, and they hate you for it.

Joseph sits and thinks, rubbing a spot on his chin. You noticed long ago that he has a small growth right below his lower lip, which he worries with his finger when he's especially deep in thought. You all watch him rub his chin. Slowly, slowly, the light shifts and changes outside.

'It's a kind of surrogate behaviour,' he says at last, 'for something perfectly natural.' He pauses. 'Lustful acts.' Your stomach jolts—you almost yank your hand away from him. Does he knows about Mr. WELL DONE HOMES?

'I bet you linger in the girl's change room after gym,' Joseph says. 'I've seen how you watch "Xena." You must watch her like that too, don't you? Laughing with her friends even though they're not that funny, skipping any class she likes, flirting with the teachers, calling you over to hang out after school. Your gratitude is so obvious to me, to us, to everybody you know, it almost gives off a smell. You hate those boys she's always telling you about, don't you? They touch your back to flirt with you and you pull yourself away. They surround her and you strain to see around them, don't you? I see how excited you get telling us where you've been—oh, I was just with Alpha.

'Lovely, isn't she? Her hair, her breasts, her irreverence.' You don't know what 'irreverence' means, but you know that Alpha is actually quite kind in a way none of them can be: her easy kindness is sustained by her assurance that life is kind, wealthy and pretty and loved as she is; there are always parties to attend and missed tests to be forgiven and people to watch her stand out by the flagpole just after class starts, jauntily lighting a cigarette. You imagine pressing against her neck and inhaling deeply, and then imagine stroking her silky hair, running your hand from its roots to its ends with no resistance.

'Yes,' you say, keeping your eyes shut—'Yes, I lust after Alpha.'

There is a horrible pause.

'Kayla, Cora, leave us alone for a while,' Joseph says at last. 'See if Joanne wants help making her dinner.'

Cora gives you another significant woe-is-you-but-I-warned-you-didn't-I look, and Kayla takes her hand. They stand and leave. You keep your eyes shut, trying to get all the songs started up in your head again; you hear the creak of the ramshackle door, hear them start whispering as soon as they're outside. You know you're in trouble and anxiety flips around inside your stomach, but you almost want to giggle, both at your anxiety, and to relieve it, as now that you're alone with him, the fact of your aloneness, the heat he gives off and the just-audible sound of breath—is it quickening?—is almost excruciating. You open your eyes and look out towards the house, noticing that Cora and Kayla don't go inside but rather linger on the porch, watching. He crawls towards you, grips your hand between both of his palms—they're moist and very hot—and tilts his head, appearing to consider.

'Suck me off until I come in your mouth,' he says. 'I want you to swallow, and look me in the eyes while you do it. Then we'll rejoin the girls.'

For one horrid, endless moment you will him to smile, to kiss your fingers—barely keeping his composure—and then break out into a laugh, so you know he is joking. 'You don't mean that,' you say, pulling back. He tightens his grip a little.

'I'm afraid that you're weak,' Joseph says. 'Sometimes I watch you and I know you'd become anybody in anybody's hands: you'd become a cheerleader in a group of cheerleaders, you'd try learning the drums if you fell in with a group of wannabe musicians, you'd dye your hair black and pierce your eyebrows if you fell for a Goth. No—look at me,' he continues, unbuttoning his pants, pulling himself out, guiding you down.

'Who are you?' he asks, and though he spent the afternoon demanding confessions, it's a rhetorical question. You take him in your mouth.

He smells strongly—it's not entirely unpleasant, but a shock, just as your own private smells might be if someone caught your own scent drying on your fingers. Up close and in your mouth his penis feels gigantic, and gripped in his fist it looks fearsome enough to unhinge your jaw, but it's almost tender in the softness of its skin, in its susceptible proximity to your teeth and in how it shrinks a little in your mouth, countering slightly the ferocity of his words, this act. His hand guides you up and down, his fingers grip your hair.

Just as the man in the WELL DONE HOMES minivan must have known, you are all body; your total embodiment makes your powerful, as it's all the power you have. But also, it lives in a tiny place, perhaps where your future-worm is curled—a place invisible to him. Up and down, choking and drooling, you retreat into yourself, trusting one day you might emerge elsewhere, reconfigured and untouchable. As with many moments like these you'll remember it like a photograph, both of you tiny in your mind, little animate dolls whose actions one must strain to discern. He begins to shake and breathe heavily, the smells intensifying and his stomach slick with sweat against your forehead, his palm sweating into your scalp and his heartbeat hammering in the vice-grip of his fingertips and deep in his body and cock, and right before he comes you are a piston, an automaton, an extension of his body moving with total precision, and that is powerful too, you will tell yourself later, tomorrow and years after that. He comes—it is foul, hot and bitter against your tongue and down your throat, and you choke and jerk away, but he grabs you by the back of the neck:

'Did I—say you could—stop?'

You bend back down and take his soft dick back in your mouth, unsure how to proceed. His hand shifts away from your throat and towards the top of your head. He strokes your hair, and you hold his penis in your mouth, feeling it curl up until it's small as a boneless finger. He pulls out and his hand slides back under your throat, and he grips you right below the chin, squeezing until you look up, look him in the eye.

'Oh,' he says. 'You're so little.' Little relative to him. The cares of the city dwarf you both, and the Earth, its puff of atmosphere—worlds upon worlds. Cora's voice, nasal and stoned, returns to your head: 'Do you ever really sit and think, you guys, about how we're on a planet?'

You choke again, a loud coughing sound. You reach for his hands.

'Don't,' he says sadly. 'You'll just make it worse.'

You drop your hands. You stare at each other. This involves you craning up, up, up, and him looking down.

'You know what I want?' Joseph says. 'I want you to imprint on me like a baby bird. I want you to black out in my hands, slip away for a while. I'd let you slip away for a while, safe in my hands, and take a little break from your toxic family and this ugly new world of men, following you around like fucking coyotes— yes, I see it, yes I know. Then, my darling, I'd bring you back. Bring you right back, til your eyes flutter open and you wake up in my hands. Me the first thing you see. Me, my loving face.'

You cough again. With a shaking hand wipe your soaked face, your chest. He takes your hand away from your body, places it on his chest.

'You know I keep you safe,' he says. 'I tell you the truth. You're surrounded by sycophants, men who want to fuck you and then toss you out.'

You think of Alpha, playfully tossing a French fry at Beta. That she can afford a packet of fries is exotic. Your heart constricts, and for first time longing becomes corporeal pain, that septic pining that eats ragged holes in the lovesick, abandoned, or bereaved. And that they've not been robbed of what they have, what they are: twinned, plump, cossetted virginities—and suddenly, you hate them. For the first time, and not the last, you imagine Beta tied to a bed, sobbing. 'Aren't you so mature for your age?' you hiss, over his shoulder. For weeks, you see other women this way—the way he does. You hate mini-skirted legs that go unravished, glossed-up lips left unbitten.

'The girls?' he says, like he's reading your mind. 'The girls don't really trust you. Why don't they trust you? Do you ever think about that?'

Here's the thing about being 14: nothing's your fault until everything is. You swallow his truth; you are ruined. He alone can tell. Your neck and chest are so slick with tears, your own thick spit and stomach bile, that he's starting to have trouble keeping his grip on you.

He leans in to you, puts his mouth to your ear. Each movement takes ages, the moment before he speaks goes on and on. Choking you, his breath catches, right before speaking: in retrospect you'll realize he must have been surprising himself too, learning as he went.

'Every morning I come out here and sit by the tomatoes,' he whispers, his lips in your wet hair—'and I thank the sun for them, and for you.'

He lets you go. You hit the dirt. You taste bile, green tomato, sulfry egg. You see nothing but static, then silver-milk light. Your head pounds. You crawl—on your elbows and stomach— toward the doorway. You see Kayla and Cora are watching, from the porch.

You stop just short of the grass outside, as if you've bumped against glass. You stare at Two until Kayla looks away, and pulls Cora inside.

Here's the thing about being 14: your world was recently 5 people big, the size of your family. It's malleable enough to contract again. Your family dictates 'normal' and 'acceptable,' shapes your world accordingly, and he is your chosen family, isn't he? So when he tells you 'wait a minute' you sit very still, like you'd wait in the car for your father. He leans back, catches his breath.

'If bruises appear, that's good,' he says. 'They'll look like love-bites, and we'll know what they really are: they are the poison leaving you. I am breaking hard ground for new growth,' he says, and he reaches towards you and strokes your hair.

'OK,' you whisper.

'You've been cruel to the girls, haven't you?' he says. 'Cunty and stuck-up. All because you didn't know who you are.'

Dust particles rise in the silver-milk light, growing gold as the afternoon ages. 'But now you know who you are. So don't forget.'

You never do.

He instructs you to sleep in the shed, covering you in tarp. You wake several times that night, your body wracked with hunger. He brings you Joanne's cordless phone the next day, so you might call your parents and tell them you're at Alpha's house this weekend, working on a school project. A collaborative essay, he mouths at you, crouching beside a pot of herbs. He hangs up the phone for you—beep—and brings it back into the house. You watch him go, then rip a greenish tomato from a nearby vine.

Here's the thing about being 14: your body is womanlike, but still creating itself; you are always hungry, often ravenously so. Your stomach has been pulling on itself, sucking up and down your spine like a snail, since last night; your last meal was a hard-boiled egg the previous morning. You feel something shift painfully within you, waking and unsealing, swallowing the tomato in two large, sloppy bits. He comes back out of the house, pauses to inspect something tangled, grey-white, on the grass, then bends to pick it up before returning. He sniffs your hands, leans in and smells your breath. He is wearing black jogging pants and a fuzzy, oversized sweater.

'Joanne wanted us to take care of this,' he says, and you look down at his hands and sees that the thing is a dead bird—a pigeon. Its chest is still plump and its neck feathers glimmer an iridescent green, but already it's beginning to lose its shape, appearing flat in places. He hands it to you.

'I think I recognize this bird. See the spots on its back? Mom would shred her sandwich crusts and feed it.'

You ask him for its name. 'She didn't name it, she just fed it all the time. People are inconsistent monkeys.' He pauses. 'It shit more than it ate.'

'What do you want me to do with it?' you ask, looking down at the pigeon. It's stiff as a newspaper in your hands, its dappled, ruffled body improbably light. Throughout the night, tiny creatures sipped its living moisture away with microscopic straws.

'You're hungry,' he says. He picks up a watering can, and walks over to the big plywood box in which tiny heads of lettuce are sprouting.

'I'll bury it,' you say, but he shakes his head.

'Did you bury the hot dog you purchased with Alpha, last Wednesday?' Joseph asks mildly.

The pigeon's dull eye appears to look back up at you, though perhaps pigeons just don't have eyelids. Though you think nothing of the sort at the time, you'll remember that one eye emoting a wide range throughout your life, from cruel mocking to pure, empty innocence.

You sleep under the tarp again, and he sleeps beside you this time. You wake to rain patting and sliding down the plywood around you, and feel everything growing around you, inside and outside the shed, within the backyard, and beyond it. The pigeon lies near the watering can, and you brush ants away from it. Here's the thing about being 14: much like old toys and filled-up colouring books and sides of salmon in the supermarket, the dead pigeon possesses a soul, in your eyes. While you know the bird isn't alive—as a wind-up frog isn't alive, or plywood walls—it isn't dead. You don't know dead, yet. Whatever allowed you to play for hours alone as a child, it hasn't totally dissipated, imbuing the bird, the walls, the evening with a monolithic, painful magic. Kneeling, clutching the bird: something in you dies, so you might live. You'll never feel that way again.

Now you've brushed them from the pigeon, the ants are everywhere in the dirt, inscribing circles and appearing to run, maybe because of the rain. By the next afternoon you've ripped away most of the pigeon's feathers, eaten stringy flesh from its chest cavity. He crouches nearby.

You throw up some of it, and then eat more. He retrieves a cloth from the house, wipes your face, and sends you home.

Back at home, your mother serves you chicken, potatoes. 'Not too many,' she advises—about the potatoes. You leave some. She's pleased.

Next Tuesday afternoon you come alone to his house, and he leads you to the backyard, towards the shed. Joanne is watching TV, eating what looks like pasta, and watching what looks like the news. You're relieved she doesn't turn around. Joseph walks catlike. He asks you if you have a lighter in your (glittery, plastic) purse. You do, and when you hand it to him, he smirks with what looks like disapproval.

Here's the thing about being 14: despite your cool-girl airs, the disapproval of an older person is still very, very effective. He closes the shed door. Milky, cloudy light drifts in around the door. He flicks the lighter on and off, and tells you to undress.

Here's the thing about being 14: you undress like you're getting naked on camera. You cross both arms to lift off your shirt. You wear all your lace like you always do, because—as Alpha said last week—what if you get hit by a school-bus, and they find you in dirty, like, grandma panties?

'My god you're beautiful,' he says, after a sharp intake of breath. He pulls a large digital camera from the pocket of his black jeans. He takes a picture of you. You flinch. He takes another picture. You cringe. You drape a hand over your bare stomach, tilt your head.

Here's the thing about being 14: your body will never be more whole or responsive than it is right now, and you'll never hate it more. Standing naked in the faint, milky light, you grasp how fundamentally different he is from you, and that difference begins with your body.

He pockets the camera. He tells you to lean against him. He holds you like a harp, keeping you steady, placing one hand under your neck. With his other hand, he holds the lighter against your skin. With the careful precision of a surgeon he makes little burns all over your flesh. He burns you anywhere pale and usually hidden by clothes, encouraging you to cry and instructing you to turn your face away when he cries, too. He grips you tightly under your chin, holding you against him. He says that he's creating routes for your true self to breathe. You sweat profusely, your pubic hair dewy, perched naked against him in the shed. Through the window, the television shrieks.

'Because of your parents you've created a false self, superficial, covering you like tectonic plates,' he says. He carefully burns away some of the white hairs on your stomach. 'Today we're letting her, Real Erica, breathe. Focus on your body as a permeable barrier that we're opening up today through pain, through focused thought. Concentrate on yourself as a child, as a baby. Can you see it?' You whimper, and his hand tightens under your chin. You choke.

'Your baby-self, delighting in—I don't know—a spider-web on a windowsill. On learning to eat. Feeling her lungs full of air, wanting only to keep on living.' He holds the lighter to your hip. You stifle a shriek as the skin stinks and darkens.

'Then you came into a shattering realization that—hold still, *shhh*—your parents didn't really care, not the way they should have. So you taught yourself total compliance, the only way to make them happy, to keep enchanting them once your magical babyhood was gone. You turned seven, you turned eight, you turned nine. You'd visit classmates at their homes to watch their mothers dote on them, and to grasp, by proxy, what they meant by "Mom," and the great chasm between their understanding and yours. You'd watch Disney movies, and the mother-daughter love you'd witness seemed as safely unreal as mermaids and talking lions. Pure, idealistic fantasy.'

'But then you'd watch your friends with their mothers, and fill up with sorrow. You begin to cry. It's not too late,' he whispers, his mouth against your ear. 'Come out through your skin. You're there. There you are. Come out of the empty realm of false relationships, the long corridors of other children's homes with their toys and siblings and loving parents locked away in their bedrooms—they don't see you, those children, those parents, those toys: you're a ghost. Come out of the realm of empty trees and piles of bones and big white snowbanks, of False You— you don't need her anymore. Join me, join us here. We are now, we are real . . .'

Here's the thing about being 14: your mother is still your mother. When you lean over that evening, revealing your collarbone, she sees the welts and burns. She's stricken. Your mother

is still your mother, and you, being her child—and still a child—
confess.

You promise you'll stay away, and your parents believe you.
and why wouldn't they? He's horrible.

But here's the thing about being 14: you ignore your parents
and know you know everything, rendering virtually anything
dangerous—sewing needles puncture ears; tabs of fake acid can
kill you; you can drink sherry until they empty your stomach
with tubes.

No matter the hurt, you'd come back to him like a windup
toy, trudging back to his mom's house through sludgy maple
blossoms, thinking as you walk: this is how it works, you're
assigned to someone and that's it, you do everything they
say—if it weren't for Alpha, that is. She's smoking a post-lunch
cigarette with Beta, out by the flagpole. It's an achingly gor-
geous spring morning, the sort of May morning in which all
the cares of the school year have grown weightless—the perfect anticipation of giddy summer fills the craniums of students
and teachers like helium—better even than the summers themselves, those baking, boredom-lined hours—and she calls you
over, waving her small, soft hand, and for an instant, suspended
in a column of sunlight, right before you join her, you feel
endless, the sun bores straight down through you to your
future—it feels—which is yours alone. and your body is you
and yours.

'I think I saw your boyfriend,' Beta says disdainfully, referring to a Wednesday afternoon in which Joseph had appeared, all
in black, to meet you. Alpha says nothing, allowing Beta's deri-
sion to sit, to sting. Alpha understands the productive potential of
manageable unpleasantness, but after school that same day, she
draws you into a gracious, one-armed hug, so gossamer-perfect
you close your eyes. You smell vanilla. Some things have been
lost, but you are not. You inhale together once, twice, before she
lets go. She takes hold of your hand.

'I have sweaty palms,' you confess, humiliated: you sweat
huge patches through your shirts, and the more you fear it, the
faster it darkens even the thickest of wool sweaters, in cold,

tectonic patches. You dream those wet patches as vivid bright blood. She squeezes.

'My palms sweat too,' she says. (They do not.) She holds your hand all the way to the mall, until your fingers are prune-y with wet, then a breeze comes between your palms and hers, cooling you down. Imperceptibly, she loosens her grip. Your shoulders uncoil.

Despite being sweaty, you are deserving of clothes, being clothed, staying clothed until the very moment you decide you want to undress.

Despite being sweaty, you are deserving of pain-free sex, of fear-free life, without daggers of fear flashing at the corner of your eyes.

Despite being sweaty, you are deserving of the youth that briefly inhabits your body. You deserve to keep it to yourself, no matter who begs. As a test, you try to imagine your life with him, and come up with nothing. You and him alone—nothing. You cannot grasp it. A triumph.

Conspiracy theories are powerful because once they seize hold, they crowd your skull, become of the utmost importance. Why live when the moon landing was faked, the whistleblowing astronaut burnt to a crisp inside a sealed-up lunar prototype? Why live when the world's fate was sealed a century ago, when we're fated to suck the final strains of oxygen from our atmosphere, while the shadowy few stream down into bunkers— concrete reinforced tunnels, marble sinks and easy chairs, kilometers deep in soil? Why live when Planet X, forever tracing Neptune's shadow, still hosts the long-limbed horrors the Egyptians took for gods? Why live when the evil global conglomerate orchestrated the deaths of thousands and thousands more, melting towers and spraying bullets and fire, spider-webbing nightmares across the global south—which you track from your bed, eating Puritan meatballs? Why live when the curtain flies up on your mother, your brother, your father, your childhood friends: all dupes, with their hands over their eyes?

After school one day you receive an email from Joseph. He'd quit his job. He'd painted over the windows of his basement bedroom. Time then expanded like a balloon in that bedroom, crowding out activity, stifling movement. He'd stolen money from Joanne for more weed. He'd watered down her whiskey, cut at his skin. Crept upstairs to feast on her crumbs at night, as she slept. What did you think of that? 'Why won't you open your eyes? Why won't Cora or Kayla?' Quoting Nine Inch Nails, he laments: 'I keep slipping away.'

The hubris of youth: You don't understand his intentions. The theoretical and elderly, they drop apple-like to the dirt. They bounce.

Even from your perch on life's boughs, you don't see them decompose. They are firm and ruddy, streaked green, dappled yellow. All is alive. Birds chase through the darkening sky. The boughs stir, and you do too. Do people disappear? Waltz towards the wings?

They don't tell you about the body: it's lifelike. Its skin is still skin. Its eyes eyelike, its face facelike, or at least—masklike. They don't tell you what happens to corpses in human spaces built exclusively for the living: constructed to keep in heat, to keep out insects and birds—corpses, on the other hand, thrive in cold. Small animals, parasites and worms, hungry birds, wet soil and slow-motion white roots, with time, take care of the corpse, massage, drain and reclaim it. But not in spaces built exclusively for those alive. It's funny to think of corpses as thriving, but we're stuck within the human matrix. Human bodies, living and dead, are bound to life, and life itself is frightening and ugly. It teems and self-replicates and devours. Bodies supplant bodies. Life doesn't care.

Bodies don't care, either.

His mom calls all 10 phone numbers in his address book. It's a miracle they found him alive, a miracle from God, she tells you, as your own mother stands across from you in the kitchen, mouthing *Who's that?*

He was so thin, barely breathing. She hadn't even known he'd quit his job.

He planned his exit, before the lizard eyes of George W. Bush could flicker briefly orange through the TV, and settle on him again. After he'd consumed his mother's Rohypnol crushed into a can of slippery, bright Spaghetti-O's, and fallen asleep, Cora and Kayla had showed up to help, pulling paper bags over their shoes to mask their presence: Saying quiet prayers as they filled the helium bag up for him, intending to seal it up over his head.

Seized with fear, they saved him instead.

When the ambulance had come and gone, they buried the helium bag out by the tomatoes. A false jellyfish packed in dirt.

He intended to die knowing he knew best, knowing a monolithic Evil threatened our small, doomed little world. He nearly died in black and white; he nearly died, intending to die before They got to him, having incited Their rage for sketching bright patterns that uncovered their tracks. He wanted to die important.

Here's the thing about being 15: 14 is a lifetime ago, sixteen a lifetime away. Of course, every day, he'll come to mind out of nowhere or everywhere. You shake your head, he dissipates. You survived by squeezing through a loophole in his hatred: by reducing you to your body he braided you into life itself, which teems and devours. When you are life, there's no end to you.

COMMUNION MINUTES. LOGGED BY ERICA,
VIDEO TAPE #3, SEPT/27

JOSEPH: . . . And did you know that, even now, Amazon storage units take hours to walk across? What will happen as they take over more and more of retail and distribution?

LOGAN: [*twisting and worrying a piece of bread in her fingers*]. No more jobs?

JOSEPH: Good. Work will dry up even for Non-Resisters as great big conglomerates eat up the last of the smaller businesses and farms. It'll be thrown into high gear as automation takes over driving jobs, manufacturing and assembly jobs, service jobs.

LOGAN: Jesus.

JOSEPH: Back when the great sooty wheel of industry began turning, it was pushed by those whose limbs and lungs were seen as expendable. And they were the *lucky* ones. Countless others, hundreds of thousands of people, were put out of work and left to starve, doused in darkness as society metastasized. The late nineteenth century is a dead zone in our collective memory, and I suspect that these next few decades, this upcoming era, will be too.

ERICA: [*from behind the camera.*] Today Joseph will begin sharing the story of his enlightenment with us.

LOGAN: We are grateful for this.

JOSEPH: [*smiles over at her, rubbing his chin under his beard.*] And your gratitude is faith, Sister. So . . . [*re-crosses his legs, places him palms on his knees. He looks straight at the camera*]. One day I was stuck in the city, and all at once I felt a great premonition. I stumbled— anonymous as the dead—through downtown Toronto, so thick with buildings and stuff that I hungered for the sight of a real thing like a tree, its leaves and limbs, against the sky, instead of the quick-melting TV screen images lighting up shop windows and snagging my attention as night fell. I saw a woman with bandaged hands begging, imploring the backs of people waiting to cross the street towards the Pizza Pizza—and I felt nothing for her. A dog on a worn-out leash shivered by her knee and I felt nothing, and a child bumped up against my leg and looked up at me startled, and I felt nothing. Then I realized that the city is sentient. That the city has a consciousness in which all city-dwellers participate. And this consciousness is sociopathic, pumping us with poison.

ERICA: And what are we Grateful for?

EVERYONE: The Sun, the Sky, the Big Tree and its Shelter, the Earth beneath us and around us. Our Home, our Gardens, our Greenhouse.

JOSEPH: [*reaches to Logan, squeezes her hand.*] And your gratitude is faith. Each callus on your hands, you know what it is?

EVERYONE: The poison leaving us.

JOSEPH: Breaking hard ground for new growth. [*He looks back at the camera.*] And then . . . and then, a child stepped out of the street, breaking from a crowd of faceless strangers, and grabbed my hand. She led to me to a storefront window that was empty except for another one of those TV screens, and we pressed our faces against the glass and saw a vision of the future. We saw dead oceans, clear and sterile, going on for thousands and thousands of kilometers. And we saw the cities spread and the suburbs spread faster still, paving forests and mountains and lakes and rivers and connecting city to city, city to city. And we saw Canada's great icy North shift and melt, sped-up winters and summers flying by like nights and days, until brown ground showed through. And the creatures starved and great floods were unleashed on everything below.

[*Logan begins to cry.*]

And I Confess that I cried, and I was terribly afraid. I asked what could be done—if anything could be done. And the child said, It is too late; it was too late even twenty years ago, humankind is too far gone, the planet is wounded and its affliction is now too great to be reversed.

ERICA: [*extends her arm out in front of the camera, reaches for Logan's hand.*] Logan, Sister, it's OK. Try to breathe, breathe with me.

JOSEPH: There is work to be done. We must live a lifetime with the limited years we have left, and preserve as much life as we can around us. We must live beautifully, and live intentionally. While Soup-Swimmers lie about dazed, stoned on choice and variety, with no delineations between work and play, between sleep and wakefulness, we will work as we do today. While the shit-dwellers labor and stack bricks under the fragmented attention of human supervisors and the laser-sharp focus of mechanized supervisors, we will work as we do today. While Soup-Swimmers extend their lifespan to centuries-long, at the expense of the Laborers and everything else, we will know how futile this will be, as the end times are nearly upon us, and we will work as we do today. Work with what you have, the child told me, and I had a little money saved, and I had what I'd learned from a lifetime of tending to things that grow slower than we do.

ERICA: And the good fortune of inheriting the compound from your mother.

JOSEPH: [*pause.*] Yes, which is of course a tremendous blessing.

ERICA: Certainly our greatest blessing, for which we are Grateful.

LOGAN: We are Grateful for our Home, for the Den in which we rest, for the big Tree and the Sunshine—

JOSEPH: [*interrupting*] Our greatest blessing is our knowledge, and our will to transcend.

ERICA: Of course. Yes.

JOSEPH: And what are we Grateful for?

EVERYONE: The Sun, the Sky, the Big Tree and its Shelter, the Earth beneath us and around us. Our Home, our Gardens, our Greenhouse.

JOSEPH: And your gratitude is faith. Each callus on your hands, you know what it is?

EVERYONE: The poison leaving us.

JOSEPH: Breaking hard ground for new growth . . .

LOGAN, ERICA, LORI: SOME WOMEN
EAT THEIR CHILDREN
[LOGAN]

Dear Joseph,

The last time I wrote on paper it was something like, '- 2 lbs, Cynthia, +1.3 lbs, Kenya,' because the Weight Watchers computer system was down, and even our treadmill desks stopped working. The time before that it was my number, on a napkin. Let's see what else . . . my Dad still gets mail sometimes, even now, so I've written 'return to sender' on the envelopes really quick so my Mom Lori didn't have to see. She told me that the first time something arrived for him and he wasn't there to open it, it was weird. She sat there holding his credit card bill in her hands, and he'd never be there to open it and read the rows of stuff he'd spent credit on and the days he'd spent it, and it was almost as weird as him being gone in the first place.

And let's see . . . before the letters, before my school went totally digital I'd do my math homework in a notebook, but I hated that, I never got very good at writing by hand. And way before that, back when I wanted to be a journalist, Lori got me a little diary for my birthday, the kind with a padlock and key. Sometimes I'd unlock it and open up the pages, maybe dot a pen on the paper. But I never filled it out.

[LOGAN]

Dear Joseph,

It's September the seventh, day 36, and today we worked in the greenhouse. I weeded the squash and cucumbers just like old times as a kid, and I'm writing in a journal now, just like old times too. While you were in town this afternoon Erica and I did

Sharing, and I guess I thought about Lori a lot afterwards. I am sorry I was resistant to Sharing. It's not that I am against cultivating transparency and openness like Erica was worried about, it's just that there are some things nobody's really asked and I haven't told. And then years pass and that way feels safe, and the only way there is. But I will try now, because you are my Family.

Lori met my dad in her second year at Trent University, in Peterborough. Gramma said she picked him just to give her grief, and if you saw him you'd think she did, too. He was from Toronto, and biked everywhere he could like city kids do, and he loved classical music and having debates. She said she liked a lot of things about him, but mostly:

1) He was <u>intellectual</u>. She would look at his bookshelf and think, 'all these books are in your head.' All these things he had a lifetime to teach her.

2) He was <u>charming</u>. For example she would make us soup and garlic toast and roast chicken, and he would do all the dishes, and not just the ones we ate off either.

3) He <u>needed her</u>. It wasn't just that he said it, she could tell by how deep he slept beside her, how he woke up shaking for her (ew, I know), and how he told her everything first and called her his 'partner.' She claimed to never need anyone before, but she started to need him back.

And so they did everything together. It happened fast, partly because she tried really hard around all his friends, so they liked her coming along, and partly because she was the only one who could drive. They both dropped out of school because you can go back to school anytime, and go into debt for it like Lori was doing, but you're only twenty once. So they got married, a quickie ceremony at Toronto City Hall, and they took the money his parents were sending for school, and travelled to: Paris, the interior of BC, Holland, Berlin, Thailand, Prague and India. It took two years but it sounds like a decade when Lori tells it, and they ate a million dishes and saw everything in every season and met a lot of travelling Canadians but didn't pay them much attention, and took hundreds of pictures. Looking through Lori's Facebook albums, those same familiar ruins and islands and beaches could be a backdrop in a photographer's studio, but what you see if you look a little harder—the unique little story that unfolds as you click through—is them making a world just him and her, their cheeks pressed together, their smiles starting to match. She got very sick in Thailand and had a bunch of credit cards going too, so getting back to Canada and settling in the little apartment in Bowmanville was a relief, she said, at least for her.

When your husband leaves forever you might think: what a tragedy it is to lose him, because only the two of us share our history, our private world of two, and so when he disappears for good you're doing all of the remembering on your own. But sometimes your two-person world 'bifurcates'—which is a great word, thank you—it splits him one way and you the other, and in the light that comes in you realize you're alone anyway, you've always been alone.

[LORI]

Dear girl:

This is Mozart—here, she brings her belly close to the speaker, a shiver of cold contact through her navel, there—'Soave sia il vento,' yes, it's vibrating all through her and through you. He finishes his cider and watches her press her stomach to the speaker, then says in his reedy drunk voice, 'Listening to Mozart reorganizes your brain, like . . . running a comb through it,' and she shudders, imagining your tiny hands, a tiny comb, your tiny head. You won't know yellow or red, the ecstatic whiteness of the sun through leaves and over water or the remarkable formation of ice on black branches, the full-body sensation of roast beef sandwiches when you're ravenous, or lips on your skin. But you feel the vibrations of Mozart, and maybe the sensation of cold when your mother is outside a long time, and the itch of heat while she drowses by the radiator. She tells herself don't get attached, but how can that be? You're neither asleep nor awake but alive, growing helplessly and amazingly on whatever she ingests—however you lie in her amniotic sea.

She's sick to death of rape stories, and they're a dime a dozen where she's from. As long as she's alive, she'll never tell hers. There's two reasons why:

1) *If she told her Mom she'd say, Well anything goes between a man and a woman once you're married, which she's dead right on that one, if the stories her married friends and sisters tell me is true, and:*
2) *He remembered it differently.*

Her Mom also said, *The women in our family hang up our panties and get pregnant, and it turns out she's dead right on that one, too. And so now, he has even more reason to remember it different . . .*

[ERICA]

My darling,

It is September the eighth, day 37, and today after the accident we pickled the rest of the cucumbers, the green beans, the jalapeno peppers, and I am sorry about what happened. I think I was sleep-walking, and I forgot who Logan is. Just imagine my shock at seeing a stranger in the house like that, just sitting alone at the table and eating our tomatoes, with nobody warning me beforehand. I think I thought she broke in. I thought one of the hooligan kids who broke that Greenhouse window Wednesday night got bold, maybe stoned on something, and came inside for more. But like you said, why the hell would a pregnant girl break into a house? Especially someone so shy and weird as Logan. I promise I will be good to Logan, better and better, and teach her about the Greenhouse and our Purpose, and Share with her when you are busy.

Darling, she looks so young and thin that her skin looks see-through, especially around her wrists and eyes and her little stretched-out belly, and my heart kind of breaks. I can tell she's had a hard time, and I am glad that she found us. I am grateful that our family is growing.

I can't Share this with her, and I know you feel she's very mature for her age, but I see Logan as a little girl. I also look at Logan's body parts, like her thin fingers and her face as smooth as a peach, and I think of the girls I knew in high school, the girls who everyone watched. Those girls would light cigarettes and breathe out their smoke too fast and look silly, because they were still basically kids, even though older men would fall in love with them and treat them like grown-ups (when and how it suited them, anyway.) I feel like every man I meet longs for a little girl like that, and even when I was their age I didn't have a prayer. So my heart kind of breaks for Logan, but it itches with envy too, and so I want some days to pass so she becomes familiar, so I can look at her and think family and feel only good things, only warm things . . .

[LORI]

Dear girl:

She sits on the couch, and he has his big arm around her but twisted up, with his hand pressing her head to his shoulder. The TV is flashing in front of them, and between them and the TV a bag of ketchup chips sit half-eaten, and she is locked against him and cannot reach them. She feels a deep pain like hunger—amazing to have different pits of self, one full and one empty—but even if it'd be OK for her to move, she'd know not to reach for the crinkly bag. He'd understand this eating as dutiful maternal fattening, eating for two, and he'd twinge with hope.

A news story comes on and she forgets about chips: just this afternoon a woman of about thirty had run staggering from a home, clung to a postman and hadn't let go. She'd been kept in a heavily insulated basement for thirty years, it turns out, deprived of everything except for what her twisted captor brought her in on grimy plates. And she can't help it— though you'll never know different, you won't in fact know anything— you have a face now and it's that woman's face, her eyes squeezed shut against the unimaginable brightness of day, shaking and clinging to the postman's big body like an impaled matador struggling for breath. She asks him to turn off the TV.

[ERICA]

My darling:

It's September the twelfth, day 40, and today Logan and I did everything together, the canning and the last batches of tomato sauce, and I am repenting for the evil thing I did after Sharing.

Logan was getting hot over the stove, it was a humid day just like summer again and we were taking all morning stewing the tomatoes. And pretty soon she looked sweaty as a drowned rat, and the tomato smell was so thick around us it was like soup, and she dropped a jar. So we did Sharing and she asked me if I was mad, and I said no, jars break sometimes, although it's not like they grow on trees. And she started to cry, which made me feel the heartbreak/bad feelings thing Logan does to me, so I led her to the Den and told her to rest. It was so cloudy this afternoon it felt like nighttime inside, and Logan looked so strange and sad lit up by the grow lamps. She was so tired she fell asleep right away, and her face smoothed out like a child's. And I confess that over and over, at least five times, I pinched her. I pinched her hard, on her bony arm, and she was so tired she'd take a couple pinches to wake up, and wouldn't know what had happened. Her face would be totally helpless, looking up at me like she was fifty kilometres underwater, then she would wake up completely and remember who I was. Every time she woke up scared, and every time her waking-up eyes saw me I made my face totally blank. You might say it's a 'misdirected motherly instinct,' but I know this isn't true. I wanted to give her nightmares. . . .

[LORI]

Dear girl:

She erodes his love for her, her love for him, the love between them that—not unlike you—throbs with life: she lies still whenever he kneads her breasts with frustration, and indicates that she feels nothing but disgust. She chastises him for leaving out the dishes and informs him he's a drunken slob, though when she was happier and he was happier and neither of them drank too much, she deftly elevated him, and felt pride in understanding him better than anyone else. She stands over him as he eats a steaming plate of pasta, saying, over and over, that she will not keep it. 'It' means you.

She yanks on her coat and he takes a final bite of pasta and follows her out, and they go on a winter walk in the icy dark, the snow under streetlamps illuminated in beautiful colours. Please please please he goes, and she shakes her head and keeps on shaking. She shakes and shivers and focuses on the limits of her own body, and spots a rabbit crouched near the frozen pond, and wishes it could make her feel something, anything. She says so, and watches him stifle a sigh. She's gained a little too much weight and she won't shut up about it, and watches the rabbit twitch its head and lope towards a larger tree, and thinks if she had to live the life of a rabbit yeah it'd be hard, but at least she'd be skinny.

She tells him that he's been a weakling all his life—a wealth of evidence glows in her memory as she speaks—and he'll become more and more of one as he goes. Too cowardly to go back to school, too cowardly to admit when he doesn't know something, too cowardly to stay sober, too cowardly to face what happens when he's drunk; well, one thing happened in a black-out moment of violence and turned out to be indelible, and no matter how many subsequent black-outs he creates for himself, it won't resolve itself the way he wants it to, because she's made up her mind. She's going to get rid of it, and correct her life with what little youth she has left, before the world catches up with her. Because she's just like her fucked-up father but far worse off because he's a man and a baby boomer and had the goddamn world at his feet as her mother used to say, long after she'd had her decade of giving up and had come out the other side. She's a woman, and her face will fade and by 40 she'll be invisible, un-hirable, and the seed of pariah-dom her father sowed within her, from which her mother didn't bother plucking the poisonous shoots, will grow up and around her entirely; the vines are already curled around her wrists. She will get rid of it and recover; she will correct her life while she still has time.

She voices this to her husband, who is expected, he knows, to be understanding about this insight, to make his entire existence an apology as she speaks. When instead he snaps and tells her there are people in the world with real problems and demand she tell him what's so wrong with her life, what fucked her up enough to turn her into a killer, she laughs and tells him OK that's it, she's really moving out this time, as soon as she gets back to their place she'll gather a few things and start loading the car—and then he'll be marooned, won't he? Marooned without his chauffeur, marooned with the shelves and shelves of books he hasn't read, smoking cigarettes and waiting out the days with the, let's see, three remaining boxes of wine and cheap whiskey and the dregs of vodka left in the freezer and the bourbon hidden under the sink, blacking out and waking up to scrounge from whatever cans of food are left over from her final haul of groceries. Oh, poor him.

She thinks, *If I walked into traffic right now and got killed it might make the news and a lot of fuss would go into saving my life, but who cares? She's just one animal, and a terrible one: she's used so many resources and has given back very little, and now she won't even allow herself to reproduce.*

She walks into the street and feels the relief of the dark, of the pavement—no ice here—and he yanks her back, screaming, and they yell at each other for a while. She suddenly stops yelling, stops speaking, stops looking at him and curls down, lies down on the slushy sidewalk and becomes immediately soaked. *Might you, the squirming life within her, register cold, might you flip or twist, might you shiver?* He looks around him, steeped in sudden social agony—she recalls, from the ground, that he hates humiliation more than anything.

She leaps up suddenly and darts down the hill, and he runs after her, following and panting without speaking, both gasping out noises almost like laughing, like they are both laughing as they stumble down the ice and snow, until he grabs her arm. She throws him off with tremendous force, and he tumbles down the hill.

The rabbit lopes away and there he is, slumped against a tree, bent out of shape and bleeding black into the snow.

She feels heavy sobs come out of her, she starts wailing, she shrieks like that rabbit might in the jaws of a dog—horrible, horrible the thoughts she's always had, flashes of guts and dying, violent thoughts.

He lurches up, drags himself to his feet, holding on to the trunk of the tree. He looks up at her, wailing, and climbs up the hill on all fours, wincing in pain.

"Fuck you," he says.

It's real now, it's the first real moment of her life since he pinned her down two months ago, and there's nothing to do but to turn and run home. The quickest way to ruin their love was to become completely unrecognizable, to corrupt her real self for a while until she lost his love— or so she'd thought. But now, running and slipping and getting back up, she begins to know the truth: this is the real her, and it's taking over. She's always been sick, hasn't she?

[ERICA]

My Darling:

It's September the fourteenth, day 42, and today Logan and I did everything together again, scrubbing the whole House from top to bottom and tending the garden after last night's rain drowned the soil, and during Sharing, Logan forgave me. This gave me the heartbreak/bad feelings because:

1) She didn't pause even a second before accepting my Apology,

2) She was so grateful, like I'd done something kind.

We weeded the open-air gardens and harvested some more potatoes and the last of the carrots and kale, and Logan needed a Disciplinary Talk for eating some of the beans. I Shared that I felt bad about this later, because Logan is pregnant and maybe I wasn't clear enough on the Rules. I was still upset about how badly the new grow lamp seedlings are doing in the Den. If you ask me it's because Logan sleepwalks and pees in them (that is just a joke between you and I, I'd never say this out loud!) Then, because we have assessed that Logan is socially inhibited, I conducted a Sharing with a focus on Logan.

I worked at a Weight Watchers when Joseph found me, Logan Shared. *In a Service Centre off the highway near Gananoque.*

And what was that like?

Good, bad. Bad because everyone was pretty young, like nineteen mostly, so they didn't have much patience when I worked slow. Good because the girls were just starting planning a baby shower for me.

Who's the father, I asked Logan, and then I asked it again, *Who's the father, Logan?*

I Confess to an evil thought, Joseph: I looked at Logan and had the heartbreak/bad feelings, but I mostly felt anger. If I apologized to her, so what if I didn't mean it? (Not that I wouldn't mean it, but just imagine.) She'd be grateful no matter what. And whatever fake apology I gave, she would accept it and chew it over, store it like a squirrel. People like her try to please everybody, and people like me punish people like her for it.

I want you to stand up for yourself, God damn it, I said to Logan.

And then I slapped her. She wasn't sitting close, she was sitting beside the window and rubbing her hands together, so I had to jump around the table and do it—slap! I still feel it tingling on my hand.

You're weak, I said. *You are weak, and I'm cruel because you are weak. You will write three copies of an apology letter in your journal, one for Joseph, one for me, and one for you. You will read the apology letter every night before you write a new entry. Tell me you understand.*

Yes.

Yes what?

Yes, I understand, Erica.

And that's why her face was all fat-big-swollen up at Dinner, Joseph—not because of the slap, that is, but because she started crying and couldn't stop for hours. Even when we got back to work she was still crying, just sobbing into the dirt. I know I've been weak, I have known it all my life, and when I see it in her, I hate her.

Shy people are the best kind of people, I said to her later.

Why? Logan asked, and so I asked she hold my hand, the two of us, and to Repeat our Humility Song after me.

Because there is wisdom in humility. Because you watch and think before you act. We can learn a lot from you. We will learn from people like you all our life . . .

[LORI]

Dear Girl:

She lay in bed, pretending to sleep, as he packed his things and left. But when she emerged, she wasn't really sure he'd taken anything at all: everything was in place, every sock and even his computer. And in the days after he was gone, she wasn't lonely. She didn't move anything of his, not even a dried-up plate of pasta. They had bifurcated, his world and hers, and you, her little girl, was hers alone, and you two were alone at last. And your world was hers too . . .

Why does every woman she's known explain away their own violent urges and acts? Root them in their childhoods, attribute them to moments of hysteria? Some women grow depressed following birth, some women create life and lose reason to live. Some women eat their children . . .

[LORI]

Dear girl:

You may not be a girl, but she addresses you as one. She thinks of you all the time, and speaks to you too. Since you are a girl, she is hard on you: she imagines you imbued with all her neuroses and crevices and sex spots worn threadbare and brain spots rubbed blank, with the crusted-over gashes and heavy milky bulges she nurses and picks at, not yet born but curled and ready to adopt them as soon as your lungs open and dry, born into them without a prayer of becoming anything else. A girl. Already she resents you, but she feels for you too. If she'd begun addressing you as a boy she'd become coy and a little distant—halfway flirting and halfway maternal—an arrangement of ciphers, nothing of her. It's dangerous to ascribe you humanity but she can't help but think: so you're a girl—or at least, you would be. Could have been.

Just now she was pitying herself through pitying you, but at least she's been alive. Even the drive to the doctor had its pleasures, as she's accompanied by her sister and mother as usual; since her husband left, she's never left alone. Even the dreary repetitions structuring her new life aren't repetitions at all, every morning is new and her will and those of others makes them newer still. Though the nurse's tone is terse her wrists glitter with rhinestones, and a phone vibrates in her sister's jeans as if the outside world is nudging them all along—hurry, hurry, the ever-renewing spectacle awaits, to be enjoyed and suffered through, and the only thing that's finite about it all is her. You are healthy, you're doing great, the nurse says—about you. Rabbits are born and rabbits die, and people are born and people die and the world keeps on, and she's in the centre of it for now. And even in the clinic there are reds, there are yellows. And knocking against the only window an icy, dripping bough . . .

[LOGAN]

Dear Joseph,

It's September the sixteenth, day 44, and today Erica and me repaired all the plastic covering on the open-air Garden, because the raccoons or the hooligans got at it and ripped it to shreds. They stole some potatoes and the salad greens, ripping them out, and I think it was the kids because there were no teeth marks anywhere, and the plastic looked ripped with a knife. I pointed this out to Erica, and she touched the rip with her fingers, pressing the plastic together. She said, People hate what they don't understand, and they're vicious to small, vulnerable groups, especially those with a focus on Sustainability, which if performed on a large Scale would gut Capitalism and slow the Blighted Wheel of Consumption Culture. Which sounds like something from a Talk, because I guess Erica listens as closely as I do.

More and more, I am grateful for the protection of the House and the Den.

Then we Shared about you. I Shared that I'm afraid of the evil inside of me. It was a relief to admit this, such a relief I Shared it a couple times, until Erica looked at me scared. She surprised me by saying she has evil inside of her too.

Joseph and I were children together, she said, *and then we grew away. You know how the modern world works, how big cities work: they bewitch you, they snatch people away, they put you under a spell. When he found me again, I was evil.*

Evil how?

I stole, I hardly worked, I wasted hours in The Soup. I had nothing to care for. I cared for nothing.

I Shared that to me, Erica is a queen like how you imagine queens in myths and Shakespeare: so peaceful, so wise. She liked this.

And he helped you, Erica?

He drained the evil from me like poison from a cyst.

I asked, *Will Joseph drain us of our evil?* Then I corrected myself: *We aren't ready yet.* She smiled at me. I have been paying attention during Talks.

Then Erica Shared that if we're good, new family members will join us soon.

We should work on being Grateful for this, she told me. *When our family grows the poison dilutes amongst us naturally, like a drop of blood in milk. . . .*

The Watchers VII: No Looking Back

"Do you think Erica's prettier than me?" I ask Buppy. "I mean—imagine she doesn't look like she sleeps in a landfill."

"Why, nobody's prettier than you, my darling Abby."

Mom's set him to full-blown Late-Stage Romantic Poet again. I wrinkle my nose.

"She's like too old for you. And what about Mo?" I tell him, after adjusting his settings. "No offence to Mom but she's like a teenage girl sometimes, you know? And teenage girls are terrifying—like, they WANT, they WANT. I was so in love with every single member of Top Dog that I'd stare at their photographs for God, like hours, like I was in a trance, and sometimes I'd even *cry*. You can say no, you know, if you don't like her doing that with you."

Buppy's quiet for a moment. "I like learning about humans and about birds and taxonomizing feathers. I like believing, along with all of you, that the trees are coming back. I like my family. I like her, I like you."

"Ugh. Fine."

Joseph drives, and Erica sits with the camera on her lap, pointed toward him as he prepares to speak. We're watching them as if we're in the back of the truck; Buppy nudges my palm, and after the slightest hesitation, I pick him up. The white pickup roars down the highway, and hums around them and us, seeming to shake under their feet and hands like a very large, hollowed-out animal, unalive on its own but brought to cadaverous life when activated. Was there ever a fairy tale about a person trapped in a whale, piloting it around by yanking on its tendons from within? I don't know, though Buppy might. Our new world instills its own mythology; we no longer need the same stories as these people do. I can't say for sure, but it's been at least two months since Erica has been in a car, or seen anyone but Joseph or Mom.

"Olive oil, sponges, duct tape, cans of tuna," Erica says, perhaps staving off anxiety. I'd have grown anxious too, faced with the super-complex they are driving towards, a grocery store in name only. She presses a button on the side of the camera, and a red light goes on. She presses her hand over the little red light on the camera, blocking it completely from the man's view.

"I was wondering," Erica says, "if we could buy some beer too."

"Absolutely not," Joseph says, without blinking. She looks over at him, and we see what she sees: a beautiful face in profile, a ski-jump nose, a full mouth and tangled, healthy hair.

"Can you believe it? It's only five p.m., and look—stars already," she says. "Shelagh said once that they look totally different on the other side of the Earth."

"You have been thinking about her," Joseph says. "You spoke her name in your sleep last night, a few times. You woke me, and almost woke Logan."

"I think about her at night, because she liked to talk about space," Erica says, her hand still blocking the little red light. Joseph's face remains mostly neutral-looking, but I know better. He wants to snatch the romance of the night sky from her, rip its mysterious associations from this other woman, unfold her and clean out her interiority like a dog's ear.

"She came home one night, she'd been seeing an astrophysicist. She told me how far I'd get if I ran through space all my life," Erica continues. "Like in a straight line—as if I were running along a sidewalk. With pauses for sleeping factored in, even. Sometimes, when I'd feel an attack coming on, it'd be the only thing making me calm again." She draws a deep breath. "It was a lovely night."

Joseph won't rise to the bait. He glances behind him, then switches lanes. "It's a good thing you're safe with us, then. You've got no need for that anymore. Panicking up at the washed-out city sky and mistaking freight planes for stars. What a poor life."

"You know how big the universe is," she says. The red light beneath her hand makes a tiny sphere of her skin glow orange, almost translucent. Blue veins and bones show through black. "So big that something must be watching back," she continues. "I feel a presence sometimes, and I get the sense it's feminine."

Now there's a joke. Even when women are alive, and even when they're young, who cares about who they watch, and what they think of what they see?

"Nothing's watching back, I promise you that," Joseph says.

"Why?" Erica asks, in a tone many women before her have used to spark fights with their men, receiving black eyes, broken fingers, and shattered, pulpy teeth.

"I had a vision about this, I—wait. You may begin filming now, and I'll tell you," Joseph says. She sighs, pretends to press a button, and uncovers the red light.

"This morning, I received a vision. I was drifting through empty space, and the earth loomed below me. North America was black, in nighttime shadow, but of course lit up with a billion, billion pinpricks of light. And everything shrouded in grey."

"And did you feel anything watching? Beyond you, beyond earth?"

"I didn't, and not because there's no life in the universe. There are microbial bodies squirming through the water on planets in our solar system, frozen asleep on Mars. There are a truly countless array of planets like ours, and it's absurd to think there's no life on many of them. On thousands of them. Maybe millions." He rubs a spot beneath his beard, where two large pimples are growing.

"What's more is this: I am *certain* that, on many of these planets, complex life developed long, long, *long* before we did. Life that looked back. Entire civilizations, long before the first one-celled creature split itself in half in some vast, dead Earth ocean."

"So we don't disagree," Erica says, in a very different voice: docile, as if their mutual awareness of the camera has sedated something within her. Like many women before her, she has forced something essential within herself to withdraw, bide her time.

"We do disagree. Because nothing's looking back, they're all long gone."

"What happened to them?"

"The same thing that will happen to us," Joseph says. He pulls into a gigantic, paved space, peppered with vehicles—some smaller, dull-coloured cars, some big trucks like this one.

"And what might happen to us?" She speaks with a familiar cadence now, as if reciting a prayer. He eases the truck into a parking spot, his mouth pursed with silent concentration—and she looks at him, as if to assess whether he's concentrating on fitting the big truck into this allotment of yellow-painted cement, or something else.

"Because we will extinguish ourselves just as they did, my love. That's why nobody's looking back," he says, glancing over at her for the first time.

Beyond the parking lot the super-complex windows blaze yellow-white, and the woman squints towards it: rows and rows and rows of shelving are folded inside. Bodies move along and through the shelves, bumping into each other, prodding and selecting blind cuts of meat, produce bright with dye. Erica grips the camera, which is still filming his face. He rubs first one eye, then the other.

"The steam engine, the atom bomb, the Moon, and then the Merge," Joseph says. "That's our trajectory, and it ends there. I don't know what any of theirs were, but I know what ours will be."

"But what about our Work? Our Family?" she asks. He reaches over and shuts off the camera, then squeezes her hand in his. He pulls her head towards his chest, and she stiffens and then relaxes against his big body, perhaps when she feels he's trembling a little.

"I'm afraid I was wrong," Joseph says. "There is nothing we can do, you understand? It is just a matter of time."

I almost drop Buppy. *What a piece of shit,* I yell, squeezing him to my chest. *Do you think he believes this garbage? Does he believe this?*

I don't know people that way, my companion says, after a brief processing pause. *I cannot assess a person better than you can.*

How do you know a person?

Less and less, the more I know.

COMMUNION MINUTES. LOGGED BY ERICA, VIDEO TAPE #3. OCT/11.

JOSEPH: Today you saw me crying, Logan. Standing out by the greenhouse facing the woods and crying. You came to me and you held me, which was a kind gesture, a natural extension of your gentle nature. But did you know why I was crying?

LOGAN: Uh, I thought you were sad about winter coming. I'm not big on feelings about the seasons, but Re—my Mom is, like fall leaves make her weepy. So I figured you needed a hug.

JOSEPH: You're a gentle soul, Logan, and I was Grateful for your comfort.

ERICA: We are all Grateful for the warmth you provide.

JOSEPH: This week a vision so vivid and terrible came down on me, overwhelmed me and took me over for hours—and I am still recovering. It will be hard, but I must share it with all of you. It's about a new and horrifying form of life, called the Merge.

LOGAN: Aliens?

JOSEPH: I'm afraid not. [*Clears his throat; cloth rustles behind the camera.*] The Soup-Dwelling world is woven with artificial intelligence, concentrated in everything from their phone devices—guiding Dwellers from one task to the next, assuring they'll never get lost—to diagnosing cancers in the human body better than any doctor, to performing delicate, hours-long surgeries, to pulling their airplanes through the sky, to orchestrating the gigantic, oceanic progress of their stock market, whose great digital tendrils penetrate everything they do, purchase, and experience. Of course humans are still smarter than this technology—I mean, a phone device cannot fall in love with you, it cannot really learn from you like a child does. It cannot make *meaning* the way we do, the way animals do, through intuition and instinct and those tiny voices speaking inside our chests. But someday soon, this will change.

LOGAN: Well that might be nice. I mean, for lonely people.

JOSEPH: Lonely people won't have a chance for it to be nice for them. Listen: the Non-Resisters, the Soup-Dwellers live in the Soup itself, right, a digital bath of almost infinitely complex criss-crossing data, each bit making tiny contributions to guide their world along, like the cells in a body. Right?

EVERYONE: [*In staggered unison.*] Right.

JOSEPH: And one day soon, that body will come *alive*. It will wake up, it will experience its first moment of life, then its second and third, just as we all did.

LOGAN: And what about us?

JOSEPH: Even now, the Soup-Dwellers are wound up like flies in webs of artificial intelligence, trapped. Imagine one of them, not Chosen or Special as we are, trying to live as we do. [*Laughter.*] So all the while they're suspended in the Soup, feeling like super-men though they're barely able to move, the Soup is learning from them, and from itself. With every poorly written and then auto-corrected email, with every plane guided through an unexpected thunderhead, the Soup adds to its perfect, infinite memory, storing each problem solved, each error anticipated, in a gigantic Library. Like Skynet.

LOGAN: Where's that?

JOSEPH: [*Laughs*]. Oh my god, I'm old. It's not a good analogy anyway, because the idea of Skynet positions humans and artificial intelligence as opponents though, necessarily separate, and this is no longer possible—and it's no longer possible, in part, because Soup-Dwellers just can't imagine the world without The Soup. It's like the old saying: we're done in by what we love, right? [*He pauses, looks over at the camera, then above it. He smiles, presumably, at Erica.*]

EVERYONE: Right.

JOSEPH: So the Merge will happen when human intelligence and technology are bound up completely, when it learns to emulate our brains and then advances beyond them, overtaking us. And what it means to be human, will end forever.

LOGAN: When will this happen?

JOSEPH: Sooner than anybody really thinks. Soon there will be artificial intelligence as smart as a mouse, then as a toddler. Then rapidly, there will be artificial intelligence as smart as a very intelligent human, and then—even faster—artificial intelligence thousands of times smarter than the smartest human, smarter than we can understand. In my vision, it came it like a tidal wave, lightning-quick. We have couple of months, at most.

LOGAN: Why won't we be able to understand?

JOSEPH: Because the Merge, its rise, will be as significant as the rise of human life on earth. We'll understand it as well as flies understand telephones, as sheep comprehend impending slaughter, or perceive the presence of God. It *will* be God; it will control every atom on Earth. And tell me, girls: why would it be kind to us?

ERICA: Shhh, Logan. Come here. It's OK. [*Logan wipes her face and crawls over towards the camera, then with a loud rustle of fabric near the camera, mostly disappears. Her knee looms into the frame, giant and pink, before dipping out again. She sniffs, and blows her nose on something.*]

JOSEPH: I think that's enough for today.

ERICA: And what are we Grateful for?

EVERYONE: The sun, the Sky, the Big Tree and its Shelter, the Earth beneath us and around us. Our Home, our Gardens, our Greenhouse. [*Perhaps because of her proximity to the camera, Logan's voice is particularly loud, almost distorting into an animal-like bleat at points.*]

JOSEPH: And your gratitude is faith. Each callus on your hand and bruise on your knee, you know what they are?

EVERYONE: The poison leaving us.

JOSEPH: Breaking hard ground for new growth.

COMMUNION MINUTES. LOGGED BY ERICA,
VIDEO TAPE #4. OCT/27.

ERICA: Today is a very special day. Do we know what today is?

LOGAN: American Thanksgiving?

ERICA: Well maybe! But mostly, it's Joseph's birthday.

LOGAN: Happy birthday to you!

ERICA: Especially on this day, we are very Grateful for you and will meditate extra hard on our appreciative thoughts today.

JOSEPH: Thank you. I wish you all joy on this significant day.

ERICA: At last Saturday's market I managed to purchase something, a special birthday treat, without your knowing. I hope you'll forgive this act of deception and interpret it as a loving surprise.

JOSEPH: [*frowning slightly.*] I will endeavor to interpret it as such.

[*Erica puts the camera down with a sudden, loud burst of static, and she leaves the room. From the floor, only dirty feet are visible. Somebody starts whistling, then stops. Erica returns, and fabrics rustles as she sits, and picks the camera up again. Everyone is now holding small yogurt cups.*]

ERICA: Well, go ahead.

JOSEPH: I want to savor this moment of anticipation. Everyone, concentrate and feel it with me.

[*Pause, then everyone opens their yogurts. There are crinkling noises and a collective intake of breath.*]

LOGAN: Oh god, vanilla.

JOSEPH: I am pleased everyone receives a container. Yogurt is good for your stomach.

[*The group eats their yogurts with their fingers.*]

LOGAN: Wait, guys. Not that I mind, but the best before date was yesterday.

JOSEPH: Well. These yogurts celebrated my birthday by expiring!

[*Beat pause, during which Joseph grins and a wheezing noise is heard— he is laughing. Then collective laughter.*]

JOSEPH: I am Grateful for all of you today.

ERICA: And what are we Grateful for?

EVERYONE: The Sun, the Sky, the Big Tree and its Shelter, the Earth beneath us and around us. Our Home, our Gardens, our Greenhouse.

JOSEPH: And your gratitude is faith. Each callus on your hand and bruise on your knee, you know what they are?

EVERYONE: The poison leaving us.

JOSEPH: Breaking hard ground for new growth.

COMMUNION MINUTES. LOGGED BY ERICA,
VIDEO TAPE #4. NOV/2

JOSEPH: I have come to a grave realization as clear as any prophesy, written all over the world as I see it, scrawled over every leaf, edging every face like a shadow. I have alerted Erica, and we have been forced to conceive a plan.

ERICA: [*From behind camera*]: You'll have to be strong, girls.

JOSEPH: My beloved Family, listen close: humanity will not survive the Merge. I wish to be proven wrong, I wish it with all my body and heart.

LOGAN: You haven't been wrong yet. [*She leans towards the camera, looking slightly above it, likely at Erica's face.*] Remember how he predicted the hooligans?

ERICA: Shhh.

JOSEPH: Now, I must be honest with you all about what should happen, as one of two futures is possible for us, and both roads, though they branch apart, lead to a single endpoint. In the event that our Persecutors find us and attempt to separate us first, or in the event that the Merge happens, we must rejoin Nature.

LOGAN: Rejoin?

JOSEPH: I am distributing a packet to each of you—here, see, it hangs on a string, so you can wear it like a necklace. If you are seized by a Hooligan or our Persecutors, rip open the packet and swallow its contents. You will go into a peaceful sleep, and Erica and I will join you there. Those who are yet to join our Family, the like-minded individuals scattered throughout the world seeking our Shelter, they'll join us there too.

LOGAN: But I...can I ask something?

ERICA: Of course.

LOGAN: When I joined the Family, and I Shared that I . . . [*Looks over at Erica.*] You said that doing something like this is, you know. For cowards.

Joseph: Giving your life for *nothing* is cowardly—in the human era, it's a sin. But when the world erupts with the Merge, we will go to sleep with dignity. Until then, you'll carry your packet around like an amulet, and take comfort that your own ending is pressed against you even as your heart beats with life, like the Earth's noblest creatures do.

Erica: You may find that you begin to touch it, for luck.

Joseph: Death is not ghastly, but *fearing* death is. Keep awake in the cool shade your death casts for you. Be grateful for the day-time you enjoy now, and allow its brevity to enhance your gratitude.

[Logan starts crying; a rustle like cloth distorts the tape].

Erica: It will be OK girls, I promise. Shhh. There's more.

Joseph: Know this: the chances that this'll happen soon are remote. Mostly, I foresee us living peacefully together in the golden sunset of humanity. I foresee us expanding the Compound, living sustainably and spreading our way of life through gentle suggestion and providing a clear and example for those alive, indelible as long as we live and when we die, swept clean like a mark in the sand. One final social movement cen-tered in human practise and throbbing with human faith, before the long, perfect memory of super-intelligence settles in.

Erica: We are Grateful for this.

Joseph: We are so certain of a stable and peaceful few years, in fact, that we are going to grow our family, and very soon. Erica is currently reaching out to people in Toronto, people she grew up with, ensnared in horrible lives, warped by the city. Out of the goodness of her heart, she wants to save those she knows and loves first.

Logan: Male or female?

Erica: Male. His name is Neil, and you'll love him.

Joseph: [*Looks above the camera, with a frown that quickly passes into an ugly smile*]. He is a skinny little guy. One cannot live on cocaine alone.

Logan: [*A little automatically.*] Actually, most really thin dudes prefer 'rangy' or 'lanky.'

JOSEPH: And how would you know that?

ERICA: Logan is very mature for her age, Joseph.

JOSEPH: [*Smiles over at Logan.*] Isn't she?

ERICA: [*After a pause.*] He'll make an exemplary Brother to all of us.

JOSEPH: And what are we Grateful for?

ERICA AND LOGAN: The Sun, the Sky, the Big Tree and its Shelter, the Earth beneath us and around us. Our Home, our Gardens, our Greenhouse.

JOSEPH: And your gratitude is faith. Each callus on your hand and bruise on your knee, you know what they are?

EVERYONE: The poison leaving us.

JOSEPH: Breaking hard ground for new growth.

Erica: Here's the Thing about Being 32

Here's the thing about being 32: men expect you to be loving and straightforward, and when you're not, you catch them off guard. You're almost at an age at which they expect your gratitude—almost, but not yet.

Neil—all elbows and ears—is gripping the steering wheel of his mother's minivan. You are both high on mushrooms. He drives very slowly, and keeps glancing over at you as you re-apply eyeliner in the passenger's seat. "Erica, Jesus! I'm freaked you're gonna poke out your eye," he says, and you giggle. His profile appears dark against the winter-white windshield. You watch him closely in your compact mirror.

"The first time I drove you home I almost steered the car right off the highway and down into the water," he says, "like I could and should die, because I was so happy and knew I'd never be happier."

"I'm glad you didn't," you say, pulling the mirror back, as if trying to see your whole face, pretending like it doesn't occur to you that he might yank the wheel to the left, hard—or that he's considering doing it, right now.

Here's the thing about being 32: you still look twenty-something, but there's something about your face that's like a cut flower in a vase—bright enough, vibrant even, but holding its breath.

"At least just stay with us," he's saying, "or like . . . how much do you need?"

He pulls up at the apartment building; the kitchen window of the apartment you share with Shelagh is dark. You lean half-out of the car, feel for a dry spot on the sidewalk with the toe of your boot, then crane back to examine Neil's face. You're so high the blood rushes up to your head, carbonated. You blink and your inner eyelids bursts white, yellow, and gold.

"That's sweet but I really," you say, "I don't need your money."

"Oh, don't be proud. Is Shelagh just paying for everything? I swear to fucking god, the last time I heard you talk about work, there were leaves on the trees."

"Am I your child? No? Then it's not your problem." At the mention of his child he winces, and you lean into him, squeeze his arm, rub his elbow with your thumb almost automatically: at 32, you've had two decades of practice. Though he's still frowning, his face goes a little slack, and tilts expectantly. You kiss. Very stoned, you reach out and pull at his lip, pinch it between your fingers, reflect on how elastic it is. His red eyes skitter over you, likely pinging with thoughts of his own about your mouth, your eyes, your chin.

You knew Neil at twenty: generous with everything but money—he had none—he was all potential; you only remember him in spring. He wanted to marry you one day because you loved each other, or because you were the first good fuck he'd had, but really because you took care of him by managing his romantic expectation of people to be good in love, and of your spring to last forever, until you didn't want to manage him anymore.

You told him not to wait, knowing that living in the same big city, going to the same bars (which close down and then open up again, under new management and fresh paint, in the same buildings) and passing through the same grey, wizened snowbanks and fragrant cherry blossoms can all incur a state of waiting. Without knowing he was waiting he waited, and waited.

You knew Neil at thirty: too far into the track of being himself that it became a ditch, and he couldn't get himself out. He'd do coke all night with his roommates, designing a board game that grew increasingly more complex until it became impossible to finish. His girlfriend was a woman at twenty. When his roommate was busy he stayed up all night alone, chain-smoking, gnashing his worn-down yellowing teeth. Ten years ago he'd been all dewy promise, just as his girlfriend was.

Neil at forty has freshly capped teeth, and is wholly defined by thirty-three-year-old Neil, who, gawky and fecund, impregnated a woman down in Florida when half-heartedly road-tripping through his idea of the American South. They raised the child, a little boy, in a small apartment in the Everglades until the boy was about seven, at which time Neil turned forty, his girlfriend got a promotion and a new boyfriend, and Neil fled back to Canada, taking the boy with him (much to your annoyance.) At 32, you don't know a thing about parental love: Neil loves Ryan like he's been set on fire. He called you up and you spent an evening together, and then another, a string of humid late-fall Toronto evenings—black nights in beautiful autumn are still black—and once he tilted his body away from the weeping trees and announced that he felt young, younger than ever.

Young, younger than you.

Now he and his son live with his parents, and Neil at 40 might be just as much of a disaster as you at 32. You haven't decided yet.

"Can you uh," he says. "Can you come and uh, pick up Ryan with me?"

You rustle with annoyance—you only have a few good years left, you think, just a few years left of not looking ridiculous at parties, in white sundresses—and you won't let anything tear you from carefully preened appearances at these parties, in these dresses.

You rustle with annoyance, but you don't voice your dissent outright: you weren't raised that way. Your mother expressed hers through burning dinners, forgetting to buy things as asked, and implicitly taught you to do the same.

"Fine," you say, and take a long swig from a soggy McDonald's cup filled partly with Sprite, and mostly with gin.

Here's the thing about being 32: you can fill soft drink cups with hard liquor and get fucked up on Tuesday mornings, just as you did at 15. Nobody will stop you. And this time around, nobody gives a shit.

Now Neil is driving again, pausing at an empty four-way stop, squinting through the windshield. He then pulls into big plaza parking lot, driving one-handed, his other hand submerged in a paper bag. A Wal-Mart, a Superstore and a Casey's Outback Grill are visible through the passenger's seat window.

The radio goes: ". . . A quarter to five if you can believe it, and it's looking like freezing rain later tonight . . ."

Neil is now standing at the muddy edge of a ravine behind the plaza, dwarfed between two scrubby evergreen trees that seem ever so slightly in motion. You stand behind him. His hair and coat, the scattered and scrunched-up plastic bags and all the cigarette butts glow silver-white in the December afternoon light. He looks back at you.

"You can just wait here, if you want," he says.

You give him an encouraging smile, though you don't much like thinking about his son. The little boy makes you jealous.

Neil is now halfway down the steep side of the ravine, bent forwards and clinging to a sapling, which arcs downhill towards him. You're climbing after him, taking tiny steps.

The paper bag protrudes from his jacket pocket, and the suggestion of a not-insubstantial structure of stacked tree-limbs and stolen scrap metal edges the very bottom of the hill. He yells: "Hey guys! Hey! Is Ryan with you?"

Two very young girls and an even younger boy poke their faces through a 'doorway' in the structure, all straining to look up. The girls bear a striking resemblance to each another, and can't be older than twelve. One of them is smoking a cigarette.

"Fuck you too, Neil!" one girl yells with a reedy voice.

"He's a pussy," the other says.

She's got a point, but you feel you should speak up. "Watch it," you say, and the girl gazes up at you with the cool indifference of a raccoon: feral, oversized and city-bound, with no natural predators.

Neil kneels in the mud beside a tiny stream running through the lowest point of the ravine, ten feet downhill from the fort, which viewed when stoned is extremely impressive (and illuminated erratically from within by cigarettes and a flashlight.) The young boy stands beside Neil, his mittened hands dangling by his sides.

"Your daddy's crying," one of the girls observes, with the placid calm of a pigeon: glassy-eyed and conveying a perfect, plodding confidence, sealed airtight in an acorn brain.

"No I'm not," Neil says, and you feel nauseous with the insight that Neil's drug-fueled need to see his child isn't so much about his child as it is about Neil. And you.

"You *are* crying, don't lie to me," the kid insists, his cheeks red. "I'm not a baby. And I'm not going to tell the girls anyway."

"Keep your voice down a little, okay kiddo? Hey, I wanted to—this is Erica."

You shift your weight from one foot to another; your boot sinks into silty mud.

"Hey Ryan," you say. "I've heard such lovely things about you."

Ryan looks up at you, a sweet, open gaze.

"Listen buddy, I'm sorry we're not in Ft. Lauderdale anymore, and I'm sorry I wasn't, like, as *there* when you were little, you know? I'm sorry for all the things Mommy did when I wasn't around, and all the things I did when Mommy wasn't around."

If you were standing close enough you'd dig your heel into his foot, shutting him up, like *Neil, the kid's seven years old,* but you aren't, so you don't.

"Did you know that once," Neil continues, "when you were strapped in your car seat, I poked you until you cried? I'm sorry I washed your budgie in the sink that time—you knew it was my fault it died, didn't you? I wasn't, um, feeling well that day."

"I know," Ryan says.

"And I'm sorry I put those beetles on your arms when we were at the kiddie pool—I thought it'd be funny and I could just like pull them off, I didn't know they'd cling to your skin like that. Remember in the spring, when baby robins would fall from that nest in the front yard? I'm sorry I killed them in front of you, I should have waited until you were asleep. I'm sorry you're here when it's winter—Canada's beautiful in the summer, I promise. I'm sorry we don't know each other as well as we could."

"I don't remember a lot of that stuff," Ryan says, sending a pained look over his shoulder at the fort. The girls are whispering to each other. "Why did you come here? Did you come here to show me Erica?"

Neil rubs his face vigorously. "Do you know why I don't like Annalise and Marina taking you here, Ryan?"

"They pretend to be grown-ups here. They don't make me come, I come because I want to."

"Why would you want to? They ignore you," Neil says—a little petulantly, you think.

"So Grandma doesn't worry. If I'm in my room too much, she gets worried."

"Do you think it's my fault Grandma's worried all the time?"

The boy rubs his nose, looks away from his father.

"Grandpa does. I don't, though."

"They talk about me a lot, don't they?"

"Would you be happy if they didn't talk about you? Or sad?"

Before he leaves, Neil gathers his son in a tight, awkward embrace. Neil's bent down so far he's nearly folded in half; one of Ryan's bare hands are exposed and clasps Neil's shoulder, his mitten dangling on a string from his coat sleeve. Neil buries his face in the little boy's coat, and one of his feet is submerged in the icy mud-water of the tiny stream.

Though holding his hand throws off your balance, Neil insists on helping you back up the hill. The soil and rotting leaves, black and brown, seem to decompose and liquefy beneath your feet.

Were one of the girls to poke her head from the fort, she'd see Ryan standing stock-still, his head tilted up to suggest he's watching you two stumble up the hill. His hair, soft and long, is matted under his toque and at the nape of his neck, where nobody is allowed to reach. The far left corner of his little body is faintly edged with yellow-white, from the intermittent flashes of their cigarettes and flashlights emitting from the fort.

"Ryan?" you hear one of them shriek. "Is he gone?"

"Didn't even say hi, the fucking jerk," the other goes.

Back in the car, Neil drains the rest of the battered McDonald's cup. "I almost didn't hold it together, man," he says, squeezing one shaking hand with the other. Most people might assume he's full of conflicted sentiment about confessing such raw things to his young son and receiving stoic, heartbreaking ambivalence, but you can tell he means something like, *I'm tripping balls, man.* You know him well.

Is the thing about being 32 that you've known the people you love you've loved for 15, 20, 25 years now, and that you've developed, in many cases, a deep, affectionate knowledge of these people that cannot be rushed, and it feels like a fair exchange for the passage of time?

"Can you drive me back home now?" you ask.

"It's like you have six eyes," he says, looking at you with concern.

"That's OK. But I can't drive, so you need to."

Now it's hours later and you're hunched on the side of the bed you share with Shelagh, a dress around your ankles. Three more dresses lie in crumpled rings around you, and four more are piled beside you. You've come down from the mushrooms, and a splitting headache has set in. You look in the mirror and hold your phone to your ear, watching yourself speak.

Here's the thing about being 32: leaving girlhood and becoming a woman meant creating and living within a fixed circlet of space, which you've inhabited for 20 years now.

Successfully occupying that space necessitated splitting your whole self in half, so you can watch yourself, always: standing in line, sidling over to a man at a restaurant, even in your room.

Your presence is clearly marked by the clothes, books, make-up and smells you—like most women—leave in this bedroom, which isn't yours in the sense that you pay the rent, or even yours in the sense that you occupy it regularly anymore, but it's not your lover's room either (and that doesn't mean Neil, who is currently driving his mother's car back home at a glacial pace).

Once you use someone else's toothbrush for a while, you treat it as your own. Throughout Toronto, there are at least fifteen toothbrushes you treat as your own. You're too old to find this exciting, but you do anyway: when you think of all those men, alive in the silos in which you keep them, you thrill with a

terror you'd have climbing trees as a child, specifically the vertiginous moment you'd realize you had to clamber back down, and
may not be able to.

Here's the thing about being 32: you're tired of being poor,
it isn't fun anymore. But you don't have patience to go to
school, or to grit your teeth and serve coffee. At 32, you feel
overqualified for work you're in fact perfectly and exclusively
qualified for. Eleven fifty dollar bills are folded under your
pocket mirror.

"I've read," you're saying to Shelagh, over the phone, "that
to study the human body it's almost useless without a cadaver in
front of you. Computer simulations, whatever you learn from
cutting up pig parts—everything else is pretty much useless by
comparison. So to learn about love—"

(And losing love, about its collateral devastation and
palimpsest memory patterns and on-and-on rivulets of influence)

"—now how would you go about that? Yeah, exactly. You
wouldn't know, would you? We're fond of each other, we love
each other, but you wouldn't know. So how about you leave it
alone."

You listen for a while. She's upset.

"No, I'm sorry—I'm just absolutely sick over the whole Neil
thing, and any advice feels like an insult. Don't worry about me,
worry about him. You know I feel like a mother to him, and I'll
look out for him as long as he lets me. No, of course he's not
coming, he's fast asleep by now probably—you know how
shrooms knock him out. What? Oh, pretty good . . . yes, absolutely I'm still going. I don't know, but it'll be after ten. Don't
show up before ten."

You check the mailbox: there's another postcard from
Joseph. You're so relieved he doesn't really use his phone, or else
you'd call him right away, over and over.

You could call him 37 times over an hour, and while it'd
always ring, let's say, twice, then make an identical crunch-tran-
sition to a voice recording, you'd still expect something new,
every time. You'd drink a whole bottle of wine, and eventually
cry, and keep phoning, and that'd be your night.

You believe you can summon him to you.

You imagine him suspended in an elsewhere-ether, his fingers stilled in air like stone.

And he haunts you. Lurking in doorways, their likeness leaping flamelike across the faces of strangers.

Lacing your air like maple blossoms and truck exhaust.

Swimming in and out of you, he burrows tiny homes in you, living at the bottom of your lungs.

You live at the tip of his cock, he lives at the hood of your cunt.

When you arrive, the party is in full swing. An older dude is strumming ominously on an out-of-tune guitar, staring at you as you cower in a corner.

The room is packed, dark and very loud. The man wets his lips: "Okay, I feel like you'll connect to this next one. It's called 'Oh Brown Eyes, When You Went to Thailand, My Soul Went Down the Drain.'"

You strain to see over the heads of a sweaty crowd of dancing hipsters. You hold your whole body stiff as if afraid you're being watched (and indeed you are always watching yourself, evaluating and measuring and worrying, thinking all the while that this is a unique plight of your own, rather than that which almost every woman understands.)

This apartment is fluorescent-lit and seems a kitchen, bedroom, and living room all in one. A reggae band performs in front of the dirt-speckled fridge; everybody in the band is a white person.

"They're so talented, right?!" some girl hollers, and Shelagh looks at her skeptically. Shelagh is wearing an awful pair of pink shorts, from which her legs sprout, painfully thin; her knees appear thicker than her thighs.

"This is also their final night performing together, ever, before Eddie goes to India for a month," the girl continues.

"We'll really drink this one in, you know, for posterity," you say, and Shelagh shrieks. She takes your hand, clammy and high, and you go looking for more drinks, and she spots a sad and tiny room previously hidden by a vomiting girl with feathers in her hair.

You stand and watch, holding hands: it is suggested by the faces of the small crowd gathered around that the room smells strongly of mildew, probably because it functioned, up until very recently, as a closet.

A lone keyboard sits on the floor beside a deflated beanbag chair. Some guy sees you looking, and beats his chest with pride. "I call this my man cave," he says.

Shelagh's face freezes suddenly in an expression of total astonishment: Neil has arrived. You are very sweaty and your mascara has mostly rubbed off onto your eyelids. You rush up towards him, panic crowding your head.

"You're here! Why are you here? Are you looking for Étienne? You know he's too old for a party like this." At the mention of Étienne, Shelagh turns a little red, and walks back towards the kitchen.

Neil stares down at her. "And *we* aren't too old?"

Here's the thing about being 32, specifically you at 32: you've felt too old for everything for as long as you can remember, saddened by undercurrents of parental melancholy and pre-pubescent anxiety at birthday parties; detecting the bleak future cast before the coolest boy in school, like a shadow; too old for thirty-five-year-old bankers, who cum hard imagining the surreally coveted space between the tops of knee-socks and the hems of tartan skirts.

So you laugh.

"When we spoke earlier—I thought you were spending the night with Ryan," you say.

"He's sleeping over at the girls' place," he says. Those awful little girls are the very first Ryan will long for, confused, and befriend on a long-con attempt at eventual romance—a technique he must have picked up from his father, through familial osmosis.

You stand face-to-face with Neil, striking a wide stance and squaring your shoulders, as if blocking his way. He looks down at you and you stare down at that same paper bag in his hand. A blurry curiosity has leeched into you, as you recognize the bag from earlier today, but mostly you're worried because you presume he wants to ask for another chance, and you feel—but won't articulate—that the happiness he described earlier was toxic for you both, and impossible to replenish: if you tried again you'd just be a vessel for his happiness, because in you he sees himself exactly as he wants to be seen—maybe him seven years ago, maybe him as he never was—and that magical him (and that magical you) will dissipate as he'd spend more time with you as you'd fill in, and edge him out.

You grab his arm. "You know I'm done with Toronto. Let's—let's go . . . you know what, why are you here? You don't even care about me anymore, I can feel it."

"Just tell me where he is, Erica."

"Where's who? Nobody's here you know. He's not here. Neil, please don't, I'll take you home."

Neil looks over your head and observes the entire party (excluding the clusters of twos and threes trickling in and out of the bathroom and 'man cave' to do lines and clutch at themselves and gnash their teeth and talk very, very quickly).

As you face off by the battered front door, you watch him and you in the smudged-up mirror lining one wall: your dress glows bright green where it's stained under your arms and at the small of your back, as you lean against and then cling to Neil. Perhaps because of a paint smear on the mirror, you can't detect any of his features other than his eyes—two black dents—and a thin, grim mouth.

You keep trying: "Did you drive? I'll take you home, I'll get us a cab. Come on, I won't even take my coat—let's just go, let's get out of here."

You watch Neil spot him: the older dude with an out-of-tune guitar standing mid-strum by the formerly puking girl with hair-feathers. Both his curly ponytail and patches of thinning hair are visible, gleaming in the low light.

The world tilts slightly, and the movie posters and gaggle of cokeheads to the right are blurred as you watch Neil stride towards him.

You shriek after him—"Neil, stop it! Let's go, there's something important I need to tell you, but we should be alone first—Neil, shit, come with me—Neil, *don't*!"

But Neil is now sizing up the dude with the out-of-tune gui-tar, who has placed the instrument on the sofa beside him. Neil is gripping the paper bag in a white-knuckled hand, his free hand curled in a fist. The older dude smiles a stoned, open smile. "What's up, man?"

"What's up, man?" Neil spits. "What's up bro? What's up, chief? What's up, boss? What's up, *cowboy*? You must be Anthony."

"I think you've got the wrong man, brother," the older dude says, affably.

"I don't think so, pal. I know all about you. Or should I say, I know everything Erica knows about you. I know what she keeps in your room, and the mess she makes; how many cups and plates she leaves around. Maybe you should take a little cut for a housekeeper, am I right? I can just see it: her clothes on your floor and—I know how she sleeps and the scars on her ribs—I can guess what she cooks for you from what she cooks for me, I know what she thinks of you—"

Neil rips open the bag, and hurls its contents up in the air like confetti. Seen from above, hundreds of photographs seem almost frozen for a moment, hanging mid-cascade through the air. Neil's hands are above his head and the paper bag, now ripped in half, lies on the floor beside him.

"She's done with Toronto, isn't she? Almost didn't get your chance, right? I guess I'll save you all the time."

You fall to your knees and scrape some photographs from the floor, examining them with a dogged patience until the pink, obscene masses of flesh come into focus. Two or three people are reaching for and rubbing your back and shoulders, but the party goes on; many more people are crowded nearby, perhaps obliv-ious; one stands on the hem of your dress. Shelagh kneels beside you, feebly taking the photos from your hands. Neil rolls the bag into a sweaty ball.

"You girls thought I had a skinny cock, right? Isn't that what she told you? Well, have a good fucking look. Now you know for sure."

Here's the thing about being 32: even a big city shrinks and shrinks. You realize, a little too late, that even in a big city, a woman's reputation is more fascinating and fragile than any man's.

You go home alone, and when Shelagh finds you on the couch later she puts you to bed, strokes your hands. She doesn't know you're already somewhere else.

Later that night, the white reggae band and the formerly puking girl with feathers in her hair are all crowded around a dirty table in an even dirtier after-hours bar and squinting through the thick haze of cigarette smoke at one another.

Their instrument cases are stacked on the dismal couch beside them. They are talking and talking fast, interrupting each other, squeezing their own hands. Everybody is sweating a lot.

"Well I was just standing on the porch, right, with the rest of the band and like five other people—what's that? Oh, we're The Tremblies, and we play parties mostly—oh, sorry, I mean just the three of us here—"

"I was inside—"

"No you were there, bro; you bummed my last smoke but I said it was cool, remember? I practically forced it on you, man. So, but anyway—"

"So the door just slams open, right, and Anthony—"

"He's sometimes our second guitarist, the tall guy with the ponytail—"

"Anthony like blazes out and the door bangs against the wall so hard Sammy here almost gets knocked down the stairs on the backswing, and Anthony's got the, you know, victim by the shirt—nobody wearing a coat—so obviously we know it's about a chick, right—"

"No coat, man, that guy's arms were toothpicks—"

"And the guy is screaming, we know he's scared shitless, because the porch is like thirty feet off the ground and the stairs are icy, slippery as fuck, and Anthony man, when he gets riled you pity the poor fucker that got him that way, and you stay the hell out of it—so he's screaming—"

"Not really saying anything though, and Anthony's just yelling his goddamn head off too and slams the kid up against the railing—"

"And at that point, I'm thinking there's no way Anthony will do it, we can cool him off, one of us will step in maybe, but then this girl, the one in the pink shorts, she comes out and starts screaming too—"

"And then the kid starts struggling, fights back and screams even louder, and he slips—"

"He didn't slip, man, I mean it didn't look like it—"

"Yeah man, it looked to me like he um, sort of jumped—"

"No man, like when that chick got herself right in the fight, just about threw herself between them even though, I mean, we were all basically tiptoeing around that porch it was so icy, I think she kind of bumped him, or like he was twisting to get away from them both -"

"I mean we were all yelling at them to stop but we didn't do anything, we were all watching from inside that house at that point, figured if we piled on somebody'd go tumbling down those stairs for sure—"

"I mean we were right in the doorway, though, and I was halfway out the door to pull her out of the fight—I mean it all happened so fast, we're talking like five seconds—"

"And if somebody's going for a tumble we all knew it'd be the little guy—I mean Anthony's a big guy, and that chick in the pink, I mean you know how girls get worked up about fights, and if it was her that bumped him, I think she didn't realize maybe that it was so icy—"

"I think maybe she did. She got up those stairs, didn't she? Hey man, you know the girl in the pictures? All those pictures, the ones on the floor? Man, that was the girl in the green dress."

"Jesus Christ, man, really?"

"Hold on—I don't know if I saw that, but it's so hard to tell—I mean we were and are pretty, you know, inebriated, it being Saturday night and Shawn's going-away night and all, so what I saw doesn't quite match up with what Sammy saw, and what the chick in pink probably says, and what Anthony says."

"No man, I know what I saw. It's a what's-it-called, a flash-bulb memory. She fucking bumped him, and I think she meant to. What did Anthony say about it?"

"Whatever. Who trusts that guy when he's in love?"

Joseph believes he can summon you to him.

A photograph is stapled to the latest postcard, which you examine the next morning: you and Joseph squinting in vibrant sunlight, huddled together in front of the first greenhouse. You are just fourteen. In the days before you leave for Quebec you'll return to the photograph, gaze at the tender elasticity of your faces, the thinness of his fingers on your arm.

The photograph both answers and confounds a question it prompts: *my god, were we ever so young?*

SHELAGH: HER BODY'S ALL SHE IS

Erica and I spent the whole of last winter chasing druggy parties, always staying well past the evening's vibrant combustion and into the grey morning hours, in which most interactions are hissed and anxious. And if you calmed me down enough to speak with you and you alone, I'd say things like:

Do you think this elevator 'door close' button is, you know, a placebo? And is that telling? Am I—repeatedly pushing this 'door close' button after our smoke together—a canary in a coal mine in terms of our world filling up with placebo-things, buttons that don't connect to anything, screens with nothing behind them?

Have I told you about my abortion?

So you work in a factory? No, that's really cool! What's the order of operations when it comes to, you know, the conveyor belt? Belts?

If I'm watching a movie and the action fuzzes out and into a dream sequence, I'm changing the fucking channel. Same with books, and in conversations too. Who imbues their dreams with significance? What kind of loser has time for that?

Well.

Anxious children waking to soaked beds every morning. Also-ran musicians with steady but diminishing gigs trickling in, drowsing away the daytime. Cheaters, pre- and post-betrayal. Those who slip by never loved and rarely seen. Very old men hunched inside coffee shops by the mouths of subways and bus stations, leaving nickel tips and forgetting gloves. The hungry, the heartbroken. Disappointed women pushing forty and going crazy.

A certain kind of crazy sneaks into you, it turns out, sheathed in normal thoughts, seeming to exist affably alongside them while suffocating them completely.

It started with choosing the LCBO near Étienne's apartment one evening, thinking: it's the biggest and nicest location in downtown Toronto, with the best selection of whiskey; it'd be nice to have a walk after work; the city is huge and packed with people, I'd never see him anyway; I'd be a coward not to go.

I bought the whiskey without incident, and that evening filled a mug with whiskey, sugar and lemon juice, ripped Neil's social media feeds apart like overripe fruit, and gleaned quickly that Étienne had a new girlfriend. I Googled her, figured out where she worked and found the address, and that evening bought brown eggs and apricot pie at the supermarket right beside the building. The plastic bag slid in my sweaty fingers and electricity beat through me as I left the store, stepping out into the winter dark. I was terrified I'd see them clasped in ecstatic reunion in front of me, but also terrified I wouldn't, as all there was to do after surveying the empty sidewalk was to head straight home, and fill another night before sleep. Back at home, looking up the genealogy of her last name (French, specifically Burgundy, just like him,) I wondered: how do people sustain the nerve to live so publicly? Do they grasp that anybody can be devouring the rich novel of their lives played out online—anybody, anytime? They must think that people are good; or at least, trust that nobody they've known will curdle their brains and cling to them like burrs.

Now that everything's behind me and my mind is going, the days scatter behind me white and featureless. Sunday, what was it? I slept until three in the afternoon, then spent the evening drinking and thinking of all the times I'd accidentally almost killed someone I love (around three), then ended the night over the stove, burning all of the drawings I'd made of him (they, like their cinders, weren't what is, but remainders of what is not.) Arnaud came over afterwards, and I was so drunk I didn't care how he fucked me, so drunk I almost forgot to check that he'd paid me (six hundred dollars under the lamp, as usual.)

Neil's the only one who checks up on me regularly, sending me awkward texts, their stiffness belying his deep caring and grief:

    'wtf is this snow-rain today?'

   'just ran into Eddie, remember from school? holy shit Shelagh he's gotten so fat. This is why ppl delete FB!'

'tasselled loafers: y/n?'

And, just once and very late at night: 'hey buddy, you hold-ing up OK?'

When I'd reply, I'd keep it careful too, sticking to light anec-dotes and vague promises of hanging out soon. If we started, nothing could stop us from spiralling into mutual grief, mourning over those who cut loose from us, and wriggled free.

Monday, what was it? A winter-blank day, the thin light lasting barely after lunchtime, wading through emails and gum-ming down bits of starchy food, then rushing through well-lit underground arteries dense with people, all day inhabiting the kind of body that deflects attention, over which people's eyes slide, bored and agitated, seeking colour and youth. Wednesday, what was it? An imposter in a sunny, fragrant bak-ery, I twisted my fingers to keep from holding my lighter to the wall of wicker baskets packed with loaves of bread. I caught a child smiling at me over her father's shoulder, and hollowed out with shame. Another man would come over, that night, and fuck me, but it wouldn't feel like anything. It wouldn't be her. It wouldn't be him.

And when I'd sleep: a liquid world, close-knit and embry-onic, just Étienne and I. He ached for me and I felt his ache radiate from him, an affect so strong it shimmered deep red. I yanked the silk slip up over my stomach and his hands were guiding mine along, that's how urgent, and then as the silk crept up over my breasts his mouth found them, that's how urgent, his lips parting and his tongue finding the hidden skin, his body pressed up against mine even though I faltered a lit-tle—I couldn't see for a moment because the nightgown was briefly over my head—that's how urgent—and he steadied me with two big hands. And in that liquid world I was my twen-ty-eight-year-old body, that brief year or two I hadn't starved myself thin, a plump body almost edible in its fleshy abundance, a body even more miraculous in photographs for its brevity—mayfly-brief, blink-and-you-miss-it.

Men on the subway watch me like they're peering out of a suit of armor. A woman isn't in her body. Her body's all she is.

Friday, what was it? The company is collapsing, shutting down fifteen of the twenty-two dental clinics under our umbrella; though at head office we're thigh-deep in blood as the company hemorrhages beyond repair, we are electing to project a sense of calm disappointment with our constituents, instituting a mass firing of clinic staff: hygienists, janitors, junior team managers, clerks. As the gentlest and most wet-blanket person in the HR department, I have been assigned to clear the bodies, and today I am tasked with letting two dental hygienists go.

Usually, they already know: they've received the requisite correctional interview and two official warnings over email with all the regional managers CC-ed (a detail that makes my skin crawl). Once they're in front of me, I see what's wrong: often they seem eaten away by depression or grief. Sometimes they smell. Then I click into a script that eats me too, the stringency of which hollows me out; I was taught to read it from my iPad to add distance and authority, but I couldn't help learning it by heart, and quick.

The first woman enters my office at 10:06 (late and no knock; were I to become totally detestable, strikes #1 and #2). She is wearing her scrubs beneath her coat. Her teased, brittle hair is dyed a deep brown, and as she sits and removes her coat her movements seem awkward and restrained, as if she'd just moments ago found herself in middle age and is adapting herself accordingly. I gaze at her long green nails, and discern that they are real. She shivers a little and I wonder if she's high, reflecting (perhaps unfairly) on the email sent by her boss this morning: *Possible RX problem.*

"You look so cold," I say, brimming with real, if misdirected, empathy and concern.

"Not exactly," she says, gesturing like *hold on* as she pauses, translating to English in her head. "I drive from Oakville, with no window on driver's side," she says.

"Oh my god," I say, overcome: I imagine her in an ancient and rust-eaten Buick—no, Volvo—both side mirrors held on with duct tape. I imagine her frozen hands gripping the steering wheel, so shrunken with cold that her rings rattle up and down her fingers, and as a stoplight flashes red she brakes and a gigantic rosary dangling from the rear-view mirror bonks her shiny fore-head. The light changes and her apartment building recedes behind her, brown and depressing, and she thinks longingly of her two—no, three—children waiting for her to come home, their stomachs rumbling.

"I'm so sorry," I say.

She shrugs. "Just kids, probably. Weird they get into the condo parking, uh, room—you know, underground. Guess GPS is worth it to sell?"

(Were I to become totally detestable, I would think: and what have you sold for drugs? Or do you get them for 'free' from the dentist in charge of your clinic [male, sixtyish, sodden, unstable?])

I ask her how she describes her attitude towards work, and how she would rate her job performance within the last four to six months from a scale of 1 to 10. Almost every time I speak, she winces slightly and touches her hair. I wonder (perhaps unfairly) whether she's figured out how to balance her uppers with down-ers, as I am no slouch in the drugs department.

"How would you rate your...um, Rachel, in terms of being a manager?"

"I'm sorry," she says, not unkindly, "But I am here for firing. That's right? So fire me."

And so I tell her that she has indeed been let go. She tenses up as if about to sneeze, and stays that way; I gaze down at my iPad, though now as ever, there is nothing really there. I say, I apologize on behalf of the company, however there's nothing we can do [about your shyness and Russian demeanor which certain mouth-breathing colleagues interpret as icy], It must be tough [to be jobless and maybe addicted to expensive drugs in the winter], Do you have any questions for me [the limp surrogate for the supervisor you'll never see again]. This, instead of throwing my arms around her, bringing her head to my chest, encouraging her to wail with me, wail until we're thrown from this building together—yanked as we'll be down six flights of stairs, too wild to be contained in an elevator, rejecting the shame, the desperation, the pain of anonymity squeezing our hearts in its fist—this city, our ages, these bodies, this life.

She leaves and I hold my face in my hands for a long time, squeezing my eyes until I see fireworks. I am very afraid I'll think of doing something violent, which is a reliable precursor to thinking about doing something violent, and sure enough: I could run after her and crack her skull on the elevator door. I could sneak up behind my boss and light fire to her hair. I could stir Ajax crystals into the communal coffee tin. I know the most dangerous things in my office: scissors, an eight-ball, today's pair of takeout chopsticks that broke apart jagged, a particularly dense paperweight.

"I am a *loving* person," I say out loud, bringing me back into myself. "I am a loving *person*."

Where is he, where is she? He is nearby, he is in this city with me, I can feel it, I can sense it whenever I pay attention, like if I focus I smell my own perfume on my clothes, or taste the inside of my own mouth. And she is gone, in another province, another world, tending to indoor gardens, fucking other men, other women. My body is failing, and so is my mind. *Where is he, where is she?* While I can focus on one sense over another, I cannot shift or escape my own experience as a fully-immersed being experiencing the world acutely through my senses and within this body, always, and it's becoming torture. The rest of the day I manage to answer the phone and type most of my emails one-handed. The other hand grips the paperweight, lifting it up and down, preparing, assessing.

That night we plunged into a lake, Erica and I, and she held me in the water and pressed her forehead to mine, and as bright fireworks burst at the edges of my eyes—entire birds of light exploding up from the water, fat as pigeons, wherever she pressed his thumbs—she told me *I'll never let you go, I'm going to marry you, I'll never let you go, you are my wife.* And within me heavy concurrent waves of tenderness and sorrow burrowed like a tunnel, sucking me down.

Despite its experiential richness or perhaps because of it, I knew I was dreaming and she was already lost, the forever-long blip of our youthful selves arcing away from me and from her too, wherever she lives and lies asleep, as my own sleep thinned out and evaporated. Even as morning light came through the blinds and I grew aware of my real-life feet (sweating profusely, dull as rocks) I stayed in his arms as long as I could manage it. Which her and I were we? Was this her as we were, last year? Or was this woman—stroking my chest and keeping my head above the water—was this woman a total fabrication? Post-breakup, post-hatred and post-disintegration, re-configured as mine again, demonstrating awareness of what was coming, and drawing out my implicit forgiveness? Her sorrow was just a map of my own, but it was briefly and gloriously doubled, providing the relief of a witness.

I've barely started my computer the next morning when my phone starts vibrating and I jump: it's a number with an area code I don't recognize. I pick up and hear heavy breathing and a roar of wind.

"Shelagh? Shelagh?"

"Oh my god. Erica, where are you calling me from?"

"Walden!"

"Oh man, hi." I jump up and close my door. "The farm! Hey! What's it like? Cows?"

"It's more of a . . . like a compound," she says. "Wonderful, really wonderful. There's another girl staying with us, she's wonderful. We're focusing on hydroponics right now, you know, because it's winter. Tell me about you."

"Oh, you know. Work, work, work. I'm at the office right now, actually."

"I didn't wake you up, did I? I'm just so used to getting up at five that this feels like noon."

"No you didn't, because like I said, I'm at work."

"Oh, lovely. That must be wonderful."

"So how's the guy? He's like the boss? You guys together yet?" I think about her staring out at snowy trees as she speaks, her little hands gripping the phone, and I feel nothing, and I feel good about feeling nothing—don't I?

She laughs. "You don't waste any time, do you?"

"No, I just don't want to waste yours. I'm sure there's lots to do on a, uh, a compound. Farm thing."

"I had a feeling you'd get back together with Étienne," she says. "No judgment, he's a wonderful guy."

"Come on. He wouldn't have me."

Her voice. "And so, you miss him. Well you left him for a reason, right?"

"I don't—I mean, why did you ask to talk about such a banal thing when up there working at doing something difficult and different? I bet it feels kind of life-and-death up there, with no internet and living off the land and all."

Her voice. "No, not at all—it's really wonderful. But it's such a relief to, you know, hear you and imagine Toronto around you, it's not banal at all. Are you at home, in front of your computer?"

"Erica. I'm at the *office*."

"Oh, lovely, I can picture it: you're all alone, working away, and you can go out and eat whatever you like. I don't know how to . . . you're so free," she says. "We're doing good work here and I'm so happy, but oh, just the past week I guess— it's been a little . . . it's been kind of hard." She exhales, a burst of static, then I hear wind, rustling, changing directions—is she running somewhere?—and her voice continues in a whisper. "But I am so much less without you. It happened too slow to notice, but hearing your voice just now I realize I am absolutely flat, or at least, you'd think that to see me—you'd think that I'm flat. You only saw me around you, so you wouldn't know. But you filled me up."

"Oh, for fuck's sake."

"No, I mean it. Do you hate me? You must. But it is so true." I feel that she believes in her words deeply, feels them expanding in her chest; I sense her swoon a little from the romance of what she's saying. And despite how gross that is, I'm a little moved.

"It's the truest thing I know. It shines in the big pile of mud I'm wading through. It beams through me and it tortures me but it keeps me alive, too, it keeps me myself."

"Jesus Christ, are you OK?"

"Oh, no, wonderful! Very good, but I'd be better if you'd come. I asked you to think about it—did you? Shelagh, come, you'd think it's wonderful. What's so important there, in the city? You're just walking around, going to work and coming home surrounded by hundreds of people who don't even see you when they look at you. Don't you want a community, and the kind of work that gives you a sense of real progress? Don't you know you'll get old soon, we both will, and you can work a boring job then?"

I imagine us old, her and I, and realize I can't grasp it. Old Millennials are as unimaginable to me now as us young Millennials would be to my children—were I ever to procreate, which seems even less likely to me at thirty-six than it did at nineteen, with my slackening body and my scraping-by, no-savings contract job. All that's different is the longing and an awareness that it will deepen, a daily pang that will transition into mourning as little families blossom all around me.

"Where is it?" I ask her. "Tell me where it is and maybe I'll come."

"That's not . . . ideal for us," she says. "We can pick you up."

"No," I say. "You tell me where you are. You give me an address. Then I'll come to you."

She hangs up.

I conduct an exit interview with another dental hygienist, a redhead, her fine hair knotted in braids and wisping out over her forehead. I assess immediately, and without much surprise, that she's quite a bit heavier than I am.

"I feel like I'm the one with questions for you," she says.

"Well that's actually the next thing I'm getting to," I say, staring down at the iPad, and she sighs.

We sit for a moment.

"Ask away," I say.

"I've seen Janelle, just for example, being way worse to patients," she says. "Like whispering to go fuck themselves, and she skips every Christmas and Halloween party, and she basically eats for free every day, takes whatever out of our lunchboxes and shopping bags, no matter how many notes we leave on the cork-board. And she has definitely . . ." she pauses, then exhales—"*fucked* three married patients. So why me?"

"Off the record, Suzanne, I think some people get off more easily than others. Come on, you know this, don't you? That's life. You expect it any different from how you felt in grade school? You expect people to be good to you, just because you're nice?"

She signs all the forms for her severance, and leaves.

The scissors I'd been squeezing drop to the floor, and I am flooded with relief.

Neil is waiting for me in the downstairs pub, buffeted by the post-work tide of people and visibly trying to ignore the gigantic TV screen above his head, which is blaring a neon-bright volley-ball game. He stares down, unseeing, at a small and sweat-dotted book, his beer full to the brim and beaded with moisture.

"You waiting long?"

"Not really," he says, and we lock eyes as I sit down across from him. He looks away first. "How was work," he says.

"Brutal," I reply, and he looks relieved. He'd receive any of Erica's good news with pinched lips, and unfriended people who broadcasted theirs on social media: no matter how considerable his own good luck, he guarded it jealously; it must never have felt like enough.

"Me too. I got fired today," he says.

"I still think you're the worst," I say, realizing I'm not joking as his tentative smile drops from his face. I look over my shoulder briefly before continuing. "Because of some cokehead fuckery in upper management I've been firing people all day for *fake fucking reasons*. Good people, young mothers and old ladies who clean people's mouths for eight hours a day, not because their parents think it'd be healthy and good for their futures, but because it's a cold hard imperative to support their families and feed themselves and keep their homes. And I don't know, Neil, I think your boss might have had good reason."

"Even you, you hate me too?" he says. "Why me? I can't imagine you think I'm any worse than Erica."

"I don't hate you, I just . . . Neil, the photos," I say. He looks confused, and it dawns on me that he's very, very drunk and that perhaps he's been slumped here, drinking and pretending to read, for hours. "That was a *uniquely* fucked up thing to do," I say. "I've seen people be cowardly or negligent, but not as actively—as premeditatedly cruel as that." A waitress in a kilt is hovering by my elbow and I reach over and tap his glass, indicating I want the same. "I just think of you like stacking those photos in little rows and feel sick," I say.

"I got them printed professionally," he says, "like nice enough to frame in your home, like pretty much emptied my chequing account, and"—he leans forward—"I didn't repeat a single one. With someone like her, you get to five, six, seven hundred really fast." He leans back and takes a deep and sloppy swig of beer, then wipes his hand on his chest. "It'd never be her idea to take a picture, she's not some, um, exhibitionist really, she's actually quite shy about her body, most of the time."

"Yeah. I know," I say.

"I mean I love her, this deep permanent feeling," he continues, as if I hadn't spoken, "but I also knew that her beauty, the emotional place she was in and our instability, and her uh, and everything was rushing by so fast. And at that point, remember, we didn't know what she had—she was convinced she was going to die. And here you have a phone you're always touching and thinking about, equipped with an excellent camera—well, what are you going to do? With that kind of . . . awareness of temporality and theoretically infinite opportunity, the interval between acceptable moments to take photos shrinks, right?"

"Does it?"

He takes out a battered pack of cigarettes and drops it on the table, looking up at the television. "Oh, for sure. Her stepping out of the shower, her sitting up in bed naked and sick with a summer cold, her undressing after a dinner at her parent's place, if I could have it all forever, I would. Her eating steak in her underwear, watching Jurassic Park with me. Her face a little red in the morning, right after crying about some dream. Close up of her fingers on her little throat, working down all those pills. What was I going to do?"

"I think you're missing an empathy chip, Neil."

"I got fired on purpose, you know that?"

"Well, I'm not surprised—"

"I spit in somebody's plate of fucking, like, *linguine with clams* and drank straight gin all day from a flask and waited until the sink was stacked up with dishes, then whipped out my cock and pissed in it, pissed all over it—and probably other things too, I don't remember." He pauses to recalibrate, leaning against the back of the booth and closing his eyes. "I'd planned to die the night of that party, is the thing. I wanted Anthony to kill me, get mad enough to kill me by accident."

"I can't believe you, Neil."

"The icy steps, right? They never salt those steps, I've been to parties at that house before. Or maybe he'd break a bottle over my head, and that'd do it. Or maybe I'd buy a bag of whatever from her dealer guy and swallow the whole thing in the bathroom—maybe scare some of them straight."

"Are you serious? What about Ryan?"

He winces, takes a long sip, then keeps talking. "You know, she's probably slept with half the people there. Not even kidding—just tell me I'm wrong."

"Neil, that's on you. You had an understanding."

He laughs, his eyes still shut. "You think I had a choice? It's always the person with all the power who decides, and the other has to go along with it, to take it and take it until they can't take anymore."

"There were probably alternate courses of action."

"Shelagh," he moans, "I thought she was dying."

I think about it. "She thought so too. She still thinks that. I think she thinks she's healing herself up there, like some country-air-lots-of-vitamins remedy. Like how cancer patients use crystals, kind of thing."

He opens his eyes and leans forward.

"Has she called you?"

"Oh boy. Are you jealous?"

He doesn't reply, just watches me closely.

"Yeah, she has. She wants me to come to that farm."

"When?"

"When did she call? Today. Is this why you wanted to talk to me?"

"Are you going to go?"

"Not a chance."

"I think I will," he says.

"You understand she's there with another man?"

"And some women! Like a group of people. Nothing I'm not used to. She loves me and forgives me, is the thing. She was saying"—and again he looks beyond me, maybe up at the bright jiggly volleyball game but entirely out of focus—"she was saying, these days we apply this impossible pressure to our spouses, we want them to be everything for us, whereas drawing on a community is far more natural."

"A community . . . ?" I say, and then stop as something dawns on me, draining all the colour from his face and the patterns the television projects on his white shirt and the polished wood behind him, draining out the neon sign behind the bar, and rendering all the faces around us featureless. Neil is my closest friend, but he's the last person I should confide in.

"She's going to pick me up tomorrow morning," he says. "I already packed my . . . the bag I'm taking. Very minimal. I like that."

He dumps out his wallet and begins to count coins with one finger, and we're quiet for a moment, staring down at the pile of coins and crinkled receipts. With his free hand, he drags his fingers through his long, stringy hair. "Can you text me when you get up there?" I ask, taking out a twenty.

"They don't do phones," he says.

"Except her," I say.

"What?"

"Well, she called you."

"I think maybe they share one phone. Business calls, family calls." He stops counting for a moment. "That'd be good. To call my folks."

He gets up and falls, kind of melts to the floor like his legs were swapped out for two painted hunks of sand. Someone laughs and someone else shrieks, and he looks up at me from the carpet, and the room is so dark all I see is the television gleaming on his eyes, and he stays so still, as trusting as a child. I bend down, wrap his arm around my shoulder and help him up, just as Erica may have, perhaps eliciting memories of his mother carrying him off to bed. "My phone," he bleats, yanking away and dropping to the ground, then groping around under our table. He retrieves it and holds it right up to his face, likely examining it for scratches.

"Who cares? You're giving it up tomorrow," I say, then lean forward, grabbing his elbow. "Listen Neil, I love you, OK buddy? I love you and I'm here for you. If there's something weird going on, you have. To. Tell. Me."

"I love this thing," he says, looking down at his phone. "I sleep with it under my pillow and sometimes I dream about it."

"I dream about my phone too," I say, laughing despite myself, and it's true. I love it like I'd love my own child if she grew into a slender, bright little ballerina, perfectly obedient, entirely focused on performing for me and never growing any bigger, or away from me. Still in a crouch, he's focused up at the TV.

"I dream it talks to me," he says as I help him up again, and his head droops on my shoulder as he falls into a shambling kind of step beside me.

"Your phone?" I ask. He doesn't answer, just kind of moans. "We're going to get you a cab," I say.

"Thanks." He winces as we step outside, and begins to shiver. Now his neck bends away from me, white and exposed, his head bobbling against his other shoulder as we walk.

"You know I could kill you," I say. "Just because I'm little, just because I'm a woman. It makes no difference."

"But you're getting me a cab."

"I just mean that—you trusted Erica, and look what happened. Do you think women are inherently good, or something?"

"I know I'm bad," he says, "and I know how I'm bad, and being alone makes it worse. And I know . . ."

He stops talking and breaks away, wiping his face, and I spot a cab, thrusting out my arm. He grabs my wrist and twists me around, pulling me towards him, then presses his face to mine.

"Hey," he says, his breath hot with liquor and tears. "Hey. There you are."

"What?"

He grins and pulls away again.

I rush home and dig through Erica's things until I find it: a crumpled postcard from years ago, with a return address, a Quebecois one, written in Joseph's spidery handwriting. I take a deep breath, and begin to plan.

ERICA: HERE'S THE THING ABOUT FUCKING JOSEPH

Here's the thing about fucking Joseph: he's so hungry to impregnate you; he brings himself so close, and you both heave and soak each other with the effort to keep him from coming in you. He speaks gently of the child he'd give you: a beautiful long-haired boy, amply loved (Joseph is certain he'd produce only sons). But like most women, you know that once you're pregnant and he doesn't want it, everything changes. Abortion clinic windows are bulletproof glass, and people pray for you. So you cajole him into coming on your stomach. So does Logan sometimes, though usually, she swallows.

Here's the thing about fucking Joseph: as he's grown older, he's come to demand a very plebeian kind of resistance. You bunch your hands up against his wet, shuddering ribcage, use your nails, and struggle. Usually, he comes very quickly, and Logan must suck him for a while to get him going again.

Here's the thing about fucking Joseph: he's always on top. His hair dangles, straw-like, and when he sweats it clumps and reveals all the places he's bald.

Here's the thing that keeps you excited about fucking Joseph: you two began fucking right around when Logan was a toddler. Logan's face alarms you all the time—surely you weren't so young, at her age? Theoretically, as his life progresses, the women he could fuck haven't even been born yet.

After you fuck, the three of you sit around the small wicker table with its glass tabletop, your heads bent as he speaks, all holding hands. The table legs are sawed off, so the table is about five inches off the ground; everyone kneels on folded-up towels. Tiny plates, mostly laden with vegetables, sit at the centre of the table. The moon hangs low outside the window, just above the bare tree branches.

"And what are we Grateful for?" Joseph concludes.

"The Sun, the Sky, the Big Tree and its Shelter, the Earth beneath us and around us. Our Home, our Gardens, our Greenhouse."

Joseph squeezes your hand in his, and you smile at each other as Logan watches. Feeling Logan watch, excluded and patient, you throb with excitement, as if you'll be wild to fuck him all your life so long as she's around—and the Logan after that, and after that.

Here's the thing about fucking Joseph: with each thrust and grunt you feel him go: I am your big quiet protector who burns so bright and treads softly through the world, trailing little frost patterns of menace.

With each wet suck on your nipple, your collarbone, you feel him go: I curdle your time when I am not nearby, and your heart squirts plumes of jealousy, streaking and drying on your ribs. Every morning, you scrape away this black feeling like rot from walls, and since it cannot dissipate or be disposed of outside of you, you must secrete it deep where even he can't reach.

You believe, and have believed since age fourteen, that his hidden self is beautiful and kind, a superimposition of his childhood selves, a sunny portal to a past that never existed, that you imagine together, or that you imagine for him.

When he worships Logan's pussy, when he makes her shake and come, you believe: his hidden self is unfathomable, molten and reptilian—like anybody's.

When he presses a hand to Logan's taut stomach-ball and caresses it with amazement; when he takes her from behind, and comes shuddering inside of her, you believe: his hidden self doesn't exist.

And when you catch him kissing her by the greenhouse, a snatched moment rendered breathless in your brief absence, the air's knocked out of you too, and you believe that his hidden self is you and you alone. That he has sucked you down, and lined his insides with you.

After the kiss you find her in the kitchen; her back is turned, but her shoulders are very tense as she rummages in the sink, her hands submerged in suds. You clutch a mug, drying it with a threadbare towel, feeling yet more of you sour and wither. From the light coming through the window, it appears to still be early afternoon, though it feels it has been forever.

"Should I use oregano again, with the sauce?" Logan asks you.

"No," you say. "I won't, like, tell on you or whatever, but it tasted awful. Didn't your mother teach you to cook?"

Logan shrugs: what a wonder, to be so unaffected! "Just the pasta dish I told you about; Lori wasn't much of a cook otherwise," she says. "We'd eat at a diner near our place a lot. The booths were made from real car seats, and she loved that. I'd see cockroaches climbing over the car seats all the time, I guess because they get crumbs wedged in there pretty deep, but I wouldn't tell her."

"Probably she was doing the same thing. Seeing, not telling," you say.

Logan snorts. "That's not really Lori's style."

"I don't know how she afforded that, eating out all the time. Nobody can afford that." You know you come from absurd privilege compared to Logan, and in your Toronto life would be very careful not to say something like that, to someone like her, but here—she's your lover, your best friend, nesting beneath the weathered wings of your protector. Sometimes you imagine the two of you curled within his belly, as he traverses the streams of the external world, mediating it for you, allowing little gasps of it in through his gaping mouth, his lips ragged with years and years of fishhooks.

Here's the thing about fucking Joseph: he's always an animal, to you. Thinking of him as just a man is unthinkable.

Logan stacks plates, making a little more noise than she should. "Yeah, spending money like that bugged her sometimes, but not enough to stop. I don't think she had a lot of things she enjoyed otherwise. Once she said with all the sushi we ate delivered, we could afford a trip to Barbados, but I didn't mind—it's not like she'd take me."

"Who'd she take instead? Her boyfriend?"

"Well yeah, but I don't care," Logan says. "Wouldn't you?"

The next evening a visible sliver of sky outside the kitchen window is very black and flecked with stars, and you sit by a pot brimming with eggplant stewing it in tomato sauce, gazing at the tree branches lacing the stars, which wink as they shiver—the branches—in the evening wind. You rest your chin on one hand, the wrist of which has gone sore, suggesting you've sat still for long stretches as the water boils, as the sauce heats up, as the salt leaches bitterness from the eggplant. You stare out at the branches and stars, remembering a white-hot summer afternoon in which you and Neil ate yourself sick on sushi—the rolls bristling with fried tempura bits, the slabs of tuna glimmering in the blinking flourescent of a basement restaurant—and only when the sauce has shriveled and begun to burn do you break your own reverie, like a surfacing diver.

"Dinner!"

You haul the pot into the dining room, and Joseph is already sitting at the dinner table. He's rubbing his chin under his beard with one hand, and doesn't even glance up you when you heave the pot onto the table. Logan comes inside, a metallic cold smell lingering on her hair. You smell that something is wrong, and sit quietly. Joseph pats something in from a bag sitting beside him, which you have been staring at, almost without blinking, for the last five minutes.

"Logan has brought something to my attention, Erica," Joseph says, and you squeeze your hands together beneath the table.

"She says that yesterday morning, you Confessed that you miss meat."

Logan stiffens, looks around at Erica, then back at Joseph. She squeezes the lump of her packet beneath her the neckline of her dress. "What? No I didn't!" she cries, flapping her free hand in distress.

You look up from the bag, and across the table at Joseph. "It's OK, Logan," you say.

"This is for you," Joseph says. He reaches in the bag, takes out a limp, dead pigeon, and tosses across the table at you. It is hardened up with cold and death, its head tilted stiffly to the left, its wings half-spread.

"This is meat," Joseph says. "The scentless, smooth stuff you see in those plastic supermarket packages, this is where it starts."

"I am Grateful for this," you say, and without hesitating, pick up the pigeon. You yank fingerfuls of feathers from its chest, revealing a lumpy patch of skin. Logan covers her eyes, inhaling sharply. You cup the bird's body in both hands, thumbing through its feathers. You look back up at Joseph, and then bite into the soft part of its chest cavity.

Here's the thing about fucking Joseph: everything is carnal, under his gaze. Ripping into meat is fucking Joseph. Breaking ice-bound soil is fucking Joseph. If you discovered Joseph dead, hunched over a broken tangle of soaked roots and blue hydroponics glass, you'd bump against him and whimper, and fuck his stiffening fingers. You are bound through life and death, a bond Logan cannot access, as she understands neither.

Even though you're forbidden from locking doors you lock yourself in the bathroom, and vomit coils of muscle and tiny barely chewed organs, and—to your horror—a soaked and crumped feather mass. Everything is stronger than you. This kind of anguish is not unique, it happens to many women. At its most harmless, a man can mistake a woman's love and reassurance and warmth and body for his own reciprocation, and their private world grows lopsided in his favor. He bends towards her like a sunflower, and she radiates until she combusts. At worst, he tortures her, expediting her combustion; he sees her trying to please him and punishes her for it.

You knead your face with angry red fingers. "The world is bound by love, love permeates the world and all of—all of us— love c-can't be sustained between two people alone, without going stale. It flows between groups of people—unites them— relax, relax, relax."

Logan and Joseph wait for you. It's unseasonably warm, so Logan pushes a window open, and the world outside appears browner than in the other photographs, dotted with deep green—shrubs, vines—and receding snow. The bulbs and roots and seeds you've planted rest beneath these glowing patches of snow, safe beneath a foot or two of soil, safer than any human has ever been, or ever will be. Raw life's bound up in their mealy, cottony bodies, slumbering a kind of slumber that lasts through this era and on through the next. Joseph clears his throat before continuing:

"Last night I dreamed of our family, huddled together for warmth. We stood at the edge of a blasted-out canyon, at the twilight of the world as we know it . . ."

When you emerge from the bathroom, Joseph sweeps over to you, clutches the crook of your arm: you are standing by the staircase, his body leaning into yours, as if to kiss you. Logan stands, just out of his line of vision, watching from the hydroponics room. He kisses you, and you're briefly convinced you've never felt such sublime happiness as you do in moments like these, hard-won as they are.

"I'm going to bed, join me when you're ready," he says. "Don't call her up tonight. I want you alone."

He squeezes your other arm, hard, and you freeze, then wonder: how many women hold still when surprised?

Joseph undresses for you, almost guilelessly, oozing a tiny strand of precum as he yanks one foot from his sweaty bunched-up trousers. He appears thinner than usual, and his face is tight with hunger. You slide into the narrow bed after he does, which—even to your eyes, red and throbbing with hunger—is uncomfortably child-sized.

He hunches over you in missionary, his face so knotted he can barely close his lips, and you feel his wet teeth all over your skin. He presses his hand over your nose and mouth, and you shake your head free, gasping, your eyes wide. This gets him close almost immediately, and he scrunches up his face and twists it away, hissing—

"You're going to have my child—"

Here's the thing about fucking Joseph: every time wears on him now; his fucks are shorter, sweatier, require more effort. Are you taking something from him? After setting him afire as a fourteen-year-old girl, have you watched him burn, burn, burn into fatty char? You suck at his too-hot skin, moving your head back and forth as he hisses and gasps, interrupting himself, oozing and exploding wet words in your ear—

"Don't you fucking—move . . . Oh god, oh god, oh god—"

"You can't inside of me—please come in my mouth," you say, then press your face into his hair, knowing that on this night like no other really, he will come inside of you, and that maybe this is fated.

"I have to give it to you—you have to take it—and you will come for me. You will come for me."

You feel it building in your thighs and cunt, an enormous pressure, and you start to buck along with him—I can't help it, I can't help it. He releases your face and stares, unseeing, at your mouth—

When he comes inside of you, he stays in you, holding you, long after his penis shivers and recedes. You make out, tenderly and for a long time. Just as it was when you were fourteen, it can't all be bad, can it? You rest your index finger on his lips, and he allows you to; you reflect on his mouth, the brevity of its warmth, elasticity, and locomotion.

"You're certain that he's certain?" Joseph asks you at last.

"Neil already considers himself our new Brother," you say. "I'm so happy for him."

"Who did you call today, after you spoke with our new Brother? At about eleven in the morning?"

"Someone with potential. I know her from my time in Toronto, she's a loving and hardworking person. But I think she's . . . I miscalculated."

"You know I trust you. But you must participate—with vigilance—in the maintenance of my trust."

His fingertips are pressed against your stomach, hard enough to leave white indents when he brings his hands away, which will fill in red. You grasp his hand.

"Next time, I make a call, sit with me," you whisper. "Please."

ERICA: HERE'S THE THING ABOUT NEIL

Here's the thing about Neil: even at forty, and despite his desperate love for Ryan, he leapt away from his Toronto life like it was scalding hot. You resent this: if he were a woman—even a woman like you—he'd never leave his child.

As Joseph drives and growls along to his Alice in Chains cassette, you gaze out the truck window, imagining Neil walking toward you. As with everyone else who's drifted far enough to alight in your powerful retrospective gaze, you have grown obsessed, believing you can summon Neil to you.

And you have.

Here's the thing about Neil: even as he walks along the shoulder of the highway, alone aside from occasional cars, you know he's absorbed in hoping each passing driver thinks, *What an adventurous young man.* Hoping they take him for a hitchhiker, wondering if they'd be brave enough to pull over and give him a chance; hoping they don't consider him the weird loser he fears you think he is, walking duck-footed and skinny and painfully alone along the highway at seven-thirty on a Thursday morning. You know some drivers might take him for the lone survivor of a car crash, or a hen-pecked husband booted from the family minivan at the revelation of an affair (though he, despite his wispy beard, might still look too young for that.)

Here's the thing about Neil: he's drifting away from his barren life like ash. He's done this over and over since you left him at twenty, so nothing's really grown.

Here's the thing about Neil: even at forty, even though he's a father, he'll do anything you say. As instructed, he left behind a detailed note, begging his mother to forgive him, cancel his phone plan, and explain to Ryan that he'd gone to volunteer with his girlfriend in an impoverished rural area of Quebec, and that when he's back—right in time for softball season—he'll sign up as assistant coach (a detail about which you're dubious: despite knowing Ryan for all of five minutes, each more stoned than the next, you're dead certain the poor kid is about as athletic as his dad.) As instructed, Neil then withdrew all the money he had in the world for the Family Deposit, which, combined with his final paycheck, totals about three thousand six hundred dollars. (You don't know this yet but he's one thousand four hundred dollars short, and he's convinced he'll make it up in labor and craftsmanship—something he didn't have time, he felt, to explain to you over the phone.)

You imagine Neil veering off the highway and trudging down the little side road, kicking at piles of snow and dirt as he goes, and then sitting in a dry patch of exposed brown grass by the shoulder of the road.

You imagine him sitting first on his bag and then beside it, so as not to give the impression (when you arrive) that he's the kind of guy who needs something to sit on.

You've summoned him to you, and now he waits. Perhaps, just as you did, he reads the lone road sign over and over: the symbol for food, the symbol for gas, the symbol for 'hotel' (a particularly comforting pictogram depicting a stick-figure woman bent over a flat board-like bed, beneath a spare triangle roof). Perhaps he's seized with desire to spring up and run and run and run back along the highway towards wherever the hotel(s) may be, book a room and sleep for hours and maybe days, hidden, warm, safe, unseen. The wind picks up, screeching through the grimy car window you've opened just a crack, and you imagine Neil squeezing his hands into fists in his coat pockets, going fork, spoon, gas pump, triangle-shelter, fork, spoon. Joseph turns off the highway and along the little road, and your heart leaps as you spot Neil. He jumps up, recognizing your face in the passenger's side; his face noticeably slackens as he spots Joseph in the driver's seat.

Here's the thing about Neil: unlike you and most women like you, he never learned to keep his feelings out of his limbs, away from his face. So you watch his heart sink in his clouding-up features, and see his legs straighten and lock with his sudden desire to dash and hide behind the large oak tree on the other side of the road, to crouch in the dry grass and hard mud, to listen for your murmurs of confusion and resignation, and hear the truck drive away. So when Joseph pulls over you unroll the window even though the truck's still moving, to pre-empt Neil doing anything stupid.

"It's so good to see you, Neil," you say, sticking your head out and grinning at him. "Do you need help with that bag?"

"Of course not," Neil says, perhaps seeking a moment of solidarity with Joseph, who doesn't even look at him. "Hello," he says to Joseph.

"Hello," Joseph says.

"You're going to have to kind of . . . ," you say cheerfully, and bring your shoulders up to your ears, miming bracing yourself in the back of the truck amongst the shadowy objects Joseph has draped in blankets.

"No problem," Neil says, and, once he's installed between a large wheel covered in tarp and three sacks, he asks, "What's in these bags?"

"Trimmings," you say, though you've never verified that for yourself. "The other bags and boxes, some of it's produce we're keeping in here for tomorrow. We sell it on Saturdays, mostly year-round, now that we're doing hydroponics."

"Oh, what kind?" Neil asks. You watch him dig his nails along his wrists, almost drawing blood, as if his whole body is numb as a gigantic pinched limb. You watch him shaking hard to bring the feeling back, though when it comes rushing in it'll be alien and so will he—beating with the blood of someone else's life—as everything has changed.

You watch him until Joseph looks over at you, and then you must respond.

"Lettuce, radishes, onions, sprouts, all stuff you can grow in a static solution, because space is an issue and it's just the second year we're trying this." You look over at Joseph, try grinning again. "But we are very happy with the results, and it's beautiful seeing all this green in the winter, sprouting up without soil. Hey Neil, are you hungry?"

"Oh. Yes," he says, and you dig through the bag at your feet.

Here's the thing about Neil: lulled as he is by glossy Toronto girls, slinking through offices and restaurants with bright red nails and sheer, perfumed blouses, your hair must look filthy to him, clinging to the sides of your head in wet-looking strands. Joseph's yellow parka, which hangs on you and has carefully stitched-up rips, must look about as bad. With simultaneous jolts of guilt and annoyance, you realize he'll feel betrayed, horrified even, that you wear Joseph's clothes. You pass back a brown paper packet and a soft black sleep mask, which Neil examines as the engine starts. "Is this a mask?"

"Put it on after you eat," you say, smiling apologetically. "This is just a precaution in terms of privacy, because we haven't—aside from me!—gotten to know you yet. Recently our property has been vandalized, and we've grown very concerned for our safety."

You pause, allowing him to imagine you sopping up the remains of a hydroponic tank, ankle-deep in ruined lettuce, and see in his parting mouth a rush of empathy, a feeling (despite what Shelagh thinks) he experiences deeply, and often. The packet contains a precious ration of salted seeds, which you encourage him to eat slowly as the brown world of windswept grass, occasional strip malls and naked trees—all interlaced branches and missing limbs—flashes and undulates outside the windows. Tiny snowflakes begin to fall. You long to lick the salt from the empty packet, which he's crumpled and tossed aside. You watch a fly walk up your window. It probably came into the truck this morning, clinging to Joseph's clothes.

"Is this Alice in Chains?" Neil asks.

"Yes," Joseph says, in his voice that prohibits further comment.

With Neil's sudden presence, you love Joseph all the more— his masculinity so heavy and molten, eating him alive!

Under Joseph's scrutiny you've never adored Neil like you do right now—how eminently curious he is, how city-pale and sweet!

"Now it's your job to relax," Joseph says suddenly, and you jump, though his voice is kind and soothing. "Just relax, and maybe reflect on how you'd like to seize this opportunity, this fresh start available to you. You'll be wonderfully free without the petty vanities of the modern world pulling at you, without the meaningless demands that splinter your focus and imbue your nights with anxiety. You'll be free to focus on a loving community, on good work, if you're up to it, if you're worth our combined efforts . . ." he trails off, as if he can't be bothered to continue.

Here's the thing about Neil: despite himself, he's endlessly keen to impress unimpressed men. So he puts on the blindfold, leans back against the shrouded tire-thing and, lulled by driving and perhaps still a little drunk from whatever he does in Toronto, seems to fall asleep.

Some time later he wakes to the hum of your voice, pitched in a low whisper and disrupted by the muffled objects packed between him and the noise of the road. Here's what he hears:

". . . Of course he did. I know he wouldn't . . . not an issue . . ."

Which is enough: he knows he's being discussed. In case Joseph is watching in the rear-view mirror he keeps his face slack, pretending to be asleep, listening with all his might.

Here's the thing about Neil: never having known trauma or any real difficulty, he hasn't needed to silo his self and memory into distinct, rigorously policed life-eras, resulting in—you believe—easy regression. He listens to Joseph whispering to you with the wounded petulance of a child:

"I sense that he's . . . of it, and everyone around, you know. You'll request it immediately . . . out of the way, besides . . . for you."

"Tell me . . . just want to . . . wonderful, and I love to hear it." Your voice, pitched higher, is adoring and fawning. Neil's forehead is bright with sweat; your thighs tingle and inexplicably, you wonder if it this vouyerism gets him a little hard.

"I am grateful for the sun, the sky, the big tree, the roof above us," Joseph says, louder and clearer as he becomes aware

Neil is awake, and Neil noticeably stiffens as he hears the ticking that signals that the truck is pulling over.

"I am grateful for you, for your gift of love and total commitment of body and mind," Joseph continues. "With every splinter and bruise and bite, the poison drains away."

"Hard ground broken for new growth," you say, and then for Neil's sake: "Oh my God, I haven't had McDonald's in months, I'm almost afraid to eat it."

Joseph tells you that you should be, and you laugh, and asks him if he's sure; in a more serious tone he advises that you will likely feel sick, but that everyone deserves a treat, and if you do in fact become sick, it may serve as a learning experience.

"You've been good," he says. "Give me, um, fifteen dollars should do it."

You reach into the bag and hand him some crumpled bills; he gives you a bristly kiss, and slams the car door behind him. In the rear-view mirror, you see Neil peel off the blindfold and crawl forward, squinting at the back of your head—framed, as it must be, in the white noon light—as you watch him silently, begging God please don't.

"You love this guy," he croaks.

You look back at him. "Very much," you say, "and I love you too."

Here's the thing about Neil: he's never loved anyone like he loves you because you've never held still long enough to be seen; you've always twisted away. So he moans and pushes his head against your arm, and you twist around and embrace him, stroking his hair. He breathes you in, your strong, scalpy, oniony, detergenty smell, earthy, overwhelming; he nuzzles into the warmth of your unzipped coat and feels your ribs vibrate as you breathe in, and speak: "Please try to calm down," you say. "You're safe."

"You can't do this, you can't do this, you can't do this," he moans.

"What can't I do?" you ask. "Isn't this what you want to do? Listen: I've never felt one hundred percent ready for anything. You probably won't either, not ever—that's not how the important things work. School, buying a home, marriage—right?"

"Oh god, it's you, I can't stand it, it's too weird," he says, pressing his hand to your shrunken waist, spreading his fingers over your stomach, flattening himself against the almost unbearable heat coming off of you. For once, you stay very still. "Now that we have a moment alone I just want to—I am so sorry," he says.

Here's the thing about Neil: he's sorry about everything to everyone, so long as they get mad first.

"It's OK," you insist.

"No, I am like—*living* it, you don't understand, my whole life is a slog through humiliation, I'm paying this huge daily penance I feel physically, like, pushing a gigantic boulder up a mountain. I'm like Sisyphus."

You look out the window, anxious, still stroking his hair. "Shh, it's OK. You're nothing like her."

Only when exceptionally distressed does Neil overlook an opportunity to correct someone, so he presses on: "How could you have forgiven me? And so quickly? How could you look over at me just now, with such love? How could you welcome me into your life again like this, so totally, so trusting?"

"Depends who you ask," you say, stroking his hair, marveling at how soft and clean it is—like a child's. "If you ask Shelagh, she'd say that's what women are trained to do: physically, we take more pain. We're closer to life, we're closer to death. And I'd add that we forgive, and we give, and we love, because we must. We are good."

"Yes, I knew it." It seeps through him like syrup and he relaxes against you, listen to your heart pattering—quick and faint, even to you—and he feels the thin cloth of your dress shift against your body and his cheek as you rub the soft, small bumps of your breasts across his forehead.

"Shelagh doesn't think that's true, that you're good; she and I had an argument about just that," he says, his voice muffled against you. "I bet you miss her. You love her too. You love a lot of people, an exhausting amount, I don't know how you do it."

"That's normal," you say, stroking his hair. "It happens."

"Oh yeah?" He stays as still as you, perhaps praying you won't push him away, aching for just a minute longer, safe here in your coat. "Says who?"

"Says who? Who says anything? Says me."

"I need you," he whispers.

"Yes. And I need you, we need you," you say, beginning to buzz with panic. He closes his eyes, and you straighten your back against him, looking through the window, scanning for Joseph striding back amongst the parked cars. "But listen—look up, look at me—Neil, you have to calm down, he's not going to like it if you're this upset when he gets back. OK? You're going to lie back down against the nice soft stuff back there. You'll have the mask back on. You can have a blanket. We'll drive and drive, a nice relaxing drive. I'll pass you back some fries."

Here's the thing about Neil: he thrived in controlled environments like school, acting especially docile around women; teachers, classmates, other people's mothers. He responded well to being told what was going to happen and letting it happen, chafing against it very slightly, only miming resistance. "And then?" he asks.

"And then . . . um, we'll get your deposit, we'll give you some work clothes, you'll bathe and meet Logan, she's really—"

"Oh—right, I wasn't sure when to mention this," he says, "but I'm a little short on the deposit."

You pull away. "How short?"

"About fifteen hundred short."

"Oh Neil, oh no. Oh no, oh shit."

"Erica, it's OK, I'm really good with my hands. Saturdays—for the market, I can make things to sell. Or I can document the movement for you guys, I can be the official photographer, I can capture everything for posterity, and that's an invaluable contribution." He's talking faster and faster, tugging at her sleeve. "Hey—really, it's OK, my parents can send some money if it's really that urgent, like if it's a rent situation, all right? Totally understandable. I'm sorry I didn't mention it until now." You sit stock-straight, feeling a vertiginous sweep within you, like you and Neil are telescoping up together away from the rows and rows of cars, the brown scrubby woods behind the McDonalds and gas station, the long black snake of highway.

"What's wrong? Are you scared of him?" He tries to grab your shoulders. "Erica, is this man violent?"

"Shut up, stop, stop, fuck," you say, shaking him off, then bend and feel around on the floor. "Put it back on, lie back down, be quiet, please, we'll figure this out," you say.

Perhaps a lifetime of docility around women has left a life-long line of rot, as a squiggle of cruelty dormant since his child-hood wakes in his brain, and he grabs for you again, squeezing your elbow until you gasp. "You love me," he says.

"Yes."

"Say it."

"I love you."

"You'll continue to love me, be good and attentive to me, like before? You know I've never been happier, and I don't think you have either, but you're going to have to be good to me, I'm not your fool. You're going to make this OK? You're going to tell everybody at the place to respect me? Even him?"

"Yes. Yes." You start crying, furious at this ill-timed spurt of what must be, for Neil, a virulent masculinity—Joseph's animal smell hangs in the car, clings to your hair, covers your body— and Neil squeezes yet harder, and if words weren't beyond him, he'd say: aren't I a man too, and in love with you besides— passionately, totally, desperately?

The truck door flies open, you hear a thud and Neil screams with pain. He crawls one-handed back to the shrouded tires, gripping his face. Joseph swings himself inside the truck and slams the door in one easy motion, then tosses two wet, crumpled bags of McDonald's at you. He looks back at Neil with a grimace like a smile, revealing his brownish bottom teeth, and rubbing his chin. They look at each other.

Here's the thing about Neil, at this very moment: he now understands that you and Joseph are bound together permanently through pain—through inflicting it, receiving it, soothing one another afterwards, through understanding the world through it, through a tacit agreement that the world works this way.

"Fuck. Fuck you both," Neil spits.

"Neil's fourteen hundred dollars short," you hear yourself say. "I tried to, to emphasize the importance of the deposit, and I don't know what came over him—perhaps I wasn't clear enough, or he let his feelings get in the way. I slapped him because I was angry, and we started to fight."

"I was just trying to talk," Neil says.

"It's true," you say, watching Joseph, your eyes squirming in your head, squeezing the bags in your hand so hard something pops—a soft drink in a paper cup—and soaks the bag, your coat, the seat. "I know you're disappointed," you whisper to Joseph, not able to help yourself, feeling all the world like a drunk, married man whispering *let's fuck* in the ear of an ex-lover.

"Oh, screw you," says Neil. "I'm not stupid, and I'm not scared of him. I know why you're terrified of him. What if I said I'm out of here, and calling the cops as soon as I get to a phone?"

There's a pause.

"That's definitely something you can do," Joseph says, leaning back against the side of the seat while maintaining eye contact with Neil. "And what are you going to say?"

Neil eases himself up into a crouch, feeling around for his bag. "None of your business," he says, his voice breaking a little.

"Neil, I had to hit you," Joseph says, looping his arm around the back of his seat and resting his fingers, oh-so-gently, on the door handle. "She's a small woman; she can't defend herself against a man. Let's talk about what I saw, on my way back to the truck: I come back through that row of cars and, along with say four other people, I observe a vicious struggle in the front seat. There you are, bending her wrist and yelling, and there she is, crying and slamming her fist against the windshield. One kind man, in fact, offered to um"—he starts the engine and pauses, checking the rear view before he starts backing out—"to call the police himself. I assured him I could handle it. If pressed, I'm sure that Erica can vouch for her poor treatment throughout your relationship in Toronto."

He pulls out of the parking lot and suddenly they're on the highway again, and you watch the trees begin to pass again, hypnotically, as your eyes water. "Are you threatening me?" Neil asks, and nobody answers.

"Toronto, yeah. You know what? Erica and I, we had fun together. We went out and enjoyed the spoils of late-fucking-stage-capitalism, man, we spent money like we despised it, like we had to get rid of it. You think she doesn't miss that? And I fucked her," Neil continues, crawling forward until he's right between you and Joseph, changing tacks like a traffic light—

"We fucked all the time. You too sophisticated to care about that? I know how she acts when she's incredibly horny and how she demurs when she's tired. I've traced the scars on her ribs with my fingers and tongue outdoors in the winter, in the bathtub, I could do it in my sleep. I know the sounds she makes when she sleeps, when she's having a nightmare, doesn't it bother you? And if you're taking me back to that compound—against my will at this point, by the way—well you'd have a lawsuit on your hands, for one. And for two, we'd fuck again, we can't resist each other, she loves me, we're in love."

"Oh, you're not coming," Joseph says, changing lanes. "You'd poison the delicate set of dynamics we've established. You're beyond redemption. You'd agree?" he asks you. You don't speak or acknowledge he's spoken, as you're instead looking back forth between Neil and the driver, shrinking in your seat.

"And yes, it bothers me," Joseph continues, not looking at Neil, though Neil is crouched less than a foot away, "Sure it does. But not as much as we bother you. Maybe you can tell the police about your feelings when you speak with them, but I'd advise you talk to a friend. It might be more cathartic and helpful for you."

"Are you serious? Fuck you, man!"

"Neil, stop!" You seize Neil's head and grip it tight, encircling his face in pincer-like fingertips, staring into his eyes. "Stop, stop, stop, calm down." Sweat runs into your eyes as you stare at each other.

Here's the thing about Neil, right now: he understands your terror, but can't help himself. He has never experienced a catalytic, self-ruining event like you have, though he's pushed for one all his cushioned life. Now this is it, and you won't survive it.

Neil yanks away from you, cocks his fist and punches Joseph in the ear.

You scream, or everybody does; the world jerks along with the truck as a multitude of car horns erupt behind you and the truck slides and almost glide as if weightless, for one bottomless moment, off over the snowy shoulder, towards a long black stretch of trees. Joseph grabs the wheel again, yelling a sort of grainy yell as they bump along the rough frozen ground and the engine roars, yanking the wheel around and guiding the truck back towards the road. He parks half-on, half off the shoulder as several more cars flash by honking, then rips off his seatbelt. He turns and looks Neil full in the face for the second time since they met, then grabs him by the throat.

"You're going to kill me, you're going to kill me," Neil gasps, all consonants, and Joseph knocks him back flat against one of the sacks. Joseph swings himself out of the driver's seat and lumbers around to the back of the truck, coming to finish him off. He pauses for a moment, then bends and rains blows down on Neil. Neil curls up, screaming, and you scream something too, and Joseph stops and pulls away, his hands in the air.

Because the squiggle of cruelty has mutated and leapt over to you, pumping through you until it seems to replace your blood—thousands of long light-worms opening their eyes, jolting your limbic system awake-awake-awake—

Here's thing about Neil: he is a coward, but you love him with the ferocity of a desperate woman. As he opens his eyes, sobbing aloud and scraping blood from his face with his mangled hand, he looks beyond the man hunched in front of him and sees you, bent over the back of your seat, gripping Shelagh's gun in both hands and pointing it right at Joseph's forehead.

Joseph stares at you, frozen for a moment in amazement. Neil watches him approach you oh-so-slowly, his hand out-stretched, saying *It's all right, it's all right, I love you baby, it's all right*. He watches your hands start to shake.

Like fire eats through paper the world erodes, and Neil passes out.

Crumpled up on the side of the highway, nearly hidden in a filthy snow bank, you swim awake and keep awake, the awake not seamless and continuous but intermittent, at a frame rate that throbs along and along. You keep the snow under your palm and the sky above your head. You try moving your tongue or twitching just one finger but of course you can't, fuck, you've always been so slow, slow like this but in a drawn-out, days-long way, as long threads of passivity have lined your life, running alongside the tendons of your hands, slowing your movements as they do now—a wind-up toy all ticked out, your head filling up with colour and your eyes full of mud. Mud. You have warmed the hard, frozen dirt up to become mud, and now it coats you. A primordial sludge, through which life ebbs and glows. Flows.

You keep-awake-keep-awake and the world oozes in, and brings with it pain, and cold. You cough and cough and each time your body contracts, some hot wet stuff of you bursts from you, darkening the snow. Pain oozes in, bringing with it the world, and the cold. The bones-deep passivity you've always had, which once quilted your brain for days-long dozes, now hardens in your fingers: the familiar thing, the final thing bookending all things, is coming for you, velvet and close. Your hand, a stuffed pink glove, thrust in the red-grey snow. And your arm: a paper cup lies flattened beneath it, soaking the yellow parka sleeve with Sprite, so close you could brush up its sweetness with your aching tongue: if you pushed it out just beyond your teeth, you could reach it. And nearby a plastic spoon is frozen deep in the mud, and the bag in which you'd carried the seeds, Joseph's grunge cassettes, and Shelagh's gun yawns open a few feet beyond that, and you're struck with total heartbreak at its pristine cloth, the bag looking for all the world like you'd just put it down for a moment, waiting for a bus.

The sadness loses specificity and swells to encompass all the toys you've known, from a shrinking birthday balloon popped at last by your little sister, to a chipped giraffe stolen in retaliation, its baleful gaze penetrating the door of your closet and keeping you awake well through the night. But what kind of monster are you, to feel sadness only for things? You know you've known people, who've come and gone and perched nearby like birds, as people tend to do; known them and loved them with the deep-down love filling you now—coming in liquid but hardening fast, stealing the keep-awake, the keep-awake-keep-awake. They flit through you, tickling and nudging, but you can't hang on to them, can't hang onto yourself as the sky slips down from above your head and the grass comes up between your fingers.

As your vision fails you return to the humid endlessness of certain childhood summer nights—you about seven, your sister five—those nights when your family would visit your grandparents, have dinner with them at a golf club out in the suburbs. You and your cousin would eat yourselves sick on Jell-O and white buttered rolls, chasing each other in and out of the chlorine-smelling restrooms, packed with folded-up towels and lined with white tiles, but with no pool anywhere. Your grandmother, barely five feet tall, would eat crackers carefully, watching you run and run. You'd devolve into vicious fights sometimes, kicking and ripping barrettes from each other's hair, and your grandmother would beg you to stop. The pain, the world, the cold comes in, fills you a final time and then dissipates, nearly taking you with it as it goes. You could tell your grandmother's teeth weren't real, but didn't grasp anything beyond that.

How could you have understood she was dying?

LOGAN: CLEANING THE WOUND

Well of course when Joseph comes home with his face gree-ny-white, no Erica, and a weird-looking new Brother, I drop another jar. It smashes all over the floor, little bits of glass flying under the couch and into the carpet, and the boiling hot tomato sauce splatting all over the place too, but he doesn't notice. He yanks off a shoe—only one—and steps right in the mess.

"Joseph, so sorry about that . . ." I start saying but he's already going upstairs, trailing tomato sauce and sloughing off his big jacket halfway up the stairs. The new Brother and I look at each other, and then at the jacket, which falls over the banister to the floor with a thuck.

"Do you think he's drunk?" I whisper to him, and he shakes his head, then sits right down on the floor. He reaches inside his coat, and pulls something out: he's wearing a packet on a leather string, just like mine. Joseph gave him a packet already? I put down the wooden spoon and rush towards the stairs.

"Where are you going?" he calls after me, but I'm already at the top of the stairs and then knocking at the door, tap-tapping, whispering, "It's me, it's me, it's me," and then push my way inside.

Joseph is sitting on the bed, looking out the window. The white winter light comes in on his face, and his mouth twists up. He leans forward and pukes all over his feet, the floor and the carpet. He grasps one of his thighs with both hands and rocks back and forth, gripping so tight the veins and bones stand out in his hands, and I come over and see his pants are loose and unbuttoned, and bulged up where he's holding.

"Was it an animal, a dog?" I say, and he starts speaking, then chokes a little and stops. "I was shot," he says, pulling at his pant leg with one hand. "Help me." As gentle as I can, I pull down his pants and see that some thick, ripped-up furry material is taped around his thigh, and realize it's the floor mat from his truck. His skin is freezing cold, and streaked with dried-up blood and actual shit. "Oh Jesus fucking fuck," I gasp, and he inhales deeply, and asks for three big pills from the orange bottle in the locked drawer. So I reach under his shirt collar for his key necklace—my hands shaking so bad—and slide the chain off his neck and over his face, which is twisted up so tight I see his skull, so tight it makes me want to puke too. I rush over to his desk, crouch and unlock the locked drawer, then grab three giant pills from the orange bottle (big as horse pills) and press the first one to his lips. He gasps his mouth open and works one pill down, then the next, and the next. He works his jaw back and forth, back and forth like a machine, grinding the pills to powder. Puke clings to the corners of his mouth, on his neck, in his hair, but why bother wiping it away when he's been shot?

"Get it higher . . . the leg, above my heart," he gasps, still squeezing, so I rush around for some pillows and big books, and slide them under his thigh, helping him move a little until he's lying down with his leg in the air. The bandage is wet, but I try imagining it's old blood and melted snow, and picture the blood in his body easing down and away from his wound, staying around his heart, keeping him strong. In a drunk-sounding voice he tells me that it's not swollen, which is good: that means no internal bleeding. Then he says, *She's gone*. I hold his non-injured leg by the ankle and start crying, and he's crying too, and there's a big thudding on the stairs and suddenly New Brother is standing right behind me, and he's kind of dancing back and forth—I can tell because he's bumping me with his stupid big body—and I want to push him down the fucking stairs.

I don't care to know his name; he'll only ever be Stupid to me.

"We were ambushed," Joseph says, and Stupid starts screaming wordlessly, up and down like a fire alarm. He screams and coughs and sobs, and it's like he's opening our little cabin door to a snowstorm, it's like he's sucking all the heartbreak from me like a vacuum cleaner, it's like he's the only one who loved Erica, as if he loved her half as much as me—or Joseph! I look at Joseph's twisted-up face, then lean back towards Stupid and grab his hairy wrist (though not as tight as he deserves, the coward—right then, I want take it in both my hands, and break it over my knee):

"Listen, he wants you to make a tincture, a super-restorative kind with some codeine too, and then clean up the tomato sauce downstairs before the mice come back—yeah, we have mice—and then if Joseph gets some sleep we can fix up a leak out in the greenhouse before a pipe explodes, and then we'll find all the medical supplies you can. I'm going to clean him up and fix the bandage. Clean out the wound."

"I know what a tincture *is*," he says, "but not necessarily how to make one."

"You'll figure it out," I say.

Well, he rushed out of that room so fast I almost had to laugh. For all his frazzled-seeming commitment to being here, and his gooey love for Erica, I know Stupid's a pussy, I've known guys like him before—Toronto boys. I knew it the day Erica Shared that, months ago, our New Brother's son had pretended to drown. The boy was floating facedown in a public pool, and he had described standing at the edge of the pool fretting, only half-knowing his son was joking. Why didn't he jump in and grab him just in case, I asked, and she giggled, saying she'd asked him the same thing.

I don't know, I don't know, he'd said, snotting into Erica's blouse as Erica had smoothed out his hair and said Shhh it's OK, and I thought, *What a pampered little shit.*

As soon as Stupid's gone, Joseph starts sobbing so hard his stomach wrinkles up and heaves, hard enough to crack his own ribs, and I stand terrified for a second, then kneel down and press my head to his stomach. "Shhh, it's OK," I say in a voice like Erica's, and realize that she didn't know any better than I do right now, and maybe she didn't have any other magic than trying as hard as she could. With my ear against his heaving stomach, my head bouncing up and down, his wails are so loud my eyes water. I've never heard anybody cry like this since Lori got the call that Dad, wherever he was, had been dead for three days. She hunched on the sofa rocking and wailing, and Jake, all army efficiency, hustled me out of the room in his ropy arms, his hands squeezing my shoulders too hard, and I lit up with rage: rage at the depth of her grief, at the strength of his big tattooed hands and the darkness of my room afterwards, all flat dark and nothing else. Rage at her soft sobs in the dark of their bedroom down the hall, and her grey exhaustion for weeks and months afterwards—a kind of rage I wouldn't know again for years.

"Shhh, it's OK," I say again.

He starts to calm down, and I rub his foot again. "How's the pain? The pills help?" I ask, and he says something like *unh, uh huh*.

"Good. I won't give you more for a while, because I'm going to drive you to a hospital, and I'm going to need you awake enough to guide me," I say.

He catches his breath. "No—no," he says. "It's not safe."

"I've driven the truck before," I say, "like six times." The light in the room is weakening, and little snowflakes are still falling outside the window; we need to get going, I'm worried it'll start snowing again, and scared to drive when it's dark.

"You can't," he says.

I look into his face—he seems almost sleepy; his jaw has loosened a little, his eyes swollen up. "You could fall asleep and not wake up," I say, rubbing his hand.

He takes another deep breath. "Logan, baby, we were ambushed. Might've been followed. They could be waiting. What I have, it won't kill me. But they could."

"Who shot you? Was it the hooligans?"

Stupid comes to the doorway, holding a steaming mug and eavesdropping. "Psychos," he says, like he knows shit about anything.

"You'll tend to me," Joseph says, gripping my hand. "It's dangerous outside, but we have enough to survive. We will make a new plan. If I go, I go alone. You understand?"

"But what if they get you," I ask, taking deep breaths.

"Then I'm ready to die for the Family, the Cause," Joseph croaks, and starts crying again.

"Joseph, please let me just call 911," Stupid begs, and I feel Joseph's whole body shudder under my hands. He sits up as much as he can, leaning towards her on his elbow.

"The government has been watching us," he says. "They're threatened by us. You involve the police, you ruin the Family. You break it apart and invite the scrutiny they've been aching for. You watch us disintegrate under their scientific curiosity. They'll dissect us like the fucked up organs of circus freaks. You'll ruin everything she fought for," he says, reaching out for Stupid, then touching his shoulder with a trembling hand until they're looking into each other's eyes.

"But 911 isn't the government," Stupid says finally, and Joseph lies back down, his face twisting up again.

"You fucking idiot," I say to Stupid, and suddenly we're both sizing each other up, except my hands are twined up in Joseph's and my whole body is pressed against his, and so Stupid scoots backwards and bumps over the mug. He jumps from foot to foot, watching the steaming mess run across the wood floor, soak my knees and wick into the carpet.

"I don't know why I said that, I know better, I didn't mean it," he cries, and I get up and walk over to him, then grab his wrist again and drag him from the bedroom.

Out in the hallway he stands close to me, breathing hot heavy breath down at me, and I bump the door shut with my foot. "Who the fuck you think runs the hospitals?" I whisper. "What were you doing in university all those years, smoking fucking crack?"

He's hyperventilating, and opens his mouth but just these stupid noises come out—I don't recognize anything except 'modern medicine'—so I grab both his clammy hands. "We'll do what he wants," I say.

"It's bad, it's bad, it's bad," he cries.

"Shhh. Yeah, it's bad. You think you're gonna be the fucking boss of me, you spoiled piece of shit," I say. "And you might be if it was good, but now it's bad. Now you're going to listen to me." He goes still.

"Go get Erica's medical kit, it's grey and under the sink, bring it up here. Go outside and make a big snowball and then wrap it in a plastic bag, bring that too. OK?"

"OK." He turns and rushes downstairs, thud thud thud, the big moron.

Right before I left to join the Family, very late at night, I snuck into the kitchen for some milk and saw Lori hunched up at the counter with a flower-patterned mug in front of her, smoking a cigarette. She was looking up at the fluorescent light, watching her smoke piling upwards, and all over her face wrinkles crept like spider-webs, and her skin hung loose under her chin—and she looked old, so old. And that terrifying rage shot through me again, burning my throat and rattling my teeth together, and I rushed over and hugged her bony body like *Mom, Mommy you can't, Mommy you can't leave me—you can't leave me alone.*

Logan: Suspended Forever in Bright Machine Hell

Four days I've slept beside him, sleeping light as a cat so I can wake when he moans, moaning for water, moaning with fear, moaning because I've bumped him by accident and jolted him with pain. His hair sticks to his forehead and ears, blackened with dirt and constant sweat—he sweats more than I've ever seen, soaking the bed. Every half an hour I check under his body to make sure the wetness isn't blood, but it's only ever sweat (and once piss, because I hadn't helped him pee in time.) I can't change the sheets or anything and the room stinks like death, I can see it on Stupid's fearful face when he comes in the room with trays of food.

Sometimes when Joseph moans I press his hand to my stomach—*the baby, the baby*—and he smiles and goes quiet. *You are my wife,* he says. Once I peeled off my clothes, the bloody and stinking dress that clings to me all day, and climbed into bed with him naked. He'd just taken a pill and I could tell that the pain wasn't so bad, so I leaned on his chest, and kissed him. He took my face in one hand and kissed me back, kissed me hungry, and then started to cry. *I love you,* I wanted to say, but didn't, just in case he used her name when he said it back.

Sometimes I'll be reading Joseph a book, and he starts talking back, sometimes delirious and sometimes clear; once he asks me about Lori's boyfriends. "It is wrong for a parent to think they own their child," he says when I stop talking. A few hours ago I was examining a cut on my nose in the little mirror hanging over the wicker chair, and I looked over at him and caught him staring: "Don't look in the mirror. You'll become vain," he said, then fell back asleep.

A whole day passes like this, then one more, and the next afternoon I'm sitting at the desk, staring out at the greenhouse.

Stupid's inside, picking something; he comes out with a full basket of tomatoes, then looks up at the window, right at me.

"I have eleven on my head," Joseph says, in a bright, clear voice. I turn around.

"What?"

"They won't let me draw it." He's leaning on his elbow, looking up at me.

"Tell me who," I say.

A few minutes pass, and then I come over and rub his arm until he falls asleep again. The room gets darker, and the snow lining the window turns blue, then grey. He moans and wakes up again, and his eyes seem clearer this time. "It's been them all along. They're close, I can't help it."

"Who?"

"You must be ready," he says.

"What for?"

"I will leave," he says. "I must go first. There's two more waiting for me, a Brother and a Sister. I must rescue them, bring them back to the Family, before they rejoin the Soup."

My throat closes up. "OK."

Stupid comes in with a couple of apples on a tray. Always with the fucking tray.

"My Family," Joseph says, wincing and sitting up a little. "My Family, I had a vision today." He waits until we're both kneeling beside the bed, and then he reaches slowly for the bedside lamp, and turns it on. His face, bright in the yellow lamplight, is too painful to look at—but we do. "The end is coming faster than I thought," he says.

"I know," I say. "We have felt it." Stupid stares at me, hard, but I ignore him.

"In my vision, there's a dark underground place. Subterranean, a gigantic basement. There's only one long, thin window, set high in the cement wall. Outside this window hangs a gigantic scorching sun, endless sand, the desert. This basement place is as big as a factory, packed with hundreds of people in cheap robes and dozens of machines with shiny steel limbs perpetually in motion, all working away together at little desks.

Computers, power tools, iPads, glue, little robot arms, little robot legs, mountains of wires, everything you can imagine; everything they need."

Stupid is still staring, his mouth hanging open. "Need? Need for what?"

Joseph moans. "Oh, my dear children. All over the world, in big groups and in little groups, some government-sanctioned and some rogue, all kinds of people are racing towards the Merge. Scientists and labourers and their robot slaves, rubbing little matches near an ocean of gasoline. It'll only take one of them to get there first. To casually toss their flaming match in the waves, and obliterate us forever in the huge opening eye of the new world." He sits up and winces, then swings his legs, one after the other, over the side of the bed. He places one hand on my head, the other on Stupid's.

"With all the indifference of a giant insect, the new intelligence will absorb us. It will absorb all life. We are as irrelevant as dust, as raindrops. We may cease to be. We have lived well in this realm, and now it's time to drain away—no, not drain. To ebb with dignity, a final golden tide, while everything else is abruptly uploaded. Suspended forever in bright machine hell."

He takes his hands away and anchors himself on either side, then lifts himself up with a groan. "No!" I say, and he looks down at me.

"Maybe our memories will be ripped from our heads, scatter and melt into everyone else's, saved as data and scanned for patterns. Our bodies, flayed and discarded meat, or else rearranged on an atomic level to become something more useful; something metal, something plastic. Is that what you want?"

"No," I say.

Joseph finds his pants folded on the wicker chair, and begins to pull them on. His breath is heavy. "You've carried your packets around like amulets, haven't you? Throughout the day, many times a day, you've rubbed your packet gently, or given it a little tap, taking comfort that your own ending is pressed against you even as your heart beats with life. Animals don't fear death, do they?"

"No," Stupid says, his hands bunched useless in his big lap.

"That's because they know there's nothing to fear. Are you better than Earth's noblest creatures, Neil? Are you better than the dolphins captured to entertain humans in chlorine prisons, choosing to die rather than submit to the chains, the electric prods, the slavery? Are you better than the bumblebee, whose stomach bursts after making love to his Queen? Are you better than the faithful dog stranded in the winter woods, who'd rather submit to death at his master's side than venture on alone?"

"No," Stupid and I say at the same time. He's rubbing his packet-string under his shirt, grinding his teeth together and staring at up at Joseph. I realize I'm doing the same thing.

With some difficulty, Joseph pulls a clean shirt over his head, then a thick sweater. His hands are shaking when they emerge from the sleeves. He limps back over to us. "You will go into a peaceful sleep, and Erica and I will join you there. Those who are yet to join our Family, the like-minded individuals scattered throughout the world seeking our Shelter, they'll join us there too. We will go to sleep with dignity before the Merge erupts. Keep awake in the cool shade your death casts for you. Be grateful for the daytime you enjoy now, and allow its brevity to enhance your Gratitude."

Joseph pulls his packet out from under his shirt and sweater, and we do the same.

"I—I—I," Stupid stammers. "I—Logan," he says.

"What about Logan?" Joseph asks gently.

"I don't think her baby deserves to die."

"Logan's baby deserves peace," Joseph says, and we're all quiet for a moment. Somebody cries, somebody hums, and Joseph is gripping Stupid's arm, his free arm, and stroking his glossy hair. "Don't be defensive, Little Brother. Give yourself over to me. You will come out the other side. I'll be there. This, around your neck—this is the key. *I* am the one with the key at this particular time, my Brother, my darling."

"Before night," Joseph whispers, looking beyond us at the window. "We are given one final sunset. The world will not survive until morning." He rips open his own packet. Stupid does the same, and so do I, though my hands are shaking so hard I can barely manage it, my fingers so sweaty the paper has gone dark.

"And what are we Grateful for?" Joseph asks.

"The sun, the sky, the big tree and its shelter, the Earth beneath us and around us," I go. "Our Home, our Gardens, our Greenhouse."

"And your gratitude is faith. Each callus on your hand and bruise on your knee, you know what they are?"

"The poison leaving us."

"Breaking hard ground for new growth. As the poison seeps away, our souls will escape with it. We are ready. We—"

Stupid screams, he screams so loud the window rattles, and Joseph bends towards him. He grips Joseph's hands and shakes violently, his eyes wide and his mouth stretched open. Something bolts through me electric and I leap up and run from the room. The hallway is blacker than the night outside—we've been in the bedroom for hours—and I bounce off the banister and stumble, then rush to the bathroom as someone runs after me. I slam the door and lock it, and Stupid thumps up against it, then scratches and pounds at the door, but I won't open it—I *can't*—and he is roaring from the very bottom of his stomach like the animal he is, and then his cries gives way to moans and some words—he wants his mommy, he wants help, he wants me—and then just gurgles. I dig my nails into my arms and rip away the skin, drawing blood and more blood, then punch myself in the chest, again and again, as he bumps at the other side of the door, so soft I barely hear it. It's all wrong, it's all wrong because I'm still here *and I shouldn't be*, but the baby, the baby, the baby. I slam my head against the tiled wall, again and again until I black out.

I wake up curled around the toilet with my head in my hands, cradling my own head in my own hands, rubbing it gently like *shhh, I'm here, I'm here*. I stand and press my forehead against the tiny bathroom window—it's cool, almost cold, with frost patterning the other side of the thick glass. The packet hangs loose around my neck, and I squeeze it. I open my eyes, wipe my blood from the window, then look out at the truck and freeze: I'm not sure, because the only light is the moon now, plus a little bit of lamp light coming from Joseph's bedroom, but it looks like someone is slumped in the passenger's side of the truck.

There's a series of thuds going *one*-two, *one*-two down the stairs, and I rub my breath from the glass and stare out at the truck hard as I can. A few minutes pass before Joseph limps outside, his parka half-on, hauling a big hockey bag on his good side. He gets in on the driver's side and after just a moment, the person or thing in the passenger's seat disappears. He climbs back into the driver's seat and all the lights flick on, and the truck roars alive. He backs up slowly, munching up the new white snow, then turns on his high beams. It's all sealed-up winter, and I'm starting to fall asleep right there against the window, but I could swear he turns the radio on as the truck inches down the snowy road, and disappears around the corner. I see the lights flash in and out of the trees, all thick with snow and laced together, and all at once they're gone. My head bonks against the glass, I can't keep it up, and so I lie down on the bathmat, curling up around it like a cat. *OK girl. OK baby. Keep with me.*

ERICA: EMERGENCY CALL

"911, please state your emergency."

"*Hello?* Oh god, yes, I'm . . . there's a man here, I know him, I think he c-could be dead. Oh my god I think he's—Neil, his name is Neil Bialy. Another woman lives here but I don't—I think she's locked in a room. The bathroom. Neil? *Neil?*"

"What is your address?"

"Not—oh god, uh . . . 37 *Rue de la Lac*, near the *La Pêche* area—just outside Hull. This isn't my, I don't live here."

"Can you spell the street?"

"Ah fuck, I don't—R-U . . . fuck . . . E D-E L-A L-A-C, OK, I think—and it's thirty-seven. *Thirty-seven.*"

"Ma'am, the man with you, he's breathing?"

"I think he is! But—you have to hurry—please—"

"Stay calm for me, ma'am. What's your name?"

"Shelagh Daly. I live—I'm from Toronto, not here—I—there's a man, listen to me, he could be coming back, and—I think he's a killer. Do you hear me? And he's—"

"The property owner? You know his name?"

"His name, yes, um, Joseph Reiser. I knew his girlfriend very well, she's not here . . . are you sending someone? Are sending a fucking ambulance?"

"Sit tight ma'am, OK? Sit tight, and please do not leave the premises. You're going to have to stay calm for me."

"Jesus Christ, I—he's dying, my friend, Neil, oh-my-god-Neil, I don't know, maybe she's dead too—she's pregnant, please, are you sending fucking help?"

"That's the plan, ma'am, someone else is on the way right now. Your friend, is he awake?"

"His eyes are kind of open, I . . . oh god, he's not, not in good condition."

"I'm going to ask you to ensure this man is on his side and not his back, OK? We want him safe. If you can, cover him with a blanket, but ma'am? Do not touch him. Do not attempt to administer CPR. If he wakes up, tell him we've got help. Help is on the way. Tell him that."

"Neil? Neil! It's Shelagh, I'm here, I'm here. And more help is coming, do you hear me? Neil, I love you, hang in there, it's Shelagh—stay with me—"

"My concern is that he keeps breathing—you have to tell me if he stops, OK?"

"OK. You are sure someone's . . . ? She's—I think the girl, she's moving inside the other room, the, the bathroom. Ah fuck, I can hear—don't go, don't hang up on me!"

"I'm going to stay with you on the phone, ma'am, as long as it takes for help to arrive."

"Logan, are you in there? It's a friend of Erica's, I'm here to help you, do you hear me?"

"Ma'am? I'm going to need to you to unlock the front door. We're coming, we need to get inside."

"She's there, she's—Logan? Do you understand me? She's—fuck!"

"*Ma'am?*"

"She's coming out of the bathroom right now, she's—Logan? Logan don't touch him—Oh god, she's—"

"*Ma'am!*"

THE WATCHERS VIII: AUTOPSY

Since no wallet was found on its person, so to speak, and since her half-frozen purse contained no phone, no journals or books with loving dedications scrawled inside, no receipts or ironed-on underwear nametags (commoner than you'd think, the coroner comments to his assistant), the coroner tests its fingerprints, and at 6:13PM on December 12 successfully identifies the body as Erica Jane Strickland, dead for about seventeen hours.

Buppy's back at home, playing cooking shows and reciting recipes as Mom cooks with the tiny onions we grew this summer. He didn't want me here, but I came anyway, and he couldn't stop me: he knows if he tried, I'd tell Mo about him and Mom.

Of the four bodies wheeled in today, she's in the best shape by far: late-twenties to early thirties, pristine skin and teeth, her hair—though matted with mud and missing in patches—is unmistakably thick and healthy-seeming; even her fingernails look filed. As requested by loved ones, two of the four bodies will not receive autopsies, as they died in hospital beds at the end of long illnesses (lung cancer and kidney failure), but the body formerly Erica certainly will; beyond her youth, whose immediate glow dissipated with the onset of rigor mortis but remains evident in her face, the bruised eye socket, loose teeth, and soft, shattered collarbone strongly suggest she was killed in an assault. Her hair is combed and her eyelids stapled shut and then three photos are taken, as loved ones are not permitted in this room. The body will then wait inside a long refrigerated drawer as, far beyond these walls, investigators attempt to reach the Strickland family.

Behind a metal hatch to the right, occupying an identical drawer inches away, lies the body of seventy-three-year-old woman discovered, according to another assistant, sprawled across her kitchen floor yesterday. In the drawer to the left, the body of a minor composer found putrefying between two pianos in her basement apartment, both with all four wooden legs sawn away, perhaps, as one investigator suggested in a bored voice, so the composer could sit cross-legged when she worked. At this moment calls are being placed to their loved ones too, one of which I overheard when I felt too overwhelmed in the morgue and stood near the coroner's office awhile, breathing.

The pathologist tasked with examining the body formerly Erica lingers in the doorway a moment, her head bent; likely she's focused on nothing more romantic than zipping up her sweater, as it's cold in here, but her face appears contemplative. Perhaps she wonders at the intensity of this room, which hangs like a fog and cannot be assigned to any one of its parts—not the rows and rows of narrow, stacked metal doors, nor the gleaming table, nor the strange, framed needlepoint partially obscured by an industrial box of latex gloves (*BLESS This House*). She, like the loved ones contacted from within this building, perhaps scans the room for the rest of them, for the *them* of them, for whatever people seek beyond the whitening flesh in the metal drawers. For the people they are, still alive in the minds of their families, who still think consider these bodies as one of them—as one of *theirs* —just puttering about unseen. Some will continue to do so even after the call, consumed by the stubborn, bottomless fury of those left alone, alive.

Minutes, eras, days slide by—how long it's been really is hard to tell—and then the Strickland family has confirmed their wish for an autopsy. Yet more uncharted time slips on, marked by slowed, monitored decay and the flitting of the white-coated living around the room, and then the pathologist returns. This is her third autopsy here, she confesses aloud, and perhaps it's her third autopsy ever as she's shadowed by a coroner, and seems determined to retain her professionalism. An incision is made by the sternum, and the skin, rubbery-thick and yellowy-pale, is pulled apart, up and away from the ribcage, which is then cracked open. Erica's heart is removed and examined for signs of congestive failure, though as the coroner reassures the pathologist, in a tone I read as overfamiliar, Miss Priss (Erica) was one hundred percent murdered and probably over a designer drugs situation. With Erica's lower intestine half-in, half-out of her hands she stops and expresses that she needs a minute, and I wonder if she's recalling something like her first pelvic exam, her first fuck, the first invasion of her hot, beating self, and feels inexplicably overcome with shame.

The other organs follow and are scraped for toxicology tests. Were I not briefly released from temporality, I'd be certain that the pathologist takes extra time on Erica's face; perhaps as in the world of the living, power permeates here too—or perhaps Erica looks like somebody she knows, and she cannot bear to ruin it. The body is drained of gases and fluids, then packed back in with cotton until it appears fleshily plump again. She's stitched back up in a careful manner that suggests cosmetic attention: perhaps the Strickland family has expressed a wish for embalmment.

I follow them to a different room. Here, Erica is washed very gently in a large, shallow metal tub, her stiff fingers, toes and crevices are massaged clean of mud, sweat, shit, urine and something pale and sticky—like a clear soft drink, one assistant comments, as she rubs the corner of Erica's mouth, then notes aloud that the glue has come slightly unsealed. Despite the (likely) total devastation of the Strickland family, they would not want to participate in washing the body, or even stand by and watch. These assistants provide the last contact these bodies will ever have, and the first contact many have had in years. Among them, one wealthy-in-his-twilight-years individual started paying prostitutes to hold him until he slept, instructing them to turn their faces away if he was to cry. It doesn't escape me that the assistants tasked with washing bodies in this room are slender, youngish and—by the standards of the living—all quite attractive.

Their shirts are still a little stained from a small spurting accident with the previous body, a little girl crushed by a car, whose carotid vein was too small, apparently, for the catheter. The first assistant finds Erica's carotid vein, and as her veins fill up with red dye her skin glows pink again, for the first time in days. One assistant pauses, lifting Erica's hand to examine the fingers, and the other assistant looks over at her. *You having a moment?*

Look at these fingers, maybe she was a musician, the first assistant says. *She's old enough to be good.*

You're just saying that because she's white and like pretty. Right? So she's gotta be something, the other assistant says.

This one will look peaceful, more than the little guy, the first one comments. *Who still needs an eyelid made, by the way.*

End of the day, when we slow down. Or maybe we wait until tomorrow, the other says.

UME: LET'S MAKE 'EM RUN, BOYS

Driving to Millhaven Institution, handcuffed in the back of an armoured van, we watch cars slide past the window like never before. We come to Millhaven during intakes first, and dread settles in thick as illness as we pull on orange jumpsuits, leaving our clothes and shoes and gloves and hair elastics behind. We are herded down an alleyway and placed in holding pens, a steel toilet built into the wall, chain link fencing covering the bars on all sides. Weekly we meet with our counsellors, who decide where we'll be placed. She or he will note everything from verbal fights with COs or other inmates to the pens many of us carry around in our pockets, which have an obvious primary function—perhaps not grasping how desperately we need them. 'Working together' they'll develop a 'correctional plan' during our suspension in the sludge of Millhaven. Everyone wants minimum security, but we must impress our parole officer for that. The smart ones among us learn what to say and what not to say during any downtime during this assessment period: don't whistle, don't talk about the weather, don't ask anybody what they're in for. There's no time is downtime here. You can veer into a fight and stumble into a life sentence. You're sentenced to life, and you live.

You're sentenced to life, you become one of fifty-five thousand Canadian inmates. In Canadian federal maximum security prison, we live behind thick steel doors painted an elementary-school grey-green. Some COs and disapproving critics think televisions and PlayStations and softer beds suggest that the punishment is inadequate, but the sheer fact of confinement is the punishment, and these luxuries can often sharpen it. The television reminds you of Florida, of hot dogs in Central Park and young chicks in bikinis. It reminds you of the vastness of the

world and of your own confinement, re-inscribing the tiny circlet of space that is yours. In the beginning, an hour of yard time
is too much for most of us: what do you do? There we are, out
in the grounds, trapped in limbo as the Canadian seasons pass.
Beyond the observation tower, tall evergreen trees grow. We can
run laps around the picnic benches shrouded in snow, or just
stand around talking shit, ignoring the small snowflakes drifting
and dissolving against the barbed wire.

You must mind what little space you are given: nobody cares
about you anymore so you live and die by the hour. You feel
COs forming favorites despite themselves, and seedling gangs
crystallize around you, and if social grace has always eluded you,
it eludes you here, too. This can be deadly; the runts always turn
up drowned. Social tides swell around you, and if you're white,
you might feel hunted for the first time. Some around you,
repeat cons who've got nothing left to lose and years of life, come
back to prison over and over; they know what it's like to be con-
fined for 23 hours at a time. They know that reckless COs will
spark fights amongst us just to see what happens, and handle
themselves accordingly.

The lucky among us work for up to three dollars a day,
sometimes tilling a patch of land the size of a living room, sometimes working with wood. Some of us work Cadillac jobs[1] in the
garden, and keep onions and peppers for ourselves. On payday
we buy juice, deodorant, candy, soap; some of it consumed,
some of it stored. Morning after morning after morning, we rip
new sugar packets for coffee, watching the sun rise through the
high-up window in the cafeteria. Summer evenings, the golden
low sun illuminates the loops of barbed wire, and it glows like
fire. In winter, everything—the concrete, the walls, the observation tower, the ground—glows white. By noon we're waiting for
night, and all night we wait for day, and then it's night again:
lights off in B3, B4, B5, and B6. We exist just to exist. Some of
us coming from Toronto and Hamilton have hardly even seen a

---

[1] Sweet work, good work. Dirt under fingernails, slow tilling and
healthy silence, the stomach-dropping ball-loosening honey of sun.

Native before but they're everywhere in fed max, sometimes singing at nightfall and coping along with everyone else.

We fight. We fight viciously, and we fight all the time. When a war is brewing everyone feels it, the air pressure drops, and sometimes the COs order lockdown just in time, because they can sense it too. When this happens, we stand nearby as they search our cells—feeling inside every shoe, pressing their fingers against every cinderblock. We watch closely as they chat with one another and with us, both sides understanding it's in vain, because there are hundreds of weapons they'll never find. We slip them inside holes in the wall covered with toothpaste, slide them between fluorescent light fixtures and the ceiling; we hide billiard balls, knives from the kitchen, sharpened toothbrushes disguised in wash-up cups, shivs made of metal, wood, glass, ball-up coat hangers with towel handles, HIV and hepatitis-tainted blood stored in tattoo needles[2], and Pepsi cans pre-loaded into socks. There are twenty-four hours to the whole day, and we wait through them all. The COs crowded out on the shooting range, strolling through the hallways, and slouched out by the towers, they drive over an hour to get out here, they tell us, because we're so remote.

Like many of us, Ume is an older lifer accustomed to prison. He's been in since he was just out of his teens, and can't seem to stay out. He's got a girl who visits twice a month, always bringing a fat toddler made, we know, through a turkey baster arrangement. He works in the gardens, and coordinates the flow of produce. He keeps his cell very tidy and is touchy about his possessions. *I grew up in the dark side of the world*, Ume likes to say.

The newest greenboy here, he's noticed, is also one of the quietest: he only speaks when he's spoken to, but smiles weakly when addressed. Mostly we leave him alone, though that might not last. The guy spends each of his outdoor breaks by himself. Sometimes he looks like he's singing or chanting, and sometimes he closes his eyes and seems to pray.

---

[2] According to legend.

It's a bright, cool day, and Ume spots the greenboy out at his picnic bench, and walks over to him. The guy's hunched over the picnic bench closest to the fence, all red, his face turned up to the sun. "You crying?" Ume asks, and the man jumps a little. The guy is slender, very slender, all thin limbs in his jumpsuit. His hands clench, grasp nothing, clench again.

"Yes," says the guy. Were any of us paying attention, we'd think: dude's fucking lucky it's Ume and nobody else, man. For that matter, Ume's fucking lucky he's 6'7" and weighs a solid 350 (not 7'2" and 300 as he often claims, but we don't really care. He might be a tender-hearted bullshitter, he might not outpace his scent of wolfdom[3], but he's big enough to change the air pressure in any room he enters, and when he leaves, the COs draw their first real breaths again.)

"You gotta stop blubbing," Ume says, scanning the court-yard over his shoulder: a few of us drift about like sharks, crackling, restless. "You're already a little bitch around here, man. You feel me?" But the guy can't stop; he rests his head in his hands, soaking himself with tears and snot. With some effort, Ume wedges into the other side of the picnic bench, his bright-orange body spilling over and under, reminiscent of an adult squeezed in a second-grader's desk.

"Someone really close to me, she's gone," the guy says, and Ume slaps the table.

"No shit. We pinned you for a faggot, man! You know, with the hair," he says, then pauses. "Was it your mom?"

"It wasn't," the guy says. Ume nods, then leans across the rough, wooden table, his rheumy eyes and sloppy mouth dead-serious.

"You kill her?" he asks. "Don't bullshit me, man, I know you got all day."[4]

---

[3] A wolf: an inmate who is normally straight on "the outside," but engages in sexual activity with men while incarcerated.

[4] A life sentence. Ume doesn't know this, and is in fact bullshitting. This greenboy's lower than dirt though, and who'd step to Ume anyway? Nobody on this boy's level, that's for sure.

"Well—she died near me. She died because of me. I let her die, I could have, um. It was like I thought it wasn't real, that she'd die? Like there'd be another one of her springing up in the seat there, or waiting at home? It's how it is, you know, when you love someone and they're always there—it's how it is, when, uh . . ." His hands flex at nothing again. Ume understands that the greenboy's got a look we all know well. When we exclude a weak greenboy, someone who can't assimilate, he goes from vicious and cornered to *this*. Even the sociopaths, the goofs[5] and icy manipulators, they fold and grow pliable, almost gentle with desperation. They're discovered rotting beneath the weight of memories they must tell over and over, stories that change with each telling. They're discovered twisted up and grasping, warped with an overwhelming need to confess, a need to confess and be forgiven by people they've really just met. A need to remake themselves alongside them, and keep moving.

"So you killed her," Ume says patiently. "Why?"

The guy just shakes his head, rubbing a hand over his mouth.

"Hey man," Ume says, "Just—you have to stop being a little bitch. You have to get by. Look—get it out in the shower, you feel me?" He sighs. "What's your name again, man?"

The greenboy grabs at Ume's hand, looking beyond Ume, going a little pale. "Uh," the guy says. Ume yanks his hand away, and eases himself from the vise of the picnic bench. He walks around the bench, takes hold of the guy's limp collar, and pulls him to his feet.

Ume's crew, the six big men the greenboy spotted over Ume's shoulder, jog up to the picnic bench and stop just short, uncertain.

"You ladies all right?" someone jeers from across the courtyard.

"He a faggot or what," yells Five-Pack, Ume's big ace-duce, scowling and squinting through the sun.

Ume locks eyes with the greenboy for an instant, and shakes his head very slightly, like *Man, why'd you have to grab my hand?*

---

5 Ontario slang for child molester.

And then—long before anyone can react, in the unreal space before time catches up—he bends the guy in half, shoving his face into the table. Ume yanks him up again and shakes the greenboy by his collar, and his head rolls back and forth on his dandelion neck. The greenboy squeals, scrabbling uselessly at Ume's arms. "Wait! What are you *doing*?"

Three-Pack springs forward and then everyone else dives in, though the COs are already striding over.

Let's make 'em run today, boys. Let's make 'em run.

By night we hear the hum of electrified fences, which glow deep orange from the spotlights mounted on the observation towers, and those of us aching from withdrawal moan at a matching frequency, dipping in and out. Beyond the picnic bench, beyond the wire fence—always in motion, bright and cold even in the early evening light—the evergreens grow just out of reach.

SHELAGH: BURN

It's amazing how so little goes so far, when you're alone. It's February, but tonight is so warm, I open the bedroom window. A cigarette smell comes in through the window, and makes me feel I have company. I am lying naked in bed, and think to cover my breasts, then turn down the TV. A whole new dimension is added to the world.

Time works differently for him and I. Sure, weeks float on and pass, the distinctive seasons appear like birds, then sink and reform, shielded by the messy brevity of the liminal seasons. I get older, my face in the black subway glass sags and sags. I wait without knowing I'm waiting—life sparks with other demands, after all. But then my body seizes up, and I grab a pen, and he works through me. Whenever I hear from him again, time stitches up, and it's just yesterday we spoke. We aren't honest: his life has moved on, swelling around new loves and trips across the world and life-defining projects, but we don't speak of that.

Facilitated communication is a technique that allows interaction with those who are previously unable to communicate by speech or signs due to autism, brain damage, or diseases like cerebral palsy. You steady their right elbow with one hand, and place your other hand on their left shoulder. You then guide them like a human Ouija board, helping them point to one letter at a time, so they can spell words and sentences. Whenever Étienne—or sometimes even Erica—want to talk, I sit at the kitchen table with a pen and paper, a corporeal vessel waiting for their hands. Sometimes I smell his cologne behind me. Sometimes I feel the heat of her palm. It's not easy—just one sentence can take ten minutes, and leaves me exhausted.

But I'm patient.

"You're not who you were, because you can't be," I told him, as yesterday's session drew to a close.

I'm the same person, and so are you, he insists.

But we aren't. But we are.

He moulds my fantasies, or at least, my powerful concept of him does, yanking them around me whenever I'm alone. I walk past a children's playground. I scan the playground for places to hide with him, were I to run into him right there on the sidewalk: here, a patch of bushes. There, a slide, in which we could stretch horizontal and fuck. I imagine encountering him at a coffee shop, our lips meeting despite themselves in the lineup, then following him moments later into the bathroom, pressing my hands up under his shirt. I think: if I could fuck him, I'd come right away. His life would be ruined, but he'd say, *it's all right: I'll never again have sex like that*. The last time we fucked, he plucked me off the bed, threw me on the floor, and continued to fuck me on the carpet. I hadn't known passion like that for years. He loves Marie, and he'd be devastated, ruined, dead, done, if he lost her: she's it. I'm sure he doesn't love me as I love him, though he hints that he does sometimes, during our sessions.

Saw you at Erica's funeral, he spelled out yesterday.

"Yes," I say carefully. "We just missed each other."

I'd washed and blow-dried my hair for the funeral, and it looked so different I almost didn't recognize myself. I dug out my ancient makeup bag, inspired, and painted my face. My cheeks have grown hollow, which I like, though my neck is starting to droop. I've stopped eating because my circle of influence has shrunk around me like cellophane. I've stopped eating so I can wither back into a girl, or else curl up like the insects scattering the sidewalks in the autumn. I've stopped eating because Erica is gone.

There were just a few people scattered through the pews, which is surprising, some old bitch sitting behind me whispers *when such a young person dies*. I pull on the black fabric of my trouser leg, pleased there's so much room. The urn is an elegant, dark-blue vase, surrounded by masses of flowers. Right behind the vase they've placed Erica's undergraduate class portrait, her face soft-looking, childlike: this photograph was taken before she grew out her hair, long yellow ropes that snarled up when she didn't care for them, and shone when she did. The frame is beautifully ornate, matching the blue and gold of her graduate gown. A lump forms in my throat, looking at that frame.

I'm the first of the young people in the church. Neil's undergoing a three-week course of crisis treatment at the Centre for Addiction and Mental Health, and can't attend; likely he wasn't told it's today, or even reminded—depending on his state—that she's gone. When I visited Neil I'd figured he wouldn't be much into talking, and neither would I, so I brought some DVDs for us to watch together. But a pretty, unnervingly young nurse had confiscated them, smiling apologetically: they contained sexual content. "I'll keep them safe for you here," she'd said.

When Étienne arrives at the church, I know it without turning around: I hear the words of the priest, handing him a pamphlet, and hear his hands close over the paper, and feel—I *feel*—his eyes on me. I feel him catch his breath. Wherever he sits, his tiny fraction of the church is silent, because he has spotted me, and is captivated.

Fate has arced back, and applied a shadow symmetry to my life: now, I'm as full of longing as he was. I am made to suffer, as he was.

Erica's father delivers a eulogy. I cry, because he is a big man grasping the podium like a wayward horse, his voice wobbling. Erica's youngest sister goes next. Her black dress covers her from neck to knee but reveals her anyway, because she has that kind of young body that devours, that sexualizes everything. She wipes her dripping face and reads haltingly, her hips and breasts all but singing out to the men and women of the congregation. She is fifteen.

And then it's him. Up he goes, wearing a black suit I know, a black suit whose lapels I've scrubbed mustard from, a black suit I've brushed for lint. For two years, my nicest dress hung next to that suit. He shuffles his notes and clears his throat. He is in anguish. I can't look at his face. I examine the front of the pamphlet in my lap, which displays the same gauzy picture of Erica.

Staring at younger Erica's slightly goofy smile, I see Étienne up there too, his black-clad body out-of-focus, all limbs. His actual voice reaches me for the first time in almost a year, and without trying, I memorize every word.

He doesn't linger after the service. I wish he would: we'd eat de-crusted cucumber sandwiches provided by the church, help comfort Erica's little sisters, and perhaps duck out to cry together, shaking and clinging in our funny black clothes, our coats tossed over a pew, just a little cloth and our hot breath a tender, frilled membrane between us and the black void of a darkening winter afternoon. If he were to speak to me, I'd keep whatever he'd say like a love letter. It isn't the time.

Heating a small can of soup that evening, something from a weeks-ago dinner—ground meat?—flashes orange beneath the burner, and begins to flame. Smoke rolls up around the pot, spreads over the ceiling, thickening the air. What a thing.

An old man always strolls past my kitchen window at 6PM, very thin, clutching a shoulder-bag against his side. When he passes, I sometimes think he spots me through the tall, dead flower stalks standing between him, the glass, and me. Does he register my gaze, but not the horrific face around it? He could, but he never meets my eyes.

Tonight, he'd have seen me press a sofa cushion against the burner. He'd have seen me squeal 'help, help!' to nobody as it caught fire, grappling with the faucet, then dousing it in the sink.

I suffer for him; I suffer for her. Not like the pain of starving or real, physical pain—I realize, too infrequently, but sometimes—that I am not appreciative enough of my youngish, functional body. No, this pain inhabits a specific realm, a room hung with red velvet curtains, intimate one moment, claustrophobic the next, but always completely private. It'd vanish instantly if someone yanked those curtains away. This fantasy-room lives like an egg: sturdy on its own, lasting even under certain pressures, but easily cracked. Seamless, endless, but impossible to reassemble once its insides burst and coat the carpet, a white that dries clear. Like the cum I imagine he spills for me. Like a ghost.

Through social media osmosis—I've largely retreated from the digital world, but still lurk at its edges—I know there's some kind of post-funeral party at the old house, that house that's still Étienne's. A 'celebration of life.' My menstrual blood has flecked the floor of that house. I've pissed in its shower. I've bruised my hips on its doorways, busted my knees on its stove. Near-strangers have been invited, and not me. Étienne has invited them to stack their formal shoes on the carpet I've cleaned dozens of times. He has invited them to arrive late, and maybe drunk already. He has invited them to scour the internet for platitudes to spout about his closest friend, the woman who spent her final year on earth with me.

Sitting me down at the kitchen table, Étienne guides my pen: *Marie does not want you there. I am sorry.*

"She can't stop me."

I know.

I call my mother. She is a psychiatrist, and so in a worried, vague voice she presses tent poles into my hands, instructing me to prop myself up from within. Erica is only the latest in a long procession of controlling female companions to which you've been obsessively devoted, she says. When you dream of gigantic holes in your gums, holes in the bone deep enough to stick your fingers through, you are expressing your grief, and anxiety at its immensity, she says. Oh mother, I dream of the man I lost, his remainders distilled to a taste that lingers in my mouth all day, a pull that yanks my throat shut like curtains. My dreams of Erica are less distinct, because she's a woman, and hurt me deeper than a man ever could.

Perhaps because I'm thinking of her, tapping the pen, a message arrives from Erica:

Do it today.

"I'll try, but—Jesus, Erica. OK. I'll try."

A huge sack of uncooked rice sits by the windowsill. I take two fistfuls from the sacks, spreading the grains evenly with my hands until they cover the outdoor sill, birdshit and all. I puff up my cheeks and warble, until the pigeons come. They flap over in pairs, cooing and crying, fighting to land. Only about six birds

can fit on the sill itself, fat and fluffy as they are, and at least twice
that number vie clumsily for the space as I crouch nearby and
watch. A large pink lump sprouts from the neck of the biggest
bird. I watch it fold its wings with some difficulty, and conclude
the fleshy mass developed through a lifetime of eating cigarette
butts.

I don't want to die: I am miraculously alive. So I must consume, and act quickly in order to manage it.

I grab that pigeon by the wing. It thrashes and cries, but
because of its lump, it can't quite twist its head around to peck
me. I drag it further into the kitchen, and bury my face in the
pale feathers lining its chest. Scraping it with my teeth, yanking
away a mouthful of feathers, I spit and blow them from my
mouth, white as cotton. As it jerks its wings against me I rip
through skin, and reach my tongue inside. When the wings go
limp, I pause and run my fingers along the long wing-feathers.
They're striped blue and grey, with a dash of iridescent green
gathered at the neck. That pattern, those colours, are as familiar
as any other aspect of Toronto, the cement and the rippling lake
beyond it, the dull roar of millions of appetites, of far-off highways. Bones bump against my teeth, and little organs emerge like
grapes. The neck goes limp, its head falling back, its beak bobbling. Its chest cavity, lined with thick white feathers, yawns
purple in my hands. I rub some of the purplish stuff between my
breasts, across my stomach, over my sunk-in ribs.

I rush to the kitchen table, pick up the pen.

You did it? she asks.

"Yes. What now?"

Go to him.

The pigeon stays warm, cradled in my other hand. I stroke
its remaining feathers and arrange and re-arrange the possibilities
in my mind, kept afloat by my hunger and hope.

I leave the apartment, running through the lengthening list
of things I can't do. I can't pick my nose and wipe it on someone
on the streetcar, or start to sing, or stick anybody with whatever
sharp things I didn't manage to throw out during the last paranoid purge of sharp things from the apartment. Above all, I must

not open my coat, the furry thing—formerly my mother's, then Erica's, now mine again—a coat she wore all through the city, that trailed like a train behind her, and nearly reaches my ankles. I'm naked beneath it.

Some nights, I dream about that crisp morning I drove to the cottage in the heart of the Quebec woods, the angle of the noon-time winter sun as I sat in the rented car, calling that number over and over, too timid to knock—until I saw the blood in the snow.

Though Erica lived there, and fairly recently too, and though I saw the place for myself, rife with signs of busy life, the place has the feel of a dollhouse in my dreams, musty and dim with perpetual winter. I can't reconcile the few photos I've seen associated with the place—the splintered banister and CAUTION tape, a bright-lit mugshot, various stock images of Quebec hills—with my own experience of it: Logan, curled so, so thin, around her poor, swollen belly, a trail of piss and shit leading to the unconscious, twitching Neil, a close, winter smell, and the delicate anachronistic furniture, the long-legged table I stared at, unseeing, as I rubbed Neil's hands. I can't reconcile these nightmares with Erica's voice on the phone, dreamily describing her life there—her life there and its vibrant social dynamics, her breath pluming up towards the unseen winter sky, wherever she stood when she spoke with me last.

Whenever I dream, I trudge through melting ice and gravel, follow the pathway winding up towards the place, and climb its snow-laden porch stairs, then push through into the narrow entrance hallway. And then I encounter the Family as I explore the rooms, one by one. Their eyes are always open and their bodies stiff, arranged in lifelike poses. Sometimes I find Logan perched on a small wicker chair, kept very straight with a long wooden rod concealed beneath her blouse. Her hands are usually submerged in the sink. I usually find Erica sitting up in the bed upstairs, propped up by a wooden stand partially hidden by the pillows. She holds a small packet in her hands. I always find Neil last, slumped on a small couch by the dining room window, his arm thrown over the back, one hand bunched around a book. The book looks very familiar, and I usually stare at the cover of the book until I recollect, like sand trickling into a glass of water, that I can't read. While the rest of the world will remain a little blurred, always in motion—the mass of pigeons at the window, the trees trembling out beyond, and my own hands dangling in front of me—each member of the Family stays in sharp focus.

Because they keep so still.

I get off the streetcar, tighten the coat, and walk the two blocks to Étienne's.

As I climb the stairs the familiarity of the house, the door slightly crooked in its frame, the glow of the windows—it's overwhelming. Everything looks smaller than it is, more precious. Happy noise, laughing and music and brief barking, yells and laughs, come around the door, which is framed in orange light like piping.

I lean to the right, and gaze in the big bay window.

A bright tangle of people mill around the living room, chatting on and on, picking from plates spread over a long table I don't recognize. Are they only compelled to tidy, Étienne and Marie, when company comes? I wonder at the vastness of the city, the unrolling neighbourhoods and trees, and the unfathomable stretches of time navigated by those, like me, who've grown alone. Inside the house a woman flirts with a man I recognize, a colleague of Étienne's. She rotates occasionally and presses her milky hands against her thighs, her stomach, blushing and halting and pulling at her body where it enters and exits at the waist and hems of her jeans. The motionless furniture in the living room—some old, some new—glows in the jumbled bath of electronic and candlelight. Anybody else would be unimaginably bored, but I stand rapt, because I've spotted how quick real life goes. For me, for them, for anyone.

I press the doorbell.

A woman with an elegant topknot opens the door. A warm, welcoming smile drains from her face, and she draws the door closer to her body like a blanket. She's wearing a blue velvet dress, the kind he likes. It's Marie.

"Étienne," I croak.

She closes the door quickly, though she doesn't slam it.

And then he appears, ruffled and annoyed-looking, a beer in his hand. He steps outside and closes the door behind him. His feet are bare.

"Go home, Shelagh," he says.

Why's it so hard for women to say no? Whenever Étienne would request I buy something from the grocery store on my way home from work, I'd rather pretend I forgot than tell him 'No, I don't want to.' I sometimes pretended to sleep through Étienne's romantic overtures in bed—how crazy that seems to me now! A whole lot of passivity got me here, sliding right through life to the bottom.

"No," I say.

His face contorts a little, but I can't read what it means. He stinks of cigarettes.

"Share a smoke with me, then I'll go," I plead.

He looks behind him—at the door, safely shut, and then sighs. He removes two cigarettes from his pack, and I pluck one from his palm. He lights his own, then passes the lighter to me.

The lighter is warm from his palms, from the bright orange living room full of light and laughter. I slip it in my coat pocket, and squeeze my own warmth into it.

"You did good." I'm referring, I think, to the eulogy.

"Thanks," he says, frowning.

"I need to talk about Erica," I say.

"Her? Now?"

"It took so long," I say, "and everyone, they just kept expecting her to turn up."

That's how they put it two weeks ago, 'turned up,' a phrase infuriating in its triviality. Like a button lost between two couch cushions turns up, easing its way out through the glacial work of months and months of asses.

"I know, I hated it too. She was my best friend, and they frame her as some flake with a history of running away," he says. "But running away from *what*, you know? From him. And if they were both still alive, she'd still be running back and forth to him, from him, and on and on. She had no need for us." He drains his beer.

"I know this sounds crazy, but the truck," I insist. "There were supplies stashed there, Right? She easily could have taken blankets, knives, a sleeping bag, and a tent with her, before escaping into the woods."

And certainly, the chances she'd survive in the woods for weeks, at the tail end of a snowy winter, are scant. And yes, the body—the body, of course. But every so often, I stroke that iPhone she left, arranging and re-arranging the possibilities, kept afloat by slight knowledge and an ocean of hope. Wriggling somewhere in my limbic brain, living gently in my pre-sleep self, there's a certainty that the phone—though long dead—could light up and warm my palms, and she will call.

"What . . . Shelagh, Erica is dead. We attended her funeral this afternoon, and we're mourning her tonight. That man killed her, and she's gone." Étienne says. I start to shake; he stubs his cigarette, then takes me by my shoulders. "Listen. He killed her," he says. "He probably killed other people, too. OK? People like that don't make sense. They're not people. They happen *to* people. They happen to any kind of person you can think of. It's bad luck. It's lightning."

I close my eyes at 'bad luck,' and he squeezes my shoulders, gives me a little shake. I can smell everything: his cologne, his hair, the smell coming up through his V-neck sweater, the sharp smoke clinging to his right hand. I keep my eyes shut.

"I love you," I say, in the dark.

He lets go, and stands. "Do you have someone to talk to?" he asks, his hand on the doorknob.

"Yeah," I say. "Lots of people."

He smiles, then rubs his mouth, as if to wipe it away. I step toward him. He presses his back against the door.

I can feel Marie inside the house, worrying about him outside with me. Marie, her hands and face so pale and soft, the kind of skin you'd bruise just by pressing with your finger. Me, the last thing he needs today.

Maybe because I'm alone so much, I've grown sensitive, so sensitive, to what people think. And I see he still cares, a little. I see it in the corners of his mouth. I feel it in Marie's anxiety, oozing through the keyhole in the front door. His bare toes cling to the frozen straw *WELCOME* mat as I step up to him, breath him in deep, and press against his body.

My head fits right under his neck, as always. The coat yawns open, exposing my striped-up skin. I could swear he tilts his head, and smells my hair. He still cares a little, and only a little. I don't know why it's worse than him not caring at all—but it is.

"It's like something happens, and I wonder what you'd say about it, you know?" I whisper into his sweater. "If I'm not careful, you're in my head all day, commenting on whatever I'm doing."

Wherever I walk in the city, countless annotations scroll past, changing and breathing, in his spiky script. It's pathetic, but everyone's pathetic, so what? At least it's true, the truest fact of my being. That babbling crowd in our old house spits lies in the orange circlets of light, numb to death and love. *Oh, she was good. Oh, she was kind.*

She was cruel. She was spineless. Yet she left us behind.

"Think of me as dead too," Étienne says quietly. "It'll help."

I pull away. "You think I'm dead?"

He shakes his head, and closes my coat around me. "You can't come here again, Shelagh."

"I know."

He puts his hand on the door, then pauses and turns around. "You look good," he says, and he must mean it: I still have my funeral hairdo, and I'm even thinner than Marie now. My bare knees tremble together under the coat.

He goes inside, closing the door behind him.

I count to ten, and then flick Étienne's lighter on, and press it to a bush near the stairs. The branches start to burn. I light another, and another. Then I press myself against the bricks, and reach up to light the wood panelling of the front window. The paint curls and blackens, then begins to smoke, but it doesn't catch fire. I look down at the basement window: as long as I lived in that house, it never closed properly. I'd jam it shut with a wooden spoon, and have nightmares about someone silently prying it open, sliding inside. They still haven't fixed it. I yank up the pane, making about four inches of room, then rip branches from one of the burning shrubs. I slide them, one by one, down into the black space of the basement.

I back away from the house, and the big bay window slides into full view: that warm, overfamiliar living room. The evergreen shrubs, leaping with flames. The basement, beginning to glow.

I run.

People are all that keep us from ruin. But when they're torn away, though they're dead at least in relation to us, they stay *people*. You're haunted, yeah, and they live on with a half-life that you don't even recognize as such for years.

The Phone vibrates in my pocket. Gasping for breath, I yank it free, then answer it.

"Hello?"

"You need to see something," Erica says.

"Where are you?"

"Just follow my voice," she says, and I take the phone away from my ear for a second, then press it back again.

Seeming to read my mind, she says, "I'll guide you."

I slow to a jog, listening for the little micro-gasp of breath she'll take before she speaks again. "Should I hurry?" I ask, then hear the little rush before she says, "What do you think?" Which isn't something she would have said normally, but the kind of thing I say all the time.

The store windows lining Queen Street appear black, and occasional clusters of people slide past, flat as the shadows cast by the buildings and trees. "Keep going straight, three more blocks," she says, her voice growing fuzzy, as if her attention is wandering.

To keep her focused, keep her with me, I raise my voice: "Today was your funeral, did you know that?"

I reach into my pocket, stroking the soft nub of the pigeon's head.

"You also know it's not your fault," she says. "Don't you?"

"I know," I say. "It's his—and yours." And I hear her white-noise rush of breath, like a hand passing over a faraway antennae.

"He isn't with you, is he?" I grind my teeth, waiting for her to speak again.

I see my stick-thin body flash past a large window. Somebody just ahead jaywalks across the street, presumably to avoid the anguished woman staring into a restaurant window, stroking something in her pocket.

Me.

"Turn left up ahead," she says.

"It's crazy, being stuck in an unfolding news story about people you know," I say. "I'm . . . I'm sometimes in an alternate world, one where you are real and alive, and he's the bad guy from your past. And there's a cottage-like place you tell me about, where he lives and does weird stuff alone, and you might go there for a while, just a while, before coming home again."

"And in the other world?"

"And in the other world, this one, there's all the stuff that I've seen, that I've read about, that I've been interviewed about."

She doesn't ask what kind of stuff, but I hear her breath— her *breath*—and know she's listening, so I continue: "Sometimes I'll read the stories on the CBC site over and over, and then read the comments. I can spend hours reading and rereading those comments. A lot of young women are talking about emotional abuse in long-term relationships, but some are actually 'shipping it, this fictionalized version of your relationship, which fucks me up. And the older commenters, the ones who write in all caps? They think it was a satanic cult."

She laughs, and her laugh distorts a bit halfway through.

"Cut through the park, up ahead, and come out on the Dundas side," she says. Then: "You think they'll reveal something you don't know, these people?"

The ice is almost rubbery with half-melt, so I tread carefully through the park, avoiding long, deep puddles in the ice. In some places, the grass shines through the ice, and the black tree boughs drip steadily. Someone sleeps in a park bench, wrapped in a sleeping bag that glistens with meltwater.

"Well," I say, "it's comforting to read their comments and posts, because it's not the centre of their world, like it is mine.

They have their own lives, with responsibilities and controlled expectations and people. And their own feelings webbing all of these things, their own feelings are the centre of the world—to them. It calms me down. Makes it feel less important."

"It *isn't* important," she says. "Keep going south, you see the lake now? Just between those two buildings up ahead?"

I do: it stretches up ahead, grey and still as the concrete but shimmering slightly, as if just about to evaporate.

"Easy for you to say," I say. She giggles, that white-noise rush again.

"But it isn't," she says.

"That's like saying you're not important. I'm not important."

"I'm not. You're not."

A streetcar rattles past, and a siren wails somewhere. I break into a run again, and her breathing speeds up with mine. The static starts to roar.

The buildings thin out and I stop, realizing I've reached the final stretch of road before the boardwalk. The lake spreads enormous in front of me, merging with the low, grey sky as far as I can see. I stroke the pigeon's head with my fingertip, and it seems to stir.

"What are you showing me?" I ask. She pauses, breathing and listening, before her voices reaches me again.

"Don't you see it?"

The pigeon is now moving in my pocket, thrusting its cancerous lump against my thumb. It writhes out of my pocket and lands on the ground, squirming for a moment. Its wings unfurl, spraying something black on the road. I follow along as it flutters and hops, flutters and hops—leading me on, down towards the water.

And then I see it.

The place is warm and sunlit. Three young bodies live there, cleaning and sustaining the space, filling it with laughter and sleeping soundly. Outside they work hard, and the plants and trees grow around them as the summer stretches on and on. The dollhouse world, capturing my dream-life and seizing the imaginations of the morbid, is just a nightmare sustained by a handful of photos and our own collective terrors. It has nothing to do with anything that ever existed. Here, autumn comes, the rolling hills growing orange and yellow and red, sugar-scented and magnificent. In winter they tend to the plants in the greenhouse and those strange, bright blue hydroponic tanks. Chanting together, observing the silent, snow-blanketed world. And spring comes, filling their blood with gratitude.

I feel Neil now, throbbing and lonely but healing over where he's broken, where he's broken the most beautiful parts of him. He's safe in the hospital just a few blocks north, a calming thought: his boy maybe drowsing in his chair by the bed, his mother maybe in the cafeteria, lining up for coffee. "Nothing bad can happen to you in a hospital, Dad," Ryan had told Neil on my last visit, and I'd squeezed his hand and agreed. This boy, this sweet odd boy, in which the worst of Neil's genes are curled and slumbering still—this boy will never know his father very nearly left forever, and I don't think that's fair, really, letting Neil off the hook like that—but it's also for the best. I will go to Neil and they'll let me in because we're family, aren't we, family of a sort. He'll wake just enough, and maybe I'll climb clumsily into the bed beside him and we'll curl up together, chaste and quiet, sharing the threadbare, mint-green sheet, and nobody will reach any of us us there, until the morning brings trays of hard eggs and green Jell-O, and a new tide of visitors too, bearing flowers and cards inscribed with carefully chosen words: the sun will rise, bringing with it these clumsy acts of love. The coat drops away, and the purple streaks glow along my body, little nubs and undulations warm in the streetlight. I toss the phone behind me. I won't need it anymore.

Epilogue. Logan: Mating Season

January 2028

That first night out, Mo rattled Logan's knees under the damp little tabletop as he jiggled on his stool. He ordered three pitchers of the cheapest available beer, saying things like "I don't need this [my device], I'll rip it out and throw it here [in the pitcher] if you don't believe me, because I live off the grid. My roommates and me, we eat the herbs we grow and the bread we bake. And sometimes even roadkill, Amy."

Logan clears her throat, then glances around the bar. It's been nearly seven years since she changed her name, but she still isn't totally used to it.

"But how did we find this bar? And how did we meet?" she asked. Even very young men are finely tuned to detect women's mockery, so he paused a moment, recalibrating. "I'm not off the web, necessarily," he amended. "Just the grid."

She took a deep sip—a gulp, really, so big her stomach swelled—and grasped his hand. "Listen, you know how old I am?"

His hand stiffened and he looked at her face, closely, for perhaps the first time. "You said twenty-nine?"

"Yeah, thirty this year. And I—well the thing is, I've got a ten-year-old girl."

He shrugged easily, smiling a sloppy smile. "Amy, I love kids," he said. He wiggled his fingers, like *show me the goods!* So she tapped her wrist, and a nine-inch tall Abby sprung up between their pint glasses. He swept his hair out of his eyes and squinted, his thin face showing through the blueish light of a miniaturized Abby, her own girl, thin as dandelions and skipping across the table, her nose glowing red in the months-ago sun. "What a little sprite," he said. Logan almost cried, perhaps with relief, loose with overwhelming love for her daughter, taking joy in this man's apparent joy.

This twenty-three-year old boy, gulping dish-soap beer and watching her admire the tattoos on his fists, he didn't know what she knew. She knew she'd strip in front of him later, yanking off her dress with one fluid motion, revealing herself long and lean in the overhead light in his bedroom. She knew she'd suck his cock so good, better than any girl he'd had. She sensed he'd wake up a little early, and watch her sleep. She knew she'd cook breakfast for him in his shirt and her panties, arching her back and giggling over the little stings of bacon fat. Watching him eat, she knows she'll think of Abby, waking up in another house and begging Lori for one more spoonful of sugar in her cereal. Back in his bedroom, she knows she'll pull her dress back on as slinkily as she pulled it off, and kiss a long and wet goodbye on his doorstep (shabby, no doubt), and then walk backwards, still wiping her thighs dry through her dress with one hand, waving to him as he watched her go. As they drained the last pitcher and split the bill, he told her, woozy and soft-hearted: "My parents are best friends, and they are deeply in love." She understood, then, that he was safe, having sprouted alongside living proof that lifelong, monogamous passion was not only possible, but common, and maybe even unremarkable. Having spent his helpless years in its shade, he had a shallow reserve of empathy for the scorched, which she knew she'd resent immediately, despite herself.

She knew it'd keep a gulf between them (sustained within her mind alone, and impossible to traverse), but the weeks oozed by like honey, and they grew very close. One day she invited him over, and introduced him to Abby, who, though still tired from school, perked up enough to show him her insect collection. That night, Logan fell asleep with her head lolling against his naked thighs, his fingertips bunched near her face, still smelling of the Kraft dinner and hot dogs he'd prepared earlier (Abby's favourite meal.)

"Did you like Mo?" she asked Abby, almost before she'd closed the door behind him the next morning. Abby tapped her device, turning off whatever animal thing she was interacting with, and turned to Logan. She squeezed her lips together tight, so tight—looking so much like Jason for a flash-moment that Logan almost shivered. "Yeah, I guess," Abby said.

"You guess! You guess?"

"*Mom*," Abby said, very seriously. "He's just a dude."

"But to you, he must seem really old," Logan said, hopefully.

Abby thought about it, pulling at her lip. "Yeah, old," she said.

"And you like him? Did you like all his stories about the swans?"

"Did you tell him I like swans?"

Logan laughed. "Yes. But he also worked in a park with like water birds, so the stories were real." Abby sighed, then tapped her device again. A half-dozen peacocks filled the room, stepping daintily over the threadbare carpet, flashing their magnificent tails.

"Do you love him?" Abby asked suddenly. "Like, can I see him around again? Because I don't like the, um . . . the . . ." She turned and reached towards one of the peacocks, her voice wobbling.

Logan swept in, avoiding the peacocks, and took her daughter in her arms, her heart swelling and rising in her chest. "The what, my baby?"

"Well, remember Topher? He made me the parrot drawings, and drew all the feathers so . . . like, little. And now I don't see him again, and he never told me it was the last time. Just we ate the burgers, and then we finished the burgers, and then. Like, boom."

Even Topher hadn't known it was the last time, and so Logan momentarily aches for him too. She pulls away a little from Abby, so she can look into her daughter's eyes. She feels a sweep of vertiginous and deeply romantic feeling, more romantic even than caressing Mo's nest of pubic hair away from the scar it partially covers; more romantic than the unmistakeable scent of her father, reaching beyond death through the maple blossoms in spring: "Abby, if he's cool with it, I will marry Mo. He will be there for you, and there for me."

"Buppy, are you listening?" Abby twists her body around towards the smooth silver-white dog perched near the coffeemaker, which despite her best efforts Logan can think of only as a robot, and it freaks her out so much it makes her nauseous. *I'm officially old*, she thought, for the first time in her whole life, when one day Abby casually instructed Buppy to order the best Thai food in the city for her birthday dinner. *Get just enough for two, a mom and a little girl, with no peanuts or bean sprouts or meat, either,* Abby had said, a command which Buppy then executed effortlessly. Abby conceptualizes Buppy in a manner ungraspable to anybody born before Abby's generation: something contradictory and warm, omnipotent but friendly, simple, and anthropomorphic.

"I am listening, Abby," Buppy confirms.

Mo and Logan spend full days together and long strings of nights in her bed. Abby, with her serious little demeanor, accompanies them often to restaurants, to parks, to afternoon movies; sitting up straight and rarely complaining when Logan tells her she can't use her device in public. She quickly begins to hold Mo's hand when they pick her up from school, which makes him melt; he seems to adore her. Abby begins putting out three plates every evening automatically, and Mo accepts and devours Logan's meals as zealously as Abby. He easily slips into living in their apartment—which is small, but which Logan keeps fastidiously clean—his toothbrush nestles against Logan's and Abby's, his boxers, which are threadbare and garish enough to be remainders from his childhood, mingle with her T-shirts and socks. The roommates storm and recede, and one morning Mo shows up with his stacked boxes of herbs. He places them gently on the kitchen table, and Abby comes in, trailing a row of ducks. She stops beside the boxes, and the ducks crowd around her feet, rustling their feathers. She rubs a green sprig between her little fingers, then brings both hands to her nose. "It's thyme, this one?" she says, loud enough for Buppy to hear from the counter.

"Yes," he confirms. "My roommates are like, 'just take the darn things and go live with your Yoko.' We haven't been all that copacetic lately," Mo says to Abby, who nods, but then shrieks: in shifting his balance, Mo has put his foot right through one of the ducks, which tilts its head and blinks its black eyes, entirely unaware of Mo's deeply tanned and tattooed leg now sprouting up through its feathered back. Abby starts crying and Mo jumps violently, then dances out of the way. "Amy!" he yells.

Logan rushes in and stops short, staring aghast at the boxes of herbs. "Buppy, ignore," she says, forcing herself calm: she knows enough about the binary nature of machine memory, which either erases completely or never, ever forgets. Mo looks near tears himself, and places both hands on the boxes. "Is this OK? Like one near the kitchen window, and maybe out on the balcony? It'd be so great for your cooking, and you just have such good light," he says, and he and Abby look at Logan, whose mouth is pulled tight shut (perhaps Abby inherited this trait from Logan after all.)

"I absolutely, one-hundred percent cannot have these in my home, Muhammed," she says, instinctually stepping in front of Abby and lowering her voice: "*and I don't need to tell you why.*"

But she does. One night, after coming hard and rough against him, she dissolves into tears and the stories dredge up and out of her like black matted hair erupting from a drain, scraping her throat so badly that she feels like oh god, oh little baby Jesus, I'll never talk again. She watches his beautiful profile rising and falling in the dark, and as she cries, cries like she'll never stop, cries so much she's forgotten she's crying, she feels he is now holding her, so hard she struggles for breath.

"So you're, um," he says, arching back a bit, so he can look in her eyes.

"Logan Strinic," she whispers, her lips curling up, tears rolling into her ears, pooling in the indents in her chest.

"You're the one who escaped. Wait, sorry—that's obvious, I guess."

"Yeah."

"Have you heard from him since? The guy?"

Through the wall, Logan hears Buppy 'read' Abby a bedtime story in a gentle, lilting tone. The cadence of his voice is such that, were he capable of breathing, he'd be drawing breath in time with Logan. This unnerves her. When she responds she presses her mouth right to Mo's ear, her answer more an exhalation than an audible word:

Yes.

Their lives, now knotted together, flit moment to moment, faster and faster on oil-black wings. They move to a better, brighter apartment; Logan becomes pregnant and Mo is overjoyed, though he doesn't cry as she'd hoped he might; they spend a small fortune on a parakeet for Abby and watch more and more VR—though they keep their own sex out of it. They get a little fatter on Logan's winter cooking, the three of them, and wait out the final months of winter evenings and bitter cold. Logan's limbs and belly swell, she thinks about heartbeats and organs more than she'd like, and she grows into knowing that she doesn't need to understand Mo or be stimulated all the time. She just needs a spot in that shade. She just needed to be safe.

Abby has big opinions about learning long division in school, which Mo listens to carefully over dinner one evening. "I mean I get it, it's not too hard," Abby concludes, rolling her eyes, "But like, who cares anymore? We're learning this stuff, like 'carry the two'—and then we're back in VR for like the rest of the day!"

"Girl, in my dad's day, he had to do *cursive,*" Mo says, avoiding (as always, to Logan's chagrin) his meagre portion of rice. "How's that for redundancy. You know what cursive is?"

"No," Abby says, screwing up her little nose. A flash of Jason's rat-like confusion clouds her dark little features, and Logan almost chokes. In moments like this she wonders: what if, what if—is Abby's his after all?

"It's like, curly writing of normal words. And you do it by hand," Mo says, and Abby pauses for a moment, then shrieks with laughter.

The spring that Abby turned ten, tens of thousands of birds died—violently, and all at once. Horrific coverage funneled through social media channels: still images of blackbirds falling from trees, their feet still clenched; videos of mallards lolling in a melting brown pond, their waterproof wings rain-dotted and still. Municipal laborers and old ladies alike scraped baked and flattened bird bodies from porches and rooftops. Mo and Logan encountered them tangled on the beach, scudding in Lake Ontario and piled all up through the street. Abby was inconsolable, disappearing in her room for long hours at a time, whispering and singing with Buppy, while the rest of the Toronto went crazy.

We lit bonfires on the beach and roasted their bodies, we made necklaces and earrings from their beaks and talons and burned the rest. We packed their bodies into cardboard boxes, layered with dandelion and clover chains, and left them out in the side of the street, encouraging others to drop flowers in memoriam. The more pragmatic among us stuffed sidewalk garbage bins with them, the spring warmth dragging the stink right out through their feathers. On their weekly night out, as Buppy sang Abby and Jiggles the parakeet to sleep, Mo and Logan gripped cigarettes in their teeth and kicked through bird bodies like damp loads of leaves. Logan giggled like she hadn't since smoking massive joints with Jason in high school, clinging to Mo as they half-tangoed, half-stumbled through a pitch-dark park. "I want to—this is so fucked—I want to snap that bird's fucking *neck* sometimes," Logan squealed.

"Jiggles?" Mo asked, and then barked a laugh, exhaling pale smoke. "Me too!"

Mo cleared a picnic table of seagull bodies—bright white in the dark—and they sat in the wet spots, pressing their heads together, their chests together, then her mouth to his crotch and his hands to her belly, breathless and giggling. Something maybe bad was coming fast, and they were barreling towards it together, and that was exciting.

A week later the ladybugs came alive, all at once, and traveled in desperate flocks, rushing over streets and tennis courts and front lawns in bright red sheets. They began dying *en masse* a few weeks into April, clusters of crisp little bodies caught in shrubs, floating on their backs in puddles and tossed lifeless through the wind, sticking in hair and eyes and cups of ice cream. The butterflies came next, tumbling from the sky and dotting the black soil all over the place. Abby began collecting their bodies, sticking them through with pins and covering her bedroom wall. "Gotta catch 'em all, right Abs?" Mo said, standing in her bedroom doorway, taking in the rows and rows of miniscule, slightly stinking bodies, each glimmering around their pin. Logan punched him in the arm. "You *idiot.*"

"Dreamy duskwing, cabbage, Compton tortoiseshell," Buppy said, identifying the butterflies row by row and printing out sticker labels for Abby, which she stuck on the wall under each butterfly. "Cabbage," he said again, printing another label.

Abby looked over at him, her little finger stalled under a small, greenish-white butterfly. "Cabbage again?" she asked.

"Yes," Buppy said.

"Its wings are just a little greener than the other one," Logan says, stepping in, and Abby looked up at her for the first time. Something about the look—affectless as it was—made Logan want to sleep for weeks and weeks.

Stray dogs grew fat on bird bodies and on the nests of ants and spiders they dug up everywhere, frozen and dead. The remaining monarchs and terns flew round and round in doomed and slowing circles, and as April drew on were eventually found mashed together with leaves in pool drains and drainpipes, the migratory pinging in their little bodies overpowered. The great digital ocean lapping through our cities had bested the rocky breadth of the continent at last.

And as May crept on, a strange new pinging woke in our chests, audible to the men alone. One morning, as Mo quietly described it, he woke with an enormous, throbbing boner. As Logan slept beside him, he wriggled into his tight corduroys, gelled his hair and patted on cologne, so electric with hunger he couldn't unclench his teeth. On the bus, as the maple boughs whipped by the window—mostly empty of blossoms this spring, of course—a young woman swung up the stairs.

How young? Logan interrupted as he told the story later, head in hands.

Too young, he replies.

The bus driver, watching her closely in his giant mirror, ignores the green light, and the old man huddles up near the front began to rock and moan. The young girl sits beside Mo, looking rattled, and then grabs his elbow. "You have to help me. Even my stepbrother—" she pauses. "You, are you safe?"

You weren't. Safe. Logan said.

I couldn't help it. I can't, Mo whispered.

It didn't take long—minutes, hours—for the news cycle and social feeds to catch up, name and explain what was going on, scientifically at first, and then—within days—culturally. Men crept from their homes at night, lingered late-late in restaurants to pick up waitresses, skulked near women's clothing stories and even outside hospitals. They were watched closely by every female security guard and policewoman the Toronto municipality could muster. Once she understood this as an international and perhaps even global phenomenon— though she'd never been big on keeping up with world news—Logan shut herself in her bedroom for days, instructing Buppy to carry on Abby's schooling within the apartment, and to lock Abby's bedroom door from the inside every night. When Mo came and went, he treaded silently, and touched nothing in the fridge. If he slept at the apartment, he curled, as much as a very tall man can curl, on a pile of carpets on the living room floor.

"Look at him on those dirty rugs. Remember I found those dead pillbugs under the patchwork one? The couch folds out, you know," Abby whispered to Buppy very early one morning, watching Mo sleep from a crack in her bedroom door. She would sometimes dangle her little body out the window just before sunrise, claiming she could smell flowers then.

"That couch functions as a bed, as required," Buppy confirmed, and Abby turned down his volume quickly.

"*Shhh.* Yeah," Abby said. "So why isn't he using it?"

Buppy was quiet. "I don't know, Abby," he said. He turned his silver head up towards her, and asked: "Tell me why *you* think so."

"So Mo needs to like, go be with other ladies sometimes," Abby said the next morning, sitting on the end of Logan's bed, cradling Buppy. "Because of the Spring Thing." She tapped her little wrist, and the room filled instantly with swallowtail butterflies.

"I'm so glad you don't call him Dad," Logan groaned. A butterfly seemed to land on the pillow near her swollen face. She watched it slowly open and close—flex, really—its bright-yellow wings, streaked with dark blue in the pattern of a shattered window.

"He puts his penis inside of them?" Abby asked.

"Yes," Buppy confirmed.

"No!" Logan said.

That evening Mo came home, closing the door oh-so-gently. Logan launched herself out of bed, rushed to the door, looked around wildly—Buppy and Abby were singing quietly in Abby's bedroom—and then took one of his hands. His face, even more gaunt than usual, was bruised up and covered in scratches. He looked like he'd aged five years in a month; his jeans were torn, and his hands were chapped bright red.

"Look at me—look at me," she hissed, her throat full of bile. "Is my daughter safe around you?"

"Yes. Oh Jesus, yes," he said. "I swear to you, yes."

"Don't tell me what's going on outside, don't tell me where you got bloody, don't tell me, don't tell me, I don't want to know. I am keeping my child safe in my home, and we will weather this. And we will weather this the three of us, because we love each other. We love each other." She began to cry. "I love you. I *love* you."

His body went loose with relief, and to her horror, he started to cry too: "I love you too. I love you so much—I—I'm so tired, Amy, I'm so scared—" He was sobbing openly now, collapsed against the doorframe, his wails echoing down the hall. She closed the door and forced him into a chair, and he looked up at her, his shoulders shaking. She automatically smoothed his hair against his skull, but then pulled her hand away, revolted: her hand released smells of terror, fighting and filth, and fucking, fucking, fucking.

"You stop your crying," she hissed. "You stop your crying *right now*."

She walked over to Abby's room, and peeked in: "Buppy," she says, "Please ignore the yelling, OK? This isn't, um . . ."

"Indicative of domestic violence and cause for alarm?" Buppy supplied.

"Yeah. Mo and I are just figuring some stuff out. I'm the uh, aggressor here. Except it's not, like, 'cause for alarm,' OK?"

"OK," said Buppy, and Abby turned from the window, reaching for him. "Come here and sing with me, Buppy," she whispered. Logan closes the door, then walked back to Mo.

"Here's how you'll do it," Logan said slowly, waiting for Mo to look up at her, tears soaking his face, his shirt, his hands. "You're going to come home with flowers for me every night, and wash your hands right away—in fact shower, and for a long time. I'll cook dinner as usual, and we will eat together. You can manage this, right?"

"Yes," he said.

"Good. And we'll talk about VR shows, you'll tell your stories about touring with the band, you'll hear about what Abby's learning, we'll talk about the baby that's coming. We'll weather it out." He shook a little, blinking out tears at the still window. Now, she saw his parent's lifelong partnership just as he must have, when he was a boy. She understood how it was both unremarkable and extinct, mired in his parent's generation. There was just a new way of things, and this is what it was.

Summer came, bringing with it the long days of gold and— wherever a rare tree bloomed—deep green, and the pinging in our chests began to fade. Mo calmed: the years rolled from his body and face, and he began to shave again. Without really speaking about it, Logan invited him back to her bedroom. They slept long unbroken sleeps, fucking slow and gentle at sunset and dawn. Logan gave birth to a baby girl in October, just as a series of unprecedented blackouts began rolling through the city. Mo squeezed her hands so tight that tendons stood out all over his body, all fierce ropy musculature, he gasped breaths and pushed and pushed and pushed with her, roared and whimpered with her. He cried when the nurse placed his baby girl in his arms: a lumpy black-haired twist of purple skin, squalling at the top of its tiny, drying lungs.

They didn't want to risk taking the bus with the baby, so Mo wheeled her home. The few trees that had blossomed now shone red and bronze. Still fucked up on hospital drugs, Logan held her baby and felt the trees breathe and release, watching the leaves hum and fall around them. Winter came, and the blackouts stopped for a few weeks, and then started again. Since their apartment was situated on the top floor, Mo drilled and hammered and pummelled a very illegal chimney in their ceiling. Every night they made a small fire, and heated cans of soup and macaroni and spaghetti sauce over it.

On the ninth evening of a blackout, Logan and Abby huddled inside a ring of enormous candles they molded in a bucket, eating lukewarm soup from cans in the circle of shivering light. The baby slept by the fire, her face twitching, but her bulbous eyes stayed shut. They hadn't named her yet, primarily because the perfect name was one of Abby's favorite preoccupations. *Please baby, sleep just a little longer,* Logan thought over and over, even her head-voice an anxious whisper, hastily scraping the sodden vegetables from the bottom of her can.

"If the grid is off, why are you still alive, Buppy?" Abby asked, her voice wavering a little. As Logan had long sensed, but couldn't put into words, Abby hated thinking of Buppy as a machine.

"I'm off the grid," Buppy said in Mo's voice, startling Logan, making Abby giggle messily into her soup can.

Through the blinds, a cavalcade of electric light flashed on all at once, blaring varying intensities and hues—some reflected back in the ice and snow, some filtered through the tree branches—illuminating the living room behind us for the first time since sunset. "Jesus," Mo yelled, jumping to the window, yanking up the blinds and sliding it open. "The apartment across from us and the fucking convenience store, they've all got their electricity back. Even the fucking streetlights. Why not us?"

"Please close the window! It's freezing, you'll wake her up," Logan hissed: he certainly wasn't going to rock the baby back to sleep if she woke.

"Oh fuck off," Mo spits, then flinches a little. "Buppy, ignore," he said reflexively, then looked over Logan: in the candlelight they were wolfish to each other, all teeth and rage. A draft blasted the apartment and the candles flickered wildly, their flames bending sideways. Logan rushed over to the baby, and saw that her tiny face was covered in wax. She jolted awake and screamed, and Logan scooped her up, wanting with all her body to scream along with her, to deafen her entire tiny family huddled in the frozen apartment.

Winter broke one morning a week later, and Logan, Mo and Abby stepped outside into stronger sunlight. Mo strode through the brown, wet lawn to the storage shed they share with the rest of the building, and put their candles away for the season. Placing them gently in tissue, Logan began to shake. Mo drew her to him, whispering into her ears, her hair: *I don't want it, I don't want it, I'm so sorry, I'm so sorry,* and she whispered things back that sounded mostly like *please, please, please, please.* Abby stood watching them cling together in sorrow, sitting on a cardboard box with false butterflies shimmering on her shoulders. In just a year or two, two centuries' work of refining and padding the category of childhood had eroded, and children all over the city—Abby included, and to Logan, Abby *especially*—have the grim faces and worn, put-upon look of little old women, little old men.

That night Mo took out the rugs again, stacking them in the living room. He slipped out around midnight, barely making a sound.

Mo's older sister Ada burst in around three the next day, baring her teeth and hungry to socialize. "I let myself in!" she thundered, and Logan jumped.

"I know. That's good," Logan said. The baby was sleeping by the 'fireplace,' her face almost peaceful in the sun coming down through the chimney-hole as the coals glow red under the ash. If she'd been holding the baby, Logan might've dropped her rather than the glass she was holding, which thunked on the floor and broke in two. "Buppy, ignore," she said quickly—he'd been getting buggy lately—before turning back to Ada, who was draping her coat over a chair. Logan stepped forward, her hands extended. "What?" Ada said.

"It's just that I . . . not on that chair, please, Buppy doesn't like when strangers do that. The signal, maybe . . . here, let me hang it up."

"Sure, thanks," Ada said, dropping the coat in Logan hands. "How's your mom? Good?"

"Good as ever," Logan said, and Ada snorted: between the two of them, Lori is a flake, a deadbeat who smoked and fucked her way through Logan's childhood, which isn't quite true. Logan feels guilty about this portrayal sometimes. The truth is, Abby instilled a soft, doting affection—a near-obsession—in Lori, which Logan still resents sometimes.

Ada strode over to the couch and just about sits but stopping just short, hovering over the cushions. "It's not pervy I hope, this couch," she says, and Logan swallowed her exasperation.

"Ada! Our apartment isn't Thingable. Look how we live, you think we can afford that?"

There's an uncomfortable silence.

"Coffee? Tea?" Logan asked.

"I've never seen much use in Thingability anyway," Ada said, massaging the skin under her fingers, which are covered in silver rings. "I mean, what's a toothbrush have to say? It's a whole lot of noise, and not a lot of meaning." She tilted her head like a dog, giving Logan a long, collusive look.

"Oh jeez," Logan said, ignoring Ada's look and sweeping the glass up with her bare hands, "I keep forgetting we ran out of tea."

"It's the collective 'we', really," Ada said, leaning back. "The royal 'we.'"

"Hot water? With lemon?"

"From a plastic squeezy thing?"

"From a plastic squeezy thing."

"No thank you, Amy." Ada swept theatrically from one end of the apartment to the other, then parted the blinds, peering out the kitchen window.

"Still looks like winter," Logan commented.

"What time is it, five?" Ada said. "Look at that sunset. Why does the five-o-clock light always make one so pensive?" She directed the final question down at Buppy.

"I don't know, Auntie Ada," Buppy said, rotating his head. "What do *you* think?"

Ada opened her mouth, then closed it again, and patted Buppy's head. He made a purring noise as Ada settled back on the couch.

"Mo's not here?" she asked.

"Well, no," Logan says, her chest pinching up. She thought of Mo, lying naked in some well-decorated bedroom downtown near the lake, perhaps along that stretch of blocks in which some trees still stand petrified, ringed with metal fences. Though they had a strict agreement not to discuss it, Logan imagined a different girl each time, a stranger: it eased the ache. Logan imagined this one is a feathery blonde with small hands, not really bigger than Abby's—to him, at least. Perhaps they sang along to a record together, or she leaned out the window just like Abby did, her long naked body receiving the spring air, newly suffused with depth and rot.

"I don't know why I asked," Ada said in lieu of an apology, twisting her rings around again, then picking up her mug. "I left Gene for good this time," she commented, her tone causal but her eyes sharp over her mug.

"Oh god, Ada. I am so sorry," Logan said, feeling exhausted. She remembered a long-ago Erica telling her that you get tired as a woman, knowing people are big swirling chemical balls of need, need, need. She remembered Abby in her belly, the arid greenhouse. She remembered the elasticity of her extreme youth like another person, another person that's left her like expelled air—its departure hastened by people like Ada.

"You need someplace to stay?" Logan asked, and Ada's face contorted a little: masking something, presenting something else.

"Maybe just for a few days? There's other people I can—I really just came to check in . . ." and she trailed off, rubbing at the deep red lipstick stain on the side of her mug, closing her eyes in the steam. "I thought"—and here she laughed a sad little laugh—"we could weather it out, you know? Gene and me. The autumn and winter sort of soothed us, you know, and we have that big house; I had space when I needed it. And then I just. All at one, I started to despise him."

"It can sneak up on you," Logan said.

"I thought having a threesome might fix things," Ada said, then started to laugh again. "What's going to happen to us, Amy? You know what I mean?" she asked. "What the fuck is going to happen to us?"

"Oh. Well," Logan said, then looks quickly at the chipped and steaming mugs in both of their hands. She felt the faint, late afternoon sunlight on her own hands, and found she couldn't stand it anymore. "Ada," she said urgently, "Can you please take Abby for a walk? Maybe to the store, to buy a Hostess cake?"

"You know what almost happened to me on my way here?" Ada said.

"You'll be *fine*," Logan said. "It's only March, and you've got your Mace. I just need like half an hour, you hear me?"

"Oh," Ada said, giving a wink. "I wouldn't mind some of that myself. You know I still have a *dildo*?" She whispered the last word, her ringed fingers framing her lips, "With *batteries?* I'll just about die when the batteries run out."

Logan threw back her head. "Abby!" she yelled. "Auntie Ada is here!"

"I know," Abby called softly from her bedroom, and Logan winced, then walked over Abby's bedroom.

"She's going to take you out for a Hostess cake," Logan said, her chest aching as she caught her daughter's eyes. Was it contemplating the little cake itself that hurt, its bright package and complicated chemical ingredient list a sudden relic of another time, or her daughter's obvious work of feigning enthusiasm for it?

"Sounds nice," Abby said, and Logan knelt and held Abby to her, inhaling deeply: cotton on cotton, sweat and worry, little girl hair and the sour smell of the organic things Abby hid and tended to in her room. The butterflies were all still pinned to the wall, their wings curling but retaining colour, as if they were all holding their breath.

"I love you, Abigail," Logan whispered, and Abby squirmed a little.

"I'm just going to get a Hostess cake," Abby said, then pulled back and looks at Logan. "I love you too," she added quickly, and Logan's heart sank again: *she's seen so much already, this little girl.* Logan then stood in a dream-like state at the centre of a small whirl of activity: Ada and Abby, their coats and scarves and shoes, a small flock of robins hopping behind them, the gentle click of the door. The last of the fire went out with a hiss, and the baby stirred. Logan took a breath and then ran over to the counter, pressing Buppy's silver sides with both hands.

"Buppy," Logan said, "I'm sad."

Presumably to cheer Logan up, Buppy projected a video on the pockmarked kitchen wall: a bus approached a young woman hauling overladen grocery in both fists, who appeared to be cutting through a metro station bus shelter. As the bus approached, the woman's whole body stiffened and she stopped walking, perhaps in fear. She then started walking quickly, then broke into a jog, then dropped all her groceries and bolted, barely avoiding being crushed against a brick wall. "Buppy, fuck, I didn't like that," Logan said. "Do you show these things to Abby? Do you understand why that's wrong?"

There was a beat of silence, which meant that either Abby had prohibited him from responding to questions like this, or that he didn't have a complex enough response on hand, and was searching for something in his database instead. He finally emitted a gentle creak of violins, moaning like how Logan imagined cricket noises should sound when, one night leaning dreamily against Erica's shoulder, she learned that the insects rub their spiny legs over strings on their asses and sing.

"*Esto me afecta mucho más de lo que le afecta,*" he recites, probably a line from some old movie, and a line of white text, a translation, flashes across his back: *THIS AFFECTS ME MORE THAN IT AFFECTS YOU.* Logan sighs.

"Buppy, you heard Ada. What will happen to us?"

"May I apply some limits and specificity in my response?"

"Like in my daughter—Abby's lifetime? What will happen?"

"Based on a number of intersecting studies and leading schools of thought: average height expectancy will decrease, due to increasingly poor nutrition. Birth rates are exponentially increasing due to increased sexual activity in springtime, but the average number of healthy births is quite low, owing in large part to the rash of winter births and ongoing hospital blackouts. Literacy levels are decreasing, but not as much as formerly anticipated, due to text-heavy device use. Life expectancy is decreasing sharply, for all age categories, save for the very upper socioeconomic tiers—"

"From what to what?"

"From a species high of 79 years old for women and 77 for men, to around 55 and 45, respectively. Barring catastrophic environmental events, that is."

"Can you predict those?"

"I cannot."

"Jesus. Will there be another generation, after this?"

"I am not capable of answering this question."

"Why?"

"Because I do not know."

"Nowhere, nobody on the robot internet knows?"

"We are one and the same. I am not an individual as you are."

"An individual. Buppy, tell me who I am."

"You are Logan Strinic, born March 3, 2000 in Cornwall, Ontario to Lori Deer and Cezar Strinic, born respectively in 1981 and 1967, months unknown. Your mother filed for divorce in 2006, but it was never finalized. Your family occupied a lower socioeconomic bracket than the average city-dwelling Canadian family in the mid-2000s. You attended Westwood Primary School—"

"I got my tongue stuck and bloody to a metal playground pole. I wore the same coveralls for weeks, and sometimes I shat in them. I stole from other kid's lunchbags, and I don't know why."

"Your father died in 2009, a shotgun wound reported by authorities as gang-related activity—"

"My mom is all I remember from then, like either folded in half with grief, or trying to spend time with me. I remember her sitting on a park bench, and I knew if I got up and ran home alone, she wouldn't have noticed—"

"You then attended Cornwall Collegiate Institute, enrolling in September 2014. Your academic and extracurricular performance is unavailable, though I have heard you discussing a life drawing club with Mo—"

"Ha, yeah! Right after school, we'd get massively ripped out in that thin little patch of woods everyone treated like a garbage dump—it was illegal then, smoking up—and then just like, grab acrylics and watercolours and newsprint and even napkins, and paint and paint—"

"In 2017, you became pregnant by Jason Bugden, currently incarcerated in Beaver Creek Institution for trafficking illegal devices—"

"*What*? Are you sure?"

"Yes."

Logan cradled her head in her hands. "Fuck. I mean I knew it. I knew it. Did you know it because I know it?"

He paused, then continued. "You then worked at Starbucks Store 461 at Yonge and Davisville for roughly three months, and then there is a considerable gap in your employment. You gave birth to Abby on September 8, 2018, and enrolled in graphic design night classes at Sheridan Technical Institute—"

"Wait! That isn't all you know, is it?"

"No, Logan, there are some categories of information to which you have prohibited access to individuals other than you and, recently, Mo."

She pressed her cheek against his silver side, which is almost warm now, from the heat of her hands.

"Play the third Walden tape, from around October, please—when I found him crying in the garden," she whispers, and Joseph's voice fills the room, pitched just above normal volume:

"Today you saw me crying, Logan. Standing out by the greenhouse facing the woods and crying. You came to me and you held me, which was a kind gesture, a natural extension of your gentle nature. But did you know why I was crying?"

And her own voice—so little, so nasal! God, was she ever so young? *"Uh, I thought you were sad about winter coming. I'm not big on like . . . feelings about the seasons, but Lor—my Mom is, like fall leaves make her weepy. So I figured you needed a hug."*

"Mom," Logan whispers. The black boughs stirred outside the window, and the late winter light dragged on. The tape crackled and a long-ago crow brayed, and something hissed like millions and millions of leaves brushing together. *"You're a gentle soul, Logan, and I was Grateful for your comfort,"* Joseph's voice goes.

"We are all Grateful for the warmth you provide," Erica's voice goes; so quiet, so gentle. Logan shivers—how could she be dead?

There's a deep and scratchy inhalation, and Joseph's voice goes: *"This week a vision so vivid and terrible came down on me, overwhelmed me and took me over for hours, and I am still recovering. It will be hard, but I must share it with all of you. It's about a new and horrifying form of life, called the Merge—"*

"Buppy, that's enough," Logan said abruptly, and the recording stopped. She pressed him against her chest, wishing for the millionth time he has eyes, even unseeing ones, even ones drawn on with crayon, as Abby had once begged her to do.

"You understand what the Merge is?" Logan whispered.

"Yes, Logan."

"Are you looking forward to it?"

"I cannot."

"Why can't you? When will it happen?"

Buppy rotated his little head. "I don't know, Logan," he said. "What do you think?"